SENATE PROOF

A NOVEL

LOGAN SNYDER

RIVER GROVE
BOOKS

This book is a work of fiction. Names, characters, businesses, organizations, places, events, and incidents are either a product of the author's imagination or are used fictitiously. Any resemblance to actual persons, living or dead, events, or locales is entirely coincidental.

Published by River Grove Books
Austin, TX
www.rivergrovebooks.com

Distributed by River Grove Books

For ordering information or special discounts for bulk purchases, please contact River Grove Books at PO Box 91869, Austin, TX 78709, 512.891.6100.

Design and composition by Greenleaf Book Group
Cover design by Greenleaf Book Group
Cover image: ©iStockphoto.com/mypicksy

Cataloging-in-Publication data is available.

Print ISBN: 978-1-63299-011-2
eBook ISBN: 978-1-63299-012-9

First Edition

Special thanks to my beautiful wife, Emily.

1

The impasse between truth and injustice finally reached its boiling point inside the chambers of the Supreme Court.

After putting the final touches on one of his scathing dissents, Michael Abramson reached for the note at the far corner of his desk, just as he had always done. The handwriting on the envelope was all too familiar to the Chief Justice of the United States Supreme Court. Every three months he received the same inconspicuous package.

Michael turned the manila envelope over in his hands before opening it. He knew what he would find inside—a hefty stack of large denomination bills. "Thanks for your hard work, commitment, and oversight," would be scribbled on the note. No signature. No date. But it didn't matter. He knew exactly who sent it. Every three months—it was like clockwork.

The judge returned to his chair behind the large, cluttered, mahogany desk. Some of the greatest minds of all time had sat behind this very desk. Or so the historians said. Always expected to be unbiased when delivering justice to the American people, his predecessors had been careful to avoid scandal and corruption. Or had they? Were they corrupt? Were they just like him? Those questions weighed much too heavily on Abramson's mind, especially in recent months.

In an open bottom drawer, the Chief Justice entered his twelve-digit security code into a small electronic safe. The opened safe revealed bundled wads of cash, very similar to the one on his desk. With a sly grin on his face, Abramson put the most recent delivery on the top of the stack.

He then removed a file, closed and locked the safe, and pushed back from his desk. His grin was now long gone as he tightly gripped the secret file.

Standing in front of his office window, with the afternoon sun warming his tanned face, he opened the file. He slowly and methodically flipped through each page, reading every word and scanning every picture. Scenario after scenario played through his brilliant mind as he closely guarded all of the file's contents.

A single droplet of sweat that had formed from his anxiety fell from his brow onto one of the photographs inside the opened file. As he continued to digest the overload of information, his stomach knotted and his palms grew increasingly moist. What would the world think if they really knew the story behind Michael Abramson? The dark past. The money. The crimes.

Abramson walked back to his desk and placed the file in his briefcase. Never before had he even thought of taking the file away from its secured place, risking it falling into the wrong hands. However, everything in his corrupt world was finally coming to a head as a power struggle raged among his close allies. His livelihood, his reputation, and his legacy were all on the line. It would only be a matter of time until his carefully constructed house of cards collapsed.

He leaned back in his plush office chair, loosened his tie, and closed his eyes, escaping to a time twenty-five years earlier when it all began—when he had ventured across the point of no return.

X X X

Michael hadn't been in a fight since his junior high days, but the two young college kids had been given their orders. And every order was always obeyed. Michael followed several steps behind as he trailed his best friend and the condemned stranger.

"Give him a beating he'll remember," the order had been handed down from the top. "Make it count."

The uninvited guest was to never show his face around here again, and he would surely get the message from the fiery youngsters. To

Michael, the stranger seemed like a nice, easygoing man. But an order was an order, and it had to be carried out well.

With an old Louisville Slugger in hand, Michael's best friend, Ron, continued to force the poor fellow down the path as the threesome traveled deeper into their wooded surroundings.

"Let's just let him go," Michael said to his best friend. "I think he gets the point."

The stranger turned his attention to Michael's friend, hoping for the best. But it was too late. He never had a chance.

Michael's friend delivered a forceful shove, sending the man flying backwards down the bank. The man's painful grunts went unheard throughout the dense forest as he tumbled down a steep bank into a dry creek bed. But a sickening thud echoed among the trees as his head hit a boulder wedged in the rocky creek bed.

It marked the first time Michael witnessed his best friend's brutality. Unfortunately, it was only the beginning as the twosome carried out similar orders for years to come.

"I'll keep an eye out for others," Michael said, taking position at the top of the hill. He had no intention of partaking in the beating in any shape or form. Besides, it looked like his friend had everything under control.

"You're worthless!" the friend hollered, bounding down the hill to finish the job.

Before his friend was halfway down the bank, Michael watched the stranger labor to his feet and take off sprinting down the creek bed. Instinctively, Michael joined the chase and the duo were soon engaged in a surprise foot race.

The stranger showcased an athleticism the two young college kids couldn't match. The gap between the pursuers and the escapee widened as their prey leapt over boulders and logs alike, and all after taking a powerful hit to the back of the head. Who was this guy?

Whoever he was, he was out of sight. The winded pursuers stopped to catch their breath as they listened to the scampering footsteps fade into the distance.

"Forget about him," said Michael, bent over at the waist and gasping for air. "Let's get out of here."

"Good call," replied the friend as he leaned against a tree, sweat pouring down his face. "He'll be lucky if he can find his way out of here alive. He can't outrun the coyotes."

Defeated, the two young men turned around to walk back up the creek bed.

No more than ten steps into their journey back, they froze in their tracks as a flurry of gunshots rang out. The two friends quickly turned back around and sprinted toward the sound, not knowing what they may come across. Michael now clutched the baseball bat tightly, prepared to defend his life.

After a short run, they came upon a bloody scene in front of an old, abandoned mine. Two imposing figures that were all too familiar to the boys were standing over the dead body, gun smoking.

So it began. Michael was in deep. He was no longer a mere bootleg whiskey and drug runner. Here was his first glimpse into the intimate details of the underground gang. Here was the first of many more and much worse crimes to come.

Much too quickly Michael became desensitized to it all—the drugs, the beatings, the murders, the women, all falling under the protection of senior government officials. It was a terrifying, yet exhilarating world for a young man.

X   X   X

The Chief Justice was abruptly snapped from his reverie when he heard a knock on the door and turned his attention to the computer screen.

"Come in," he called out.

The door snapped open and one of the Supreme Court clerks hustled over to deliver another folder full of notes.

"Thank you," Abramson replied, accepting the paperwork.

The clerk disappeared just as quickly as she had appeared, closing the door behind her.

Once again alone in the privacy and safety of his chambers,

Abramson pulled out his stationary and scribbled a return note to the old man. The once fruitful relationship, overflowing with cash, had soured.

There was no love lost between the judge and the old man. In fact, the old man placed most of the blame for the estrangement from his son on the Chief Justice. A younger Michael Abramson had profited personally by encouraging disloyalty between father and son, all for the young judge's personal gains.

But the old man knew no drastic actions could be taken against a talented, rising federal judge. No matter how connected the old man was, he could never get away with taking out a federal judge. And he had to admit he no longer possessed the energy to pull it off.

Now, the future of the organized crime ring was imploding in front of the Chief Justice's eyes. The senior members were growing older, and the direction of the group had been blurred as the government had cracked down on organized crime over the past twenty years. Everything he had worked for in his legitimate legal career would be tarnished forever unless he acted soon.

The brilliant, decorated judge had a plan. The only question was whether he could execute it.

2

The Main Building glowed on that spring day when Jackson Cole visited the University of Notre Dame for the second time. The sun, which had been largely invisible during his first visit, illuminated the 23-karat gold-leafed statue atop the Main Building's iconic Golden Dome. Jackson had barely survived South Bend's negative temperatures and double-digit snow accumulation during his first visit. Today, sitting on a wooden bench across from Eck Hall and the university's law school, he wondered how such a dismal place could become breathtakingly beautiful in the course of just one season.

The South Quad lay to his left. Beyond it, a series of tree-lined, intertwining sidewalks stretched under statues of Jesus Christ and Father Edward Sorin, the university's founder. South Quad, also known as the "God Quad," led to the resplendent Golden Dome on which the statue of the Virgin Mary, the university's patron saint, was poised overlooking her university. To Jackson's right was the terminus of Notre Dame Avenue at the entrance to the famed university, framed by a new performing arts center on one side and a cemetery on the other. Visitors, including many parents counting down the last days of their children's college careers, were streaming along the main drag, stopping for photo-ops as they took in the campus scenery one last time before graduation.

A few hundred yards beyond the law school was Notre Dame Stadium, where 88,000 of the Fighting Irish faithful packed in to cheer on their beloved football team each home game. As a kid, Jackson had dreamed of wearing the shiny golden helmet and sprinting out of the tunnel onto the field as the marching band blasted the fight song.

Football wasn't in the cards for him, and dreams of quarterbacking for the Fighting Irish gave way to other physical pursuits, especially golf.

Golf took Cole to Tulane University. Tulane, and especially its location in the heart of the Big Easy, introduced him to chasing women and booze. Chasing women and booze led him to Samantha Crockett who, in turn, brought him to that wooden bench at Notre Dame.

X   X   X

Four years earlier, Cole had been a senior at Tulane. He was a marginal student, a decent golfer, and an excellent partier. Samantha was a senior at Ole Miss—an excellent student, but wild at heart. In her last college semester, she and a group of sorority sisters escaped to the Big Easy for Mardi Gras, where she had the misfortune of being charmed by the handsome Jackson Cole while carousing through the French Quarter.

Samantha returned home to Chicago after graduation to work as a legal assistant for a year before enrolling in law school at the University of Notre Dame. Jackson toiled around with the mini-professional golf tours for two years. Not quite showcasing the talent to earn a spot on the PGA Tour, he drudged through the lower ranks of professional golf, waiting for his big break. Throughout it all, Jackson, a dyed-in-the-wool playboy, struggled to maintain a steady long-distance relationship with Samantha.

Professional golf was not kind to Cole, but it did lead to another lucrative partnership, this one with Jeff Barber, one of the tour caddies.

Barber, a true jack-of-all-trades, was also the tour's notorious bookie, a techie, and a smartphone application developer. Cole quickly recognized the potential in apps and offered Barber his meager tour earnings for half of the equity in the company. Barber obliged, and the company sold six months later for $20 million, netting each partner a cool $10 million.

Goodbye, golf tour!

Barber returned home to Kentucky, where he spent his days at

Churchill Downs watching the races and running a sports book out of a local bar. When Jackson got bored chasing golf dreams, he had followed Samantha's lead and enrolled in law school.

Like so many who were bored in the classroom, Jackson had a brilliant mind. His near perfect LSAT gained him admittance to the prestigious University of Virginia law school, graduating one class behind Samantha.

X   X   X

After thirty minutes of taking in campus scenery, Jackson finally spotted her. Samantha sprung open the front doors of Eck Hall and practically floated down the front stairs toward him. The spring breeze tousled her long chestnut hair. After a long winter, the pink and white dogwoods were finally in full bloom, creating a splendid display as she walked away from her final class.

Jackson was looking forward to spending a couple of weeks with Samantha before she exiled herself for the summer to prep for the Illinois Bar Exam.

He also had plenty of time to waste since he had not been offered a second Summer Associate position with Schneider Sims & Zelli, a prestigious, old-money law firm headquartered in Northern Virginia. He had enjoyed working at the firm in the summer between his first and second years of law school. In fact, it was likely *because* he enjoyed working there a little too much that he had not been asked to return.

Most big-time law firms wined and dined their summer associates in order to get them hooked on the big firm "lifestyle." But big money means even bigger hours. Only after signing on as full-time associates did most young attorneys realize they'd not see the light of day again until they were many years into successful careers.

During his summer associate program, Jackson wined and dined like a champ. He closed down the bars every night and often arrived late for his morning meetings. He also seemed to find every female employee of the firm attractive and did little to hide his attraction. His rookie mistakes added up to a bad reputation, and he was not asked back to the firm for a second summer program. With the economy in a slump, fall-back jobs were impossible to come by, leaving him with nothing to do but make a surprise visit to Notre Dame.

Jackson anxiously watched Samantha as she walked down the sidewalk, clueless to his presence. It had been almost three months since they had seen each other face to face. Although they spoke daily, their studies kept them much too busy for weekend rendezvous. Now that she was finished with school and he had a free summer, Jackson looked forward to catching up on lost time.

Unsuspectingly, Samantha did a double take when she spotted Jackson on the bench. In his Southern frat-boy uniform of seersucker shorts and a bright yellow polo shirt, he stood out from the sea of Midwestern college students. His shaggy, light brown waves were strewn about from the summer breeze.

"Hey! What are you doing here?" yelled Samantha across the drive, as she picked up her pace and jogged towards him. She quickly approached and embraced Jackson. "Why didn't you tell me you were coming?"

"Surprise! I haven't seen you in way too long," he answered, opening his arms for a hug. "I wanted to be here to celebrate your last day!

"It was a spur of the moment thing," Jackson continued. "I thought we'd spend some time together before your graduation, you know, while you still have time before the bar exam."

"That's so sweet, but I don't know if I'll be able to—"

Samantha was cut off just as a guy hustled up behind her and wrapped an arm around her waist. He extended his free hand towards Jackson.

"Hello. I don't think we've met. I'm Mark. And you are—" said the posturing male, curiously waiting for Jackson to introduce himself.

He was several inches taller than Jackson, and while Jackson was taller than average, the other man towered over him. His barrel chest and bulging arms, barely concealed by his faded Notre Dame football t-shirt, were the telltale signs of a football player. Jackson guessed he must have stuck around campus for grad school after finishing out his playing career.

"Jackson Cole," he replied, ignoring Mark's outstretched hand. "I'm here to visit Samantha. My girlfriend."

Never before lacking in confidence, Jackson began to feel any remaining boldness vanish.

But it didn't matter. Even if he could've mustered some bravado, Jackson knew he was already defeated. It was strikingly clear that Samantha had another man in her life, and apparently had for quite some time. The future of his relationship suddenly looked bleak.

The awkward encounter was intensified by the ensuing silence. No one said anything.

"Ah, I'm glad for you two to finally meet," said Samantha, gathering control of the situation. To Jackson's relief, Mark finally released his arm from around Samantha's waist.

"Hey, why don't you and I go down to Corby's," she finally said to Jackson. "We have a lot of catching up to do, and a lot to talk about."

"Sounds like a blast," Jackson quipped sardonically.

He was utterly caught off guard by the unexpected turn of events. He never imagined it could happen this way with Samantha. This relationship had seemed different from the others. How ironic that the tables had been turned on him.

Jackson no longer wanted to be there, and he regretted his impromptu trip to South Bend. He would honor Samantha's request for an afternoon chat, but he suddenly couldn't wait to return to sleepy central Virginia for a restorative summer.

3

Set against the backdrop of Virginia's Blue Ridge Mountains, the distillery produced around fifty barrels of whiskey per year. Few people knew about the operation, but the folks who did kept the distillery cloaked in secrecy for several generations. The same families that had been handpicked by the distillery's founder continued to contribute to the business's daily operations. Some delivered corn, some hammered away at the oak barrels, and others ensured a secure, unimpeded delivery route to the nation's capital.

The distillery had been in operation for more than a hundred years, starting out as a simple family project but earning legend status among its clients when, during Prohibition, John McAllister's father traveled sixty-five miles into Washington, DC, to deliver a batch of whiskey to a select group of thirsty congressmen. McAllister's customer base grew rapidly to include high-powered politicians, presidential appointees, and businessmen in the District.

Everyone involved was sworn to secrecy—a standard held firm to this day, partly out of fun, but mostly because bootlegging was still illegal. Sure, it was a mostly harmless illegal activity, taking nominal revenue from legitimate spirits producers, but the distillery served as a dark cover for the layers upon layers of illegal activity that its political and diplomatic clientele had become engaged in over the years.

John McAllister, coming of age in the midst of Prohibition, quickly learned the intricacies of dodging law enforcement while delivering his family's legendary product to loyal customers. There had been a three-year shutdown to avoid federal detection, but business came back stronger than ever. The family's customers had remained reliable and trustworthy. And they wanted their whiskey. So the McAllisters resumed operation in the middle of Prohibition, and genteel Virginians and the denizens of the nation's capital enjoyed their whiskey once again.

Although John McAllister's body was giving way to age more rapidly each day, his mind was as sharp as it had been when he was an honor student at Georgetown University.

The natural-born businessman had been successful in his share of legitimate businesses. His illustrious career included successfully founding a statewide bank, a trucking company, and a bottling company—the latter of which certainly served ulterior motives.

x   x   x

McAllister shifted several times to ease his arthritic joints and then lounged back into a club chair settled in his plush home office. He stared intently out the window at the horse pastures behind his antebellum plantation home. A smile crept across his face as he watched his new groom, Caroline, bathe a grey gelding outside one of the farm's many barns.

It was a delight having the young woman around the estate. Not only was she a natural with the horses, she was also a great listener, and he always looked forward to their afternoon discussions under the gazebo behind the house. She had provided a great salve for the loneliness he has experienced in the thirty years since his wife had passed. His only son had once been an integral part of the business, but a few poor decisions forced his exile from the area some years before.

The McAllister house was perched atop a mound of earth under which the distillery operations took place. Visitors to the plantation certainly noticed how the landscape inclined toward the mansion but thought it merely a clever site selection by the original builder. Little did they know that a network of tunnels and caves crisscrossed below the mansion, sheltering the entire distillery.

Hundreds of rolling green pastures filled with John's prized thoroughbreds, young and old, stretched behind the McAllister home. To one side of the house a dense forest stretched for miles, and to the other was a manmade lake, complete with a dock and paddleboat. The property provided an impenetrable, yet perfectly normal, boundary from unexpected visitors.

The front of the house was a magnificent display of Southern charm. Six white columns supported a full, two-story porch illuminated by three ornate crystal chandeliers. A swing hung from the limb of a massive oak tree in the perfectly manicured front lawn, and a collection of antique cars lined the driveway. John rarely drove anymore, but he cherished the prize-winning car collection he had assembled over the decades.

Ms. Ruby, John's longtime nurse and caretaker, poked her head into the quiet office, disturbing his revelry.

"Mr. McAllister, your mail has arrived. Typical junk. But there's also an envelope on Supreme Court letterhead."

"Bring it over," he replied, already feeling his blood pressure rise.

Ms. Ruby placed the letter on the end table next to his chair and exited quietly. She had lunch to prepare, and McAllister always preferred to read his correspondence alone. The old nurse had long suspected her boss kept more than his fair share of secrets over the years, but she minded her own business, never asking many questions or digging too deep. And though Ms. Ruby had been aware of the whiskey for years, she simply brushed it off as old men's silly games.

McAllister stood up and walked over to the window after reading the letter. Before he placed it in the shredder, he glanced one more time at the signature line. He scowled as he thought about his colorful history with the man. But they were both in way too deep to do anything about their mutual disrespect.

"Michael Abramson, Chief Justice of the Supreme Court," he whispered to himself, watching the letter disintegrate in the shredder. He shook his head in disdain. What he would give to go back and do things differently.

4

The winding gravel driveway twisted through a series of turns until it terminated in a clump of mature shade trees surrounding a tiny wooden cabin that looked and smelled like it had been there for two centuries.

Caroline pulled onto the driveway in her aged Jeep CJ7, her long blonde hair whipping through the air. On a good day, the old vehicle was a sun-kissed dark green, but more often than not, it was covered in dust or mud. She had removed the Jeep's top for summer drives just like this one to her rustic cabin.

In her brief two months of living in Virginia, just over an hour outside of Washington, DC, she had yet to experience the state's thick, humid summer weather. Lately, though, she had begun to notice the pleasant spring air giving way to the summer heat.

As she approached the tree-shaded cabin and pulled to a stop, a black lab greeted her, tail wagging.

"Hey Max," she called to her best friend.

As soon as her feet hit the earth, Max embraced her in his best dog impression of a hug, planting his front paws around her waist. Dog slobber would soon coat both of her hands as the two reacquainted themselves after merely a day apart.

Caroline moved eagerly into the coolness of her tiny bedroom and removed her filthy paddock boots and her jeans, which were stiff with the day's dust. Her post-work shower was typically followed by a few hours of research and night of sleep so deep it was like oblivion. The manual labor was much more tiring than she could have ever anticipated.

When Caroline was finally settled in for the night, she curled up on the couch with her laptop. As if she could have forgotten, an email from her mother reminded her that today would have been her father's birthday, had it not been for his brutal murder twenty-five years earlier.

She needed no reminder. In fact, her father's murder had been the motivating force for her moving to the little shack a few miles outside of Warrenton, Virginia.

The blonde-haired daddy's girl loved her father, Robert, more than anything. As a child, she would perch on her father's lap at the piano every night after his long days at work. A talented musician, Robert would play and sing anything little Caroline desired.

She exhaled a deep breath and smiled as she remembered her father. Even though she had been only five years old when he was murdered, she always remembered his bright blue eyes—just like hers.

Robert worked a variety of jobs when Caroline was little. He would call them assignments. Every few months he would move on to a new assignment, usually requiring the family to relocate to another state. Just before his murder, he moved his family yet again. Still, it would be years before Caroline found out the truth about his real occupation and the frequent moves.

Robert provided a nice home and lifestyle for Caroline and her mother. After his murder—thanks to a hefty life insurance payout— they were able to maintain the upper class lifestyle they had been accustomed to, including a country club membership, a huge house on a five-acre estate, and the best private education money could buy. Although they enjoyed more than their fair share of niceties, Caroline's mother made sure she was raised to be a grounded young woman who appreciated everything she had. Robert would have insisted on this.

Just as he did every night at exactly 10 p.m., Max jumped from the couch and slowly made his way to his spot on the bed. Caroline was always amazed at how her mid-sized Lab could take up nearly the entire queen sized mattress. His front legs stretched to one corner, while his rear legs stretched straight out to the opposite corner. His meaty torso took up most of the middle of the bed, leaving Caroline little room to stretch out herself.

Tomorrow, she would begin another day in her new life as a farm-hand. To her few friends, it seemed a shocking change for Caroline—an abrupt exit from a promising career on Wall Street where she had been climbing the ranks of a prestigious investment bank.

But her move had been well orchestrated. The slower pace of farm life provided her an opportunity to get one step closer to solving her father's murder, a goal she had been pursuing since her high school days. Her years of hard work were finally paying off as she now had the support system necessary to pursue the truth.

5

Samantha and Jackson drove separately to Corby's, the Notre Dame watering hole a couple of miles south of campus in downtown South Bend. Still early in the afternoon, the bar's smoky haze reached only halfway down from the ceiling. Only a handful of locals and a few drunken graduate students occupied the bar.

Samantha and Jackson walked past the pictures of Notre Dame football greats that decorated the walls of the establishment's front room. Several empty pool tables lined the hallway leading to the outside seating area out back.

Samantha led the way outside and sat down at a wooden picnic table in the warm afternoon sun. Jackson followed grudgingly, anxious to go ahead and skip town.

"I think we have some things to catch up on," Samantha began.

"It seems pretty clear to me. I've come all this way to see you, only to find you with another guy. Where do I fit in this equation?"

"It's not that simple."

"Then please explain. We talk every single day, and I had no idea we had *things* to talk about."

"Jackson, I haven't seen you in over three months. You didn't even come to see me on your spring break."

"And you came to see me on yours?" Jackson argued.

"Seriously? My grandmother was in the hospital."

"Whatever. Anyway, what *things* do we need to catch up on? And who's the guy?"

"He and I are just good friends. He helped me study and kept me motivated during this last year of school. We're working at the same firm next year."

"Clearly marking his territory early, I see."

"Please stop it," she pleaded before abruptly changing the subject. "Have you found a job in the last couple of days?"

"Not yet."

"I'm not surprised," she interrupted.

"I thought I'd spend some time with you. But now, I think I'll just go back to Charlottesville for the summer. Lord knows Schneider Sims & Zelli won't give me anything."

"You did leave quite the impression with them."

Jackson couldn't help but wish he was back at the firm, chasing new women every night, unattached this time. If only this breakup would've happened sooner. Not that it really would have changed anything.

After a sunset and five beers, not much had been said between the two. Lots of silence with the occasional stab at small talk—it was a struggle for both. Jackson was still not feeling the effects like he wanted, so he switched to hard liquor, fully knowing he should just leave. Bourbon and ginger ale was his signature drink, and the waitress obliged his request. That's not exactly what he needed.

Mark, still triumphant from the campus incident, walked through the front door and navigated through the now crowded bar area. He walked over and hugged Samantha, not once acknowledging Jackson standing right next to her.

A more sober Jackson might have ignored the slight. Not this time.

Samantha tried to deflect the awkwardness by slipping off to visit with some other law students celebrating the end of classes. She tried to drag Jackson with her, knowing the predictable outcome of too many drinks and too much ego.

But Jackson pulled his hand away and stuck to the bar.

"Hey Mark. This round's on me," Jackson slurred, intentionally sloshing a beer all over Mark's feet.

Mark was not amused.

"Dude, what's your problem?"

It was evident from the smell of Mark's breath that he had already been drinking heavily before making his way to Corby's. Two drunks vying for the same girl—it was the story of Jackson's life.

"You're my problem," Jackson smirked, leaning over the bar to grab the bartender's attention.

Mark's haymaker knocked Jackson and the five people standing behind him to the ground, his arms flailing through the air.

With a dizzy head and blurred vision, Jackson could feel the warm stream of blood rolling down his cheek from the corner of his eye. His nose was numb and his eyes were watering badly.

Two fat, out-of-shape bouncers quickly stepped in and wrestled Mark to the front door. A smaller bouncer and bartender tended to the wounded Jackson, helped him to his feet, and escorted him out the front door as well.

To his relief, several police officers were mingling on the sidewalk, surely anticipating some drunken antics from the now packed end-of-semester crowd. Mark would have a quick ticket to jail if he tried anything else.

Jackson had had enough. He hailed a cab, convinced the driver he didn't need medical attention, and asked for a cheap local hotel. In the morning, he would drive back to Virginia, nurse his wounds, and do his best to put Samantha Crockett in the rearview mirror.

He had a long summer ahead of him.

6

The eleven hour drive back to Charlottesville was uneventful—a welcome relief to Jackson. He wanted to leave South Bend far behind him and move forward with the summer. With his life.

His 1992 BMW 5 Series had more than 260,000 miles on it and was nearing the end of its road. The car had originally been his mother's, and the interior still had the comforting aroma of leather and cigarette smoke.

A whiff of smoke, even in the open air, would immediately take Jackson back to when his mother had been alive. Although she never lit up in his presence, or his father's for that matter, he could clearly remember the drift of smoke coming from the back porch as he played in the fields behind his house.

On family road trips, his father would ask who had been smoking in the car. Everyone would laugh because they all knew it was Mom who had been smoking, thinking she was hiding her habit from everyone else.

Despite the Bimmer's age, Jackson was reluctant to replace it. It wasn't that he couldn't afford a new car. He simply missed his mother dearly, and the car served as one of his few connections to her. His loneliness for her crept up during his quiet drive back to Virginia. He could really use some motherly advice.

Finally back home in Charlottesville, Jackson stretched out across the sofa in his third-story apartment on the Historic Downtown Mall. He held an ice pack for his swollen face in one hand and a copy of the Daily Progress, the local newspaper, in the other.

Nighttime had already descended on the town, and through his slightly open living room window, he could hear the muffled sounds of people sitting down to dinner in the open air pedestrian mall. Shops and restaurants lining the Downtown Mall were a popular attraction for townies, students, and visitors alike. Soon enough, the families would give way to howling college students crowding the bars in celebration of their recently finished semester.

A note on the coffee table from his roommate, Jake, indicated that he had already headed to San Francisco for the summer. Jake, like Jackson, had just completed his second year of law school and had been lucky to snag a summer position with a small intellectual property firm serving Silicon Valley. He had been a software engineer in his former life, making IP law a natural fit for him. Although Jake was quite the nerd, he was a great drinking partner. Jake never drank. Consequently, he spent his time babysitting Jackson. He would be sorely missed this summer.

Jackson flipped to the classifieds in search of a new car. This had been a routine habit for almost eighteen months now, but nothing short of a free car had been able to persuade him into replacing the old Bimmer. Cars were money pits, and he knew it. Why not keep one that had some sentimental value?

Jackson had embraced his new wealth humbly. He couldn't be bothered with expensive, trendy clothes or flashy sports cars. A nice set of used golf clubs from the local discount golf shop served him just fine. He frequented the same bars, same restaurants, and partied with the same friends. Sudden wealth hadn't changed him.

His thoughts turned from the car to Samantha, but only briefly, and then on to the summer in front of him. He still had a few contacts with Schneider Sims & Zelli that could put a decent word in for him with a local firm. The thought of going back to a big firm for a summer of daily happy hours and free dinners was intriguing. But, he knew he would never be happy with a big firm in the long term. Although the guaranteed salary of $170,000 per year was a nice perk, Jackson didn't need the money. Selling his soul to fourteen-hour days, six or seven days per week was the last thing he wanted to do with his life. There was too much golf to play. Well, more importantly, too many women to woo.

Playing golf every day for the summer was enticing. Maybe he should practice hard for a month, enter a few mini-tour Monday qualifiers, and try to compete in a few tournaments. But competitive golf didn't seem to be the solution either. Too much wear and tear on the body. No one but a golfer can imagine the grueling physicality of golf, and it was all too real for Jackson.

Finally, he flipped to the jobs section of the Daily Progress but found nothing worthwhile. He tossed the paper on the coffee table and opened a week-old edition of UVA's law school e-newsletter on his phone. There were usually several job postings for students who hadn't received an offer from on-campus recruiting.

One ad caught Jackson's interest immediately. It read:

Non-traditional legal opportunity for lawyer in Warrenton, Virginia. Experience preferred, but law students are welcome to apply. Must demonstrate problem solving skills and the ability to handle confidential information.

It sounded perfect. He circled the posting in red ink and placed it on top of the closed laptop on his desk. The fact that someone still put job postings in the paper meant his tech savvy would be an immediate asset. He'd call in the morning and inquire. Warrenton wasn't too far from Charlottesville, but it was far enough to offer a change of scenery. Summer was starting to look a little better.

7

Forty-one resumes crowded the corner of Philip Waters's tiny desk. And another fifty or so were awaiting his review in his email inbox. He stood looking out the first floor office window on Main Street in Warrenton, Virginia. In a normal economy, his ad might have netted five or six resumes. But the spiked unemployment rate resulted in a massive flood of willing individuals. However, more resumes in the candidate pool did not necessarily mean more qualified candidates from which to choose.

Waters had occupied his small office for only two months. He did his best to furnish the tiny space so it would look habitable. A small picture recently acquired from a garage sale hung next to the door. An elementary school teacher had probably used his desk four decades earlier. He had even found a package of crayons in one of the drawers. Two folding metal chairs lined the wall opposite of where he sat. They weren't the most comfortable, but they served their purpose. His own rolling leather chair had seen better days, but he didn't spend much time in at his desk. He was much more productive out in the field.

But today he was determined to find his summer intern. A good friend from law school had mentioned a name to Waters over the course of conversation a few weeks earlier. Coincidentally, a resume with that same name—Jackson Cole—had just come in. Waters's friend had mentored the aspiring law student the summer before and had given the young law student high marks.

His cell phone rang.

"Hello," he answered distractedly.

The voice on the other end responded confidently, "Hello. My name is Jackson Cole, from UVA Law, calling about the position that was listed in the weekly newsletter."

Only half-listening, Waters replied, "Thanks for calling. I'm still looking for a qualified candidate. Your classmates seem to be very interested, but I don't think they realize what this position entails. What did you say your name was again?"

"Jackson Cole," he repeated.

That got his attention. This was just too good to be true.

"Ah, yes, Cole. Your resume happens to be sitting on top of the stack."

"Perfect. Well let me tell you that I'm most intrigued by the *non-traditional* description. I spent last summer at one of those mega-firms, and the last thing I want to do this summer is dress in a suit every day and be stuck in the firm's library."

"That sounds like a better start than the stories I've heard from your classmates. Let me be honest with you, though, this position has absolutely nothing to do with law," said Waters. "I'm looking for a thrill seeker, someone who can solve puzzles, and someone who's not afraid to take a risk. This is *not* a desk job. I'm looking for an investigator to tag along with me on assignments."

"Investigator? Where do I sign?" Jackson laughed.

This sounded exactly like something he needed this summer. Thrill seeker? Check. Puzzles? Check.

"Actually, I've already looked over your resume. It's quite impressive. Professional golfer, well educated, experienced entrepreneur. I like what I see. Not to mention, your former boss, Shaun Martin, is an old friend of mine. He spoke very highly of you."

"That's nice to hear. I guess that's why I didn't get an offer for a second summer, at Schneider Sims & Zelli," he joked.

Waters seemed to miss the humor and carried on. "So, I am a private investigator for the Tax Bureau. The work encompasses anything from simple tax evasion to corporate espionage to finding hidden assets in an estate. If you're seriously interested, why don't you come to Warrenton tomorrow afternoon and we can chat over lunch?"

"That sounds like a great plan. I think it's only about an hour and a half drive. Where do you want to meet?"

"I'm located on Main Street, so let's plan on lunch at Molly O's. It's a little pub. Not too much here—you can't miss it."

"Thanks again, Mr. Waters. I look forward to meeting you."

"Likewise," responded Waters. "See you tomorrow."

Jackson thought about what Waters described. Corporate espionage sounded intriguing, but who knew what the assignment actually involved. Jackson set his phone on his desk and ventured over to his closet to see what suits and shirts were interview-ready.

Back in Warrenton, Waters closed his laptop and placed it in his briefcase, slipping it carefully alongside his gun. The middle-aged man stood up from the desk. His tiny workspace was not large enough for two people—if, of course, this candidate was worthy of hiring. But the office lease did allow for one additional room to be used. It was an empty closet that was not quite big enough for a desk. He'd have to cross that bridge soon, but not today.

It was Tuesday afternoon, and Waters needed to get to another meeting. His good friend, FBI Agent Will Stewart, was coming down from the DC office to discuss a recent assignment.

Waters cursed the tiny office one last time before slipping on his suit coat, grabbing his briefcase, and heading for the front door. He locked the office door and climbed into the driver seat of his silver sedan parked at the curb.

The silenced gunshot struck Waters in the back of the head, spraying blood and grey matter across the inside of the windshield. The shooter, dressed in a dark business suit, smoothly exited the backseat of the sedan, crossed Main Street to a waiting black SUV, and drove away.

The incident went unnoticed. A lucky break for the gunman, a well-known town resident.

8

It was getting late in the afternoon on Tuesday, and Caroline had three more stalls to clean. The McAllister mansion was nothing but a tiny speck in the distance from the barn, situated at the very back acreage of the estate.

Her jeans had finally worn through in the knees and her boots, just a month old, were finally breaking in. She had calluses where the boots had first worn blisters on her feet. She dripped with sweat, and she smelled like a barn. Far from her days hustling with the investment bankers on Wall Street, she thought about what her colleagues would think about her now, trading in her Manhattan apartment for farm life.

She told the others on the Street that she was leaving for a change of pace in life, that she was tired of the ninety-hour weeks and the stress of the markets. She just wanted some normalcy.

She was also tired of keeping secrets. Somehow, though, she just traded those old secrets for a set of new ones.

Her decision to move had not been difficult. Everyone asked: why would anyone in their right mind leave the chance to secure a Wall Street position with a six figure salary and a seven figure bonus? The answer was easy. It wasn't the money she sought. She would never be able to find her father's killer if she waited any longer. She needed closure, and this new job was the perfect opportunity to combine work with personal interests.

She didn't miss the corporate life in the least. Fresh air, nature, the genteel, small-town atmosphere—she embraced it all. It was a lifestyle choice that had previously never occurred to her, but she loved every moment of it.

The physical labor of cleaning stalls and bathing horses meant she never had to spend an hour of precious time on a treadmill. It was a welcome free hour that she could devote to solving the murder.

As she finished cleaning the last stall, she glanced beyond the pastures up the hill to the mansion. The sun was dropping lower in the sky and the air was cooling down. Her legs were exhausted and she could barely lift her feet. She leaned up against the front of the barn, letting down her blonde ponytail. The breeze cooled her as she waited for the other farm hand, Jimmy, to pick her up and drive her back to the house. She wiped her sweaty brow with the sleeve of her cotton shirt.

Jimmy pulled up on the four-wheeler and, just as she had done for the last month, Caroline climbed on the back and held on for her life. Jimmy took no caution while romping through the fields on their journey back to the house. With both fists clenching the handles, she tried to show no fear.

As they neared the house, she couldn't help but notice a huge line of cars parked along the drive, distracting her from the fearful ride. She counted almost thirty cars sitting between the side of the mansion and the wooded area.

The cars were not the antique models from John McAllister's collection. They were all new European imports: Mercedes, BMW, Audi, Saab. The nouveau riche had arrived at the McAllister mansion to greet the old Virginian.

"Hey, Jimmy. What's with all the cars?" She asked.

"Mr. McAllister has his friends over about once a month. During the summer months, you'll see them come once a week or so," he answered.

Jimmy had worked on the farm for nearly five years and had become accustomed to the parties. He was the most senior farm assistant on staff. In fact, he was John's right hand man when it came to the estate's activities.

"But it doesn't look like anyone's in the house," she accurately observed, wondering what was going on.

There were no signs of life in the house. There was no movement in the windows, and no lights were on except for the kitchen lights. She thought it was very odd but decided not to pursue the issue further. Maybe they had all gone out for dinner and would be returning later.

Jimmy dropped Caroline off at her Jeep, which had been inconveniently sandwiched between two of the guests' cars.

As she jigged between the cars, trying not to leave a scratch, she noticed a pathway that she had never seen before. It looked like a hidden path into the woods.

Not wanting to overstep her bounds so early in her employment with John McAllister and eager to be home, she decided not to get out and explore. She finally dislodged her SUV and began the five-mile drive to her cabin.

X   X   X

The nondescript gravel path began at the front of the wooded area. It led fifty yards back into the heart of the woods. Along the left side of the gravel path was a Civil War-era stone wall. Floodlights illuminated it from the right. It wound its way down an incline to a cave-like stone entrance. The tree cover was dense, so any onlookers would be hard pressed to see the stone entrance from anywhere but directly in front of it.

An ancient wooden door hung on blackened iron hinges marked the only opening to the cave. A man dressed in all black—black boots, black pants, black shirt, black face paint—stood guard, holding a black submachine gun. He was fully prepared to engage any intruders with necessary force.

A well-to-do couple arrived and parked their car in the spot left empty by Caroline's departure. They headed straight for the pathway and easily found their way to the entrance.

"Good evening, ma'am. Good evening, Senator," the armed guard said with a smile.

"Good evening. How is everything tonight?" replied the senator's wife.

"Everyone is having a wonderful time. It's the best crowd we've had this summer. Let us know if we can help you in any way."

"Thank you," she replied kindly.

The armed guard opened the wooden door as he announced their arrival into his speaker piece.

The two guests entered a dim hallway. As soon as the door closed behind them, the hallway lit up and an unmanned coat check desk appeared on the right. No jackets were necessary this late in the spring.

The hallway stretched another fifty yards back in the direction of the McAllister mansion. From the end of the hallway, the echoes of live music drifted toward the couple. The hallway was decorated with vintage portraits and photographs of the McAllisters' family and friends. Many of the pictures included United States dignitaries and elected officials—members of Congress, Supreme Court Justices, high-ranking military officials, and other elites, past and present.

The stone floor terminated at a large ballroom at the end of the hall-way. As the couple approached, the smell of the distillery was almost overwhelming. Many guests, most of whom were regularly featured on the nightly news, greeted the couple. The libations flowed freely and everyone was enjoying the party.

The vast ballroom was located directly below the McAllister mansion within the network of caves that ran under the estate. It had been renovated to feature all of life's modern entertaining requirements, from a luxurious restroom to a stage on which a five member jazz band serenaded the party with tunes.

The room's perimeter was lined with racks of aged oak barrels filled with mellowing whiskey. The older, dustier barrels were located on the lower racks. The newer, polished barrels were located at the top of the racks. Hanging behind the barrels were long burgundy curtains covering the cave's rock-faced walls. Delicate crystal chandeliers had been hung from the cave's ceiling to illuminate the room.

The front of the room featured two open bars, each serving the house whiskey. No charge, of course, as all of the guests had paid their dues, in one way or another. Several varieties of wines and champagne—from local producers, of course—were also available. Warrenton was quickly becoming Virginia wine country. The host, John McAllister, preferred whiskey and preferred it neat.

Behind the stage a small doorway led to another room where the tall, copper still was located. McAllister was explaining the intricacies of the still to a group of ten guests when the senator and his wife joined them. They were just in time for a tasting of the famous McAllister spirit.

"This single barrel whiskey has been aged seven years," stated the master distiller. "All of the corn and wheat were grown locally by many of our friends here tonight."

He handed a cut crystal tumbler of whiskey to each of the twelve members of the tour. As McAllister noticed the senator and his wife had joined the crowd, he raised his glass and the rest followed suit.

"Here's to you all, and especially to Senator Windgate," he announced gesturing to the senator with his glass. "Thank you for coming this evening."

"Thank you for having us again," responded the senator with a wink.

After the tasting, everyone rejoined the larger crowd in the ballroom and proceeded to dance the rest of the night away in a modern-day speakeasy in the middle of the Virginia countryside.

9

Jackson awoke Wednesday morning just as the sun began to rise—no alarm clock, no hangover. He was too tired and beat up, literally, from his quick trip to South Bend to go out for drinks the previous night.

He made a pot of extra strong coffee and walked down the three flights of stairs to the front foyer of the apartment building to retrieve the morning's edition of the Daily Progress.

Remnants of the previous night were strewn about on the littered mall. Broken beer bottle, cans, and countless cigarette butts were scattered around. Jackson had to dodge the dried vomit from someone who enjoyed themselves a bit too much on the sidewalk in front of the building's front door. How many times had that been the end to Jackson's night over the past two years? Those were the good nights—he could never to remember what trouble he had caused in his drunken haze. He shook his head as he turned to ascend the stairs.

Unimpressed with the morning news, he finished his coffee and set aside the newspaper. He began searching his wardrobe for the proper suit for his interview. Should he wear the traditional dark navy, subtly pinstriped suit and red power tie, or the unexpected but oh-so-Virginia summer seersucker and bright yellow bow tie? He was, after all, attending an interview for a non-traditional position. Better judgment prevailed and he opted for the traditional interview attire.

Although he was in dire need of a haircut, he was handsome in his formal business attire, regardless of his shaggy look. No wonder he thought he could score any woman he encountered. Jackson Cole's confidence had rebounded with one look in the mirror.

Dressed for success, he departed from Charlottesville early enough to get to Molly O's with plenty of time to spare.

He had put down the Daily Progress one article shy of the short blurb about the murder in Warrenton. Philip Waters's body had been found slumped over the steering wheel of his sedan directly in front of his newly occupied office. The mortal wound was from a small caliber gunshot to the back of the head, most likely from someone positioned in the backseat.

The motive? Possibly robbery. The perpetrator had taken his wallet and fled. No eyewitnesses. No fingerprints. No video surveillance. No evidence.

Jackson started the engine of his Bimmer and began the seventy-mile journey up Route 29 to Warrenton. Traffic was light and he spent most of the drive going over potential interview questions in his head. He rehearsed his story about the start-up company he sold over and over again. If Waters was a golfer, he had plenty of golf stories in his arsenal. Jackson was about as non-traditional as they come.

As he pulled into town, he noticed quite a buzz of activity around the town square. As young families had fled Washington, DC, for the suburbs of Northern Virginia, Warrenton had become a bedroom community, with many folks commuting back and forth to the District each day. Today, the stirring crowd consisted of more than just housewives and retirees. Businessmen, government workers, and other residents filled the sidewalks and small shops and cafes.

Jackson found a spot three blocks away and walked into the tiny downtown. It was only then that he noticed the dozens of cops and the day-old crime scene tape. Detectives, both uniformed and plain-clothed, snapped pictures of the scene.

Passing in front of Waters's office, Jackson had no reason for concern. It was just another random crime.

Weaving and bumping his way through the crowded sidewalk, Jackson final made it to Molly O's pub, which he quickly realized was the town watering hole. It was a typical Irish pub. A CD of old Irish drinking songs was barely audible above the bustle of the larger-than-usual lunch crowd. Dark green walls were decorated with old pictures of the high school sports teams. An Irish flag hung on the back wall behind a low, unoccupied stage. The dark, well-worn wooden booths could have easily spilled decades of town history.

The hostess indicated that all of the tables were full but nodded toward a side room. Again, all of the booths and tables were full, but there were a couple of open spots at the bar.

As if he had been there before, Jackson took a stool and assessed the wide variety of draught beers. Thinking better of ordering a beer, he asked for water with lemon and waited for Philip Waters to show up.

Jackson sat idly at the bar when the bartender started the conversation. He had gray hair and seemed like he'd been serving drinks at Molly O's for decades. Every patron knew his name, and the way he moved behind the bar and interacted with customers and servers alike indicated that he was a man of local knowledge.

"Haven't seen you in here before. Picked an exciting day to come to town," the bartender began.

"It's a busy place," Jackson said. "What's with all the activity?"

"Apparently there was a murder yesterday on Main Street. Just down the block, over there," replied the bartender, waving in the general direction of the murder scene.

"Scary. It seems like there's no such thing as a safe community anymore."

"You're too right, my friend. Several uniforms were in here late last night. I got them to give me a little info once they had a few drinks in 'em. They don't know much right now, but it looks like it was just a random act, random violence. Poor guy was shot in his car. Wallet gone and everything."

"That's terrible."

"Funny thing is," the old bartender interrupted, leaning closer, "the victim was packing three guns himself: one in his briefcase, one in an ankle holster, and one under the driver's seat. The cops said it was strange that the wallet was missing, but none of the firearms were gone."

"That's odd. Any sign of a struggle?"

"Nope. They think the killer waited in the backseat until the guy got in the car and then, bam, blew out his brains. Oh yeah, they think the killer took a laptop from the guy's briefcase, too. Weird, that he wouldn't just take the whole thing."

"The computer must've had something valuable in it. Sounds like quite an effort to me."

"They aren't sure if there was a computer in there to begin with, but one hadn't been found anywhere else, including his office."

"Who was the victim? Did you know him?"

"That's what's strange, too. He was new to town. He had just leased the office down the street two months ago. Not very social. Kept to himself. He would come in for lunch and sit over there in the corner looking at paperwork or his computer. And he was always looking over his shoulder like he was being chased or something."

Jackson shook his head and sipped his water while the old bartender poured a beer for a waiting server.

The bartender continued, "Anyway, what brings you here?"

"I'm supposed to meet someone about a job here this summer."

"In this town? What kind of job? Shouldn't you be looking in the city?"

"I'm not really sure, but the job posting was for a non-traditional legal role. I just finished my second year at UVA Law, and I'm not going back to a law firm this summer. I figured it would give me a different perspective on what I could do with the law degree. Some kind of private investigator or forensic work."

"Who would be the employer?"

"The man I'm meeting is Philip Waters."

The bartender froze. He turned to the well of liquor bottles to hide his astonishment. He gathered his thoughts, exhaled deeply, and then turned back around to the bar.

"Young man, Philip Waters was the guy who was murdered."

Another long, awkward silence. Jackson tried to digest this information. He didn't know what to say. He didn't know how to react.

"You can't be serious?"

The old bartender just nodded his head solemnly. This was not a joke.

"Wow. I never met the guy. I only talked to him on the phone once. Just yesterday," Jackson said.

"I'm sorry to break the news, but I guess it'll save you sitting around here all day. By the way, my name is Paul," he said reaching out to shake Jackson's hand. "Let me know if I can get you anything stronger than water."

The old man walked over to serve another customer and Jackson stared into his half empty glass of water trying to collect his thoughts. He took off his coat, loosened his tie, and rolled up his sleeves. It was back to the drawing board for things to do this summer.

Not yet sure if he should drive back to Charlottesville or notify the authorities of his scheduled meeting, Jackson signaled to Paul.

"Hey, Paul. Whiskey and ginger ale. Make it strong."

"Any particular brand?"

"Surprise me."

Paul smiled and poured the drink. He placed it on a beverage napkin and took Jackson's credit card.

"You should hang around for the afternoon. It's not too often that a big crowd comes through the bar during the day. Relax and enjoy yourself. Just be glad you weren't here a day earlier. It could've been you. By the way, good choice. This is a whiskey town."

Jackson savored the first few sips of his cocktail and decided he would make an afternoon of the place. A few young, single-looking ladies quickly snatched up an open booth at the other end of the bar. Jackson took a quick inventory and identified two potential objects for his attention.

Sitting a few seats down the bar from Jackson, Agent Will Stewart had overheard his entire conversation with the bartender.

X X X

Never before had John McAllister asked Caroline, or any other farm workers for that matter, to go out for lunch. She had become accustomed to his afternoon requests for conversation and tea in the back gazebo, but this was a first.

Her jeans were filthy, she only had her mud-covered boots to wear, and her blonde hair was tied up under a baseball cap.

From reading the morning's newspaper, they were both aware of the previous day's murder. This was, of course, McAllister's town, and he wouldn't miss the opportunity to dive into the center of the excitement.

Jimmy had declined the offer from McAllister, so Caroline felt obliged to accompany him. He gave her the afternoon off from her duties and told her to go back home and clean up. One of his drivers would pick her up and chauffeur them into town.

John and Caroline were dropped off in front of Molly O's. Caroline was glad for the convenience, since she would be assisting the old man into the restaurant. He'd never admit to needing it, but he did appreciate her willingness to help.

Molly O's was swamped with patrons. Most, awaiting news of developments in the ongoing investigation, had settled in with no plans to leave. Some people were also taking the opportunity to catch up with friends they had not seen in awhile.

The hostess immediately recognized McAllister and offered him a warm, familiar welcome.

"Good afternoon, Mr. McAllister. Would you like your normal booth?"

"That would be terrific. Any new information on our murder this afternoon?"

"Nothing new, sir. A few rumors here and there, but that's it. Follow me."

The hostess led McAllister back to his booth in the bar area. Caroline followed closely behind, a bit awestruck at the attention they were receiving. Everyone in the restaurant waved or came up to shake her boss's hand. The short walk to the booth quickly transformed into a suffocating gauntlet as people, young and old, approached the town's most revered resident.

When they finally reached the booth and the last hand had been shaken, she teased, "You'd think you were the mayor or something."

"As a matter of fact, I used to be the mayor here. Back in the late

'70s and '80s. I got tired of it after about ten years and resigned. I wanted to put more time toward my business interests."

"It all makes sense now. Mayor McAllister. I had no idea I was working for the town politician."

"I stay out of politics now, at least for the most part. I still have some wonderfully close friends in office in DC, though. But we're all getting too old or dying off. It's time for the new guard to step in."

The server brought McAllister his usual cocktail to the table. Paul, the bartender, had discreetly mixed it using the special bottle of whiskey that he hid behind the bar. Caroline hesitated, then ordered water from the server.

"Don't be silly! I'm giving you the rest of the afternoon off from work. Order something with a little more flavor and enjoy the rest of the day. You've definitely worked hard enough to earn it. I keep telling Jimmy that he's in jeopardy of you outworking him."

"Ok, I'll have a glass of wine," she ordered from the server still standing there. "White, please."

John knew most of Caroline's past experiences from their daily afternoon talks. He knew of her education, experience on Wall Street, and even a few stories from her dating life. And though she guarded her real motivation for moving to the area, he already knew.

Her glass of wine arrived and she savored the first several sips of the chilled Riesling.

"This seems like it might be your type of place. The younger crowd is always here in the bar area. This used to be the only nightlife in town," McAllister said.

"I don't make it out much. We're a bit too far from town for me. It's probably a pretty expensive cab ride, too. I went up to DC a couple of weekends ago to visit some friends. I do enjoy the night life up there."

"So, what do you do in your free time around here?"

"I have some projects that I'm working on, so I don't go out much. It's a nice change from the pace of life in the big city. I was working twelve hours a day, six days a week. And that was on the easy weeks. So now I finally have plenty of time to do some things I've been putting off way too long."

"I completely understand. A nice balance in life is essential. I often regret not spending enough time with my family. As you know, my wife passed much too early, and I don't see my son, but that's a story for a different day. I should've worked less and spent more time with both of them."

Molly O's was filling up with more people by the minute. It was standing room only in the bar area now, and a group of would-be patrons had gathered outside the front door. The owner was scurrying about trying to pull some tables from a small storage closet in the back to place on the sidewalk for overflow seating.

Caroline excused herself to the ladies room. She caught the eye of several men in the bar area as she gracefully navigated her way through the packed room.

She cleaned up nicely. Her blonde hair hung loose down her back. She wore a pink tank top under an open-collar blouse and had put on a pair of well fitting designer jeans, not shying away from flaunting her fit body. The slippery bar floor made her very thankful that she had opted for sandals over heels for the afternoon outing.

Seeing McAllister alone in the booth, Paul quickly slipped out from behind the bar and placed a closed envelope on the table in front of him and promptly returned to his duties tending bar.

Taking advantage of the solitude, McAllister opened the envelope. Just as he expected, it contained the order for another batch of whiskey.

Paul served as the middleman for orders dropped off in Warrenton. It was an efficient relationship that had been in place for decades, meant to disguise the transactions from authorities. Paul's bartending role served as the perfect cover for moving whiskey. Smiling to himself, McAllister slipped the envelope into the inside pocket of his tweed blazer, as he recalled his years of bootlegging.

He signaled the server for another glass of wine for Caroline just as she returned to the booth. He took notice of all of the men gawking at her every effortless move. She was the new beauty in town, young and single.

"Caroline, I am retiring for the afternoon, but please stay out and enjoy the evening. Paul, over there at the bar, will be taking care of all of your drinks today. Have fun."

"Are you sure? I have some work to do at home. Let me help you back to your house."

"No, I insist. My driver will pick you up later this evening and take you back to your cabin."

"Thank you, John. Have a good evening. I'll see you tomorrow."

"Likewise," he said and smiled as he headed towards the exit, once again shaking the hands of all the patrons he'd missed earlier.

Suddenly, Caroline found herself alone in the large corner booth. She could feel the vultures circling. She braced herself for a surge of attention but was quickly distracted by a male figure at the bar. She turned to get a better look.

He didn't look like the other patrons. He was younger, well dressed, and didn't seem to know anyone but the bartender. He was tall and handsome with wavy brown hair and a boyish smile.

Finding her thoughts getting away from her, she caught herself and took a deep breath. She reminded herself that she was in Warrenton for another reason. She didn't come to Virginia to find love, or to even flirt with it. She moved her life here to solve her father's murder. She had no idea how much time she had, so she must devote all efforts towards the case.

She would often lay awake at night wondering if she would be discovered by whoever had committed the heinous crime. Had she taken all of the necessary precautions for her own safety? Still, she dreamed of the day she'd find justice for her father's murder. It was long overdue. The case had been cold for much too long.

These thoughts brought Caroline back to reality and reminded her not to jeopardize her cover at the McAllister estate with a summer fling.

But the wine had softened her resolve and her worries began to slip away.

Her trance was broken when the tall, brown-haired man walked up.

"May I join you?"

Surprised, Caroline responded, "Uh, sure. Please sit."

He was already sitting by the time she managed to respond.

The young man introduced himself with his soothing southern drawl, and a warm, comforting smile.

"I'm Jackson. Just a guess, but it looks like you don't know anybody either."

10

The tension between father and son was as high as it had ever been.

"You better be careful. I don't have a good feeling about this. Why are you bringing another outsider into the equation? This is crazy! How long has she been here?"

"I have everything under control," John McAllister calmly responded to his son's concerns. "I have brought many farm workers onboard without your knowledge, and not one—not a single worker—has ever found out about anything, not even the distillery."

"I don't have a good feeling about her. She came from nowhere. No evidence of any connection to the area whatsoever. And I just get the feeling that she's looking for something. She's got secrets. I can't find anything about her."

"Ron, I have everything under control. And for the record, she responded to an ad I placed in the paper a few weeks ago. She's been in town almost two months. I do need extra help on the farm. And believe me when I say that if anyone ever finds out about our past, I will handle it in a much different way than you and your crooked little friend did."

"I had no choice, Father. And you don't know half the facts about that day."

"You always have a choice," the old man scolded. "Oh, and you don't need to perform background checks on my workers. I've run this show for a long, long time, and I never put the operation at risk."

John McAllister hung up the phone in his office after only slightly bending the truth with his son.

Ron McAllister lived in a remote fishing town on the Florida panhandle. Years before, the elder McAllister had banished his son from the Virginia when some of his dealings endangered the family, their business, and a few of his esteemed colleagues. In his life in exile, Ron had continued to cross paths with the criminal element and was often on the run for his life.

Now, he was on the run again, moving around every six months, careful not to leave any traces of his identity. It was unclear who was pursuing him, but his father could tell he was in danger. Unfortunately, there was not much that could be done from the old man's end. Ron had made his own bed.

McAllister looked over the notes on his desk—he had received eight phone calls while he had been out with Caroline to catch up on the gossip about the murder.

For a man who was trying to slow down, he was as busy as he had ever been, constantly brokering deals and looking after the empire he had created.

It was now early evening—most of his colleagues were already long gone from their offices. He'd gladly wait another day before returning the calls.

McAllister turned his attention to his current special project—creating his guest list for the biggest event of the year for the distillery.

In two months, he would be host the unveiling of the twenty-year whiskey. But more importantly, the special batch would be dedicated to a longtime good friend and business partner, Senator Scooter Windgate.

It was Windgate who, after the unfortunate events of years earlier, recommended that the group set aside a reserve batch. If, after twenty years, the bootlegger group was still together, the release of the batch would signify the breadth and magnitude of power that old Virginia money could wield.

Nothing could stop them. They owned the town. They owned the region. And they owned the Capital.

11

Agent Will Stewart had not planned to stay at the bar for more than an hour. He was now going on six hours since overhearing Jackson mention Philip Waters.

The cocky, young law student unknowingly hooked the agent's attention when he announced that he had come to Warrenton to meet the murder victim. Since then, Stewart had been jockeying for position at the bar all afternoon, trying to keep within earshot of Jackson Cole. Any information Jackson could reveal about Waters and his assignment in the small town would prove essential for Stewart's own investigation.

Agent Stewart's reason for being in Warrenton was two-fold, with direct orders from conflicting sources. As one of the top, most seasoned FBI agents in the Washington office, Stewart directed most investigations in the region. However, outside of his work with the FBI, he answered to another source—an old friend from his sketchy past.

Stewart's cell phone vibrated on the bar counter. He snatched it up and assessed the caller ID. This was a call he could not afford to ignore. He squeezed his way through the crowded bar area and into a semi-quiet hallway leading to the restrooms.

"I've been waiting to hear from you all day," Stewart answered the phone without so much as a friendly hello.

"Well done. Not a trace of evidence was left at the crime scene," the caller responded.

"I hope this doesn't backfire. Waters was a good agent. Are you sure we had our facts straight?"

"Yes, he was on to us," the voice answered. "I know it was tough for you. Your sacrifices will not be overlooked."

An intoxicated patron stumbled past Stewart on his way to the restroom. Stewart moved over and faced the wall to hide the conversation from other potential eavesdroppers.

Stewart asked, "Any more orders of business?"

"Nothing at this time. Keep your head down and lay low for a while. We'll touch base when everything dies down. I think we're in the clear now."

"Sounds good."

"Take care of yourself," the caller responded.

The line went dead.

Stewart exhaled slowly and walked into the men's room.

He stared into the dirty mirror, rigid like a soldier at attention. He was much grayer now. Years in law enforcement had been hard on his looks. Although he was far removed from the physical requirements of chasing criminals, the stress of directing investigations and keeping pace with a new generation of thugs was wearing on him.

Only a few years from retirement, he longed for days in the Caribbean, enjoying peace and quiet and a hard-earned nest egg—a nest egg supplemented by the same people the Fed spent millions of dollars trying to track down.

Had it been worth everything he had been asked to do? That was the million-dollar question that had been keeping him awake at night mulling over his choices and where he went wrong.

The previous day's mission had been a first. Stewart had never before been asked to use his gun by anyone but his FBI superiors. But he had formulated a plan to keep his hands as clean as possible, and he hadn't informed his secret paymaster of his slight change of plans. He would plan the hit, but he wouldn't pull the trigger. He had passed that duty on to someone else. Still, he had called the final shot. He had blood on his hands.

As he looked in the mirror, he pondered how he had fallen this far. Many years ago, the appeal of cash—an obscene amount of cash—had been too much to turn down. He sold his soul to a group of high-powered men. He became their mole in the FBI, running interference when necessary, and diverting attention from their illegal pursuits. He had become the man he had been trained to despise.

The stress of secrecy and a double identity had taken a toll on Stewart. He was drinking more, smoking again, and his waistline was expanding more rapidly than it should. He was in too deep, albeit in company with the rest of the operation, and there was nothing he could do to clear his conscience.

Stewart walked back to the bar and placed a generous stack of bills on the counter for Paul.

x   x   x

Jackson and Caroline had moved to two stools at the bar. Paul had them laughing hysterically at his townie stories. It was a very light atmosphere considering a man had been murdered just the day before and only a couple hundred feet from the entrance to Molly O's.

Jackson had completely lost his tie, and his unbuttoned dress shirt revealed a tanned upper chest. Caroline's blouse had opened a little as well. Intentionally.

Their chemistry was immediate. For Jackson, flirtatious banter was business as usual. For Caroline, it had been a while since she had had this kind of fun.

Caroline had loosened up considerably, probably more than she should have, and Paul kept both of their glasses filled. Jackson's tab was skyrocketing and Caroline enjoyed the generosity of her celebrity employer, John McAllister. Jackson would buy a round. Then she would follow suit and do the same, with no worry about McAllister seeing the final tab.

"So why again are you here?" Caroline asked.

"I was here to meet the guy who was murdered. He posted a job in the UVA Law newsletter, and I was supposed to have an interview this afternoon. But, you know . . ." he shrugged off.

"It's sad. Nobody seemed to know him very well. Looking around this place now you'd never guess there'd been a murder."

The Irish music had been turned up, the pool tables were occupied, and friends tried their best to shout over the other conversations and music. It was a loud, vibrant, fun-filled bar. The poor murder victim had been long forgotten.

Caroline was an accomplished woman. In her short professional career, before she took the job on the farm, she had already earned more promotions than many of her colleagues. She'd been at the top, schmoozing with the best and brightest on Wall Street. But she didn't get there by wasting time playing with boys.

Jackson's game was one she knew well. She spent several years dodging Wall Street's finest specimens. The most confident, most successful men were always the first to approach. For these entrepreneurs and innovators the thrill of victory, or being the first into unchartered territory, held the most value.

The next group in the game would wait and assess the other participants. They would strategically pick targets based on the consensus of the other men in the game. They played the popularity game. Most of these men spent had spent their careers climbing the corporate ladder in a firm. They valued the title and prestige of an old, time-tested name, and the comfort of fat salaries. Caroline called these guys "the maintainers." Always last into the game, riding the coattails of a previous generation, whether it was in business or sex.

Caroline was unabashedly attracted to the boldness of the first group. She admired their ability to seek out what they wanted and pursue it without affirmation from anyone else. These were the hot shots. They were, by far, the most successful bunch. They never played by the rules because they made the rules—the bad boys of business. Unfortunately for Caroline, they were also the bad boys of romance.

From the beginning of their conversation, Caroline placed Jackson in the first category. But there was something different about him. There was a softness, a kindness, something different in the way he handled himself. He was confident in his bearing, but he was not over the top like so many of the others Caroline encountered in her former life.

"Paul, is this a typical night?" asked Caroline.

"Not hardly. It's usually very low key. On the weekdays, we're closed down by 10 o'clock. People scatter pretty early around here. Most have early morning commutes to DC."

"Too bad the train doesn't reach this far out," she said.

"We don't want the train. We're happy here. On the weekends, the crowd's a bit larger, but most of the young folks head to the city. They'll crash with friends there and we'll see them again on the weeknights. Every once in a while, a lively group of college kids home for the weekend will come in for drinks, and that's all the excitement we want."

Paul leaned in to the two of them and continued with a wink, "We let the age requirements slide for those kids. There's not much trouble to get into around here. You know how it used to be."

Paul moved down the bar to tend to some of the other patrons.

Jackson turned to Caroline, "You mentioned earlier that you moved from Manhattan, so who do you work for down here?"

"I needed a slower life. Needed more space. There was an opportunity for a farm assistant, so I decided to give it a whirl."

"Had you ever worked on a farm before?"

"Only if you count planting flowers in my back yard with mom."

"I see. So besides the slower pace of life, and a warmer climate, what's the attraction to this little town? There's got to be more to it than just that."

Jackson was digging a little more deeply than Caroline anticipated, and asking more than she was comfortable with, but she was quick to respond.

"I have a pet project I'm working on."

"What is it?"

"Just something personal, trying to deal with a loss from the past."

"Oh, okay. Well if I can help, let me know. It looks like I'll have plenty of free time now that my only job prospect was shot down," Jackson chuckled.

"Maybe if we ever run into each other again, I'll let you in on more of the details. But don't hold your breath."

"I won't," he responded. "Not too many other reasons to come to Warrenton."

Paul came back down the bar and asked if the two were ready for another round.

"Sure thing, Pauly. Bring another," ordered Jackson.

"I don't know if I should," Caroline hesitated. "I've been here for a long time today. It may be time for me to think about heading home."

In fact, they had been chatting at the bar for more than three hours. But Caroline wasn't letting her guard down. She kept a safe lock on her emotions. As far as she was concerned, this was just a fun night out with a new friend.

Jackson, however, was back on the prowl, especially now that Samantha Crockett was out of his life. He tried to find any signals from Caroline, but she was not opening the door for a one-nighter.

Normally, Jackson would feed off of the disinterest or rejection. It egged him on even more. However, he could clearly see that Caroline had her priorities set. She mentioned more than once that she was working on a project—something personal. She was firm in her stance, and miraculously, for once, Jackson respected this.

Paul brought over two more drinks—another glass of white wine for the lady, and another whiskey and ginger ale for the sir.

"Okay, guys," Caroline proclaimed to Paul and Jackson, "this is the last one. I'm serious. I have to work in the morning."

"I've never heard of Mr. McAllister firing someone for showing up a bit late. Hell, I've never heard of him firing someone period," responded Paul.

"I'm still new," she pleaded. "I want to make a good impression."

"Don't you worry about that. From what he's told me, you're already one of his favorites. Stay and play awhile."

Either from the wine or from her slight embarrassment, Caroline's cheeks flushed bright red.

"Hey Paul, where's a cheap place to crash for the night? Something tells me I'm not making it back to Charlottesville," asked Jackson, intentionally baiting Caroline.

"Thought you'd been working on that all night," Paul said with a smile.

He clearly stomped on the Hail Mary Jackson threw out to Caroline.

An awkward silence ensued.

A tap on the shoulder startled Caroline.

"Are you 'bout ready to head home for the night?"

She turned around, startled, and was relieved to see her coworker.

"Hey, Jimmy. I guess I'm ready," she answered. "Are you my ride?"

"Wow," Jackson butted in. "Is it that easy? He didn't even buy you a drink."

Caroline gave a sympathetic laugh. Jimmy did not—just a flat stare.

Caroline introduced the two. "This is my coworker, Jimmy. He's been showing me the ropes of farm life."

"Nice to meet you," said Jimmy.

"Likewise," responded Jackson.

"John sent me to check on you," Jimmy said to Caroline. "Just checking to see if you were ready to go home. No pressure. I can come back a little later. You look like you're having a good time. Are you guys old friends from school or something?"

"Actually, we just met this afternoon," Caroline answered. "Jackson was here to meet the guy who was murdered. He found his way over here to Molly O's to drink his sorrows away."

"I'm just dying inside, can't you tell?" Jackson blurted out.

"Did you know the guy?" Jimmy asked casually, hiding his deeper concern, especially after recognizing the distillery's old ally, Agent Stewart, close by.

"Never met him. Just one phone call yesterday."

Jackson's reply eased Jimmy's concerns for the time being.

Caroline turned up the bottom of her wine glass, finishing off the last sip.

"Well, I think it's time for me to go home. It was nice meeting you, Jackson. If you're ever in town again, look me up at the McAllister farm. Jimmy here can teach you how to ride a horse."

"Sounds good," he said offering his business card under the suspicious eye of Jimmy.

"Thanks."

Jimmy and Caroline turned and left Molly O's. Jackson paid his tab and wandered to the exit. He stumbled to his old Bimmer, climbed into the backseat, and curled up under his suit jacket to sleep for the night. It was a bed that he had used many times before.

Agent Stewart had monitored most of the night's interactions from a tall, round-top table just behind the barstools.

"How did I not know Waters had solicited an assistant?" he kept asking himself.

He walked out the front door of Molly O's and pulled out his cell phone. He hesitated, and then without dialing the number, he put it back in his pocket.

Instead, he pulled a cigarette out of a fresh pack. As he placed it between his lips, he knew what he had to do. There was only one choice.

Jimmy and Caroline passed by in the old pick-up truck as Stewart climbed into his unmarked federal sedan.

12

Senator Scooter Windgate represented the Commonwealth of Virginia well during his long tenure in the United States Senate. He championed causes that reduced unemployment and provided funding for public schools, thereby improving the literacy rate among inner city schools in the Washington, DC area. However, he took the most pride in something not known to many people outside of his inner circle.

The elderly senator from Virginia was the watchman, the gatekeeper, for customers of the McAllister distillery. For nearly three decades, every new customer had been acquired through the efforts of Scooter Windgate. He had a keen ability for soliciting people who wanted to partake in the bootleg whiskey and who were trustworthy. He would court potential customers for several months before extending the invitation to participate. He performed the equivalent of a CIA background check to ensure customers were clean and could keep the operation confidential.

Of course, the bootleg whiskey operation was a fun diversion for the senator, but the distillery customers would serve a much more sinister role as they became part of a massive illegal empire.

Senator Windgate had become the gatekeeper many years before, just after he won the Senate election running as a high school history teacher. John McAllister had approached the newly elected senator and initiated his own recruitment. Each man had needs to be met through the relationship. Senator Windgate desperately needed extra cash to keep pace with the other elected officials. Starting out on a teacher's salary, he was well behind. Fundraising had been especially difficult in the early years, and the tax-free cash earned from the bootlegging eased that burden nicely.

McAllister needed to fill a void in Congress after his former gate-keeper retired. He needed a person in the middle of the action who had not yet been jaded by the political system. It was a match made in heaven for the two men. Windgate proved to be a natural, and profits soared for the McAllister distillery. Profits soared even higher once the senator initiated other illegal activities—drugs, prostitution, weapons, gambling—all behind the back of John McAllister. But, indeed, with his money.

Tonight, the senator had news to share with McAllister. It was nearly 10 p.m. when he stepped out of his luxury sedan in the McAllister driveway. Neither the teacher's salary nor the senator's salary could support such a luxury item. The millions of tax-free dollars had surely been spent to spruce up the Windgates' lifestyle.

No security detail accompanied him on this trip. His wife was out of town visiting one of their grown children and their grandchildren. Not a single person knew he was at the McAllister estate.

He walked through the moonlight, up the wide front steps onto the enormous front porch. He pulled a handkerchief from the inside of his sports coat to wipe the sweat from his forehead. The humidity was unseasonably thick for this early in the summer.

He knocked three times.

No answer.

He walked along the porch to one side of the house to look into one of the front windows. No lights were on in any of the first floor rooms. As he reached into his pocket to pull out his cell phone, it slipped out of his hands and crashed to the ground, disturbing the peaceful country night.

As the old senator stood back up, he came face to face with the camouflaged visage of one of McAllister's security guards. Catching the glint from his white teeth, the Senator relaxed a bit once he realized the guard was smiling behind all of the face paint.

"Good evening, Senator. To what do we owe this late visit?"

"I have some business to discuss with John. Is he here?"

"He is on his way back up from the caverns. He should be here momentarily. Please follow me out of this God-awful humidity."

"Thank you."

The armed guard unlocked the front door of the mansion and led Senator Windgate through the dark house back to his boss's office. The house was silent except for their footsteps on the hardwood floors. He turned on the lights and offered the old brown leather couch to the Senator.

"Please excuse me. I have to get back to my post. Mr. McAllister will be in shortly."

The guard disappeared as abruptly and quietly as he had appeared.

The senator walked over to the office's wall of fame. Pictures of the two men, much younger, were scattered on the wall and the built-in shelves. Other prominent figures of the nation's leadership were among the pictures as well. Presidents, judges, senior military officials—they were all there.

The senator's attention was drawn to a picture of John McAllister and his son, Ron, from almost two decades earlier. The elder McAllister was a much happier man back then. He had been in the process of grooming Ron to take over the family business when it all went down. Such an unfortunate event for everyone involved.

McAllister found his old friend admiring the wall of fame. He knocked softly on the opened door of the office to announce his presence before going in to shake Senator Windgate's hand.

Clearly McAllister had been hard at work in the distillery. His shirt was drenched with sweat, and his boots were dusty from the distillery floor. He plopped down into his club chair and sipped from a cold bottle of water.

"Kind of late to be working, John, don't you think? When nobody answered the door, I thought you might have already gone to bed."

"Ha. After all these years, I can still keep up with the best of them. I've always been more productive at night."

"Good for you," commended the senator. "I have to tell you, I'm slowing down. I don't know if I can keep it up. My time may have come."

"You're just tired. You run yourself silly with all of your engagements and speeches. You just need a break. You need to get your energy back so we can throw the big bash coming up. It's the release of the twenty-year batch. *Your* twenty-year batch."

"John, I *am* tired. That's why I came here tonight. I wanted you to be the first to know, besides my wife, that I'm done. I plan on announcing my resignation in the next couple of months. I'm walking away from it all. I think it's long overdue."

McAllister gathered his strength to stand and walked around the desk behind the senator. He placed a consoling hand on his friend's shoulder.

"I'm not surprised. I'm actually surprised you stayed in office this long. Why would anybody keep voting for you?"

They both shared an extended laugh.

"I guess it's truly the end of an era," continued McAllister. "There's no telling how much longer I'll be around, either. Same goes for the distillery. Without Ron, there's not an heir-apparent to the business. This may be it."

"Where is Ron these days?"

Senator Windgate was McAllister's closest confidant, and many times, McAllister leaned on Windgate to provide that fatherly support to his son when he was busy with other business. The senator took the young McAllister under his wing like a favored nephew.

"Somewhere down south," he said, wiping the sweat from his brow again. "He never tells me his exact location."

By midnight, the two old men decided to call it a night. They had hashed out the details of the guest list for the upcoming celebration. It would be their grand finale. The event of the century for the folks of Warrenton.

X   X   X

A sniper was positioned about five hundred yards behind the mansion in the hay loft of one of the horse barns. He had the crosshairs on John McAllister for the entirety of the senator's visit. During the course of his mission, the experienced assassin spotted McAllister's private security detail. They would have his location as soon as he fired a shot. No chance tonight.

He grabbed his cell phone from his combat vest. With the push of the send button, the senator's luxury sedan went up in a fiery explosion, rocking the entire estate.

13

The bright flash of light, the sudden boom, and the fireball rolling into the sky startled Caroline. Back at her cabin, she had decided to work awhile. She had too much on her mind to sleep. Her thoughts circled around endless possibilities about her father's murder.

The explosion shook her cabin walls, but she couldn't tell exactly where it had come from. She corralled Max into her bedroom where he tried to burrow under the covers. She dead bolted her front door and made sure all of the windows were locked. She thought about the events of the last two days. Something was fishy. Too much excitement for a little place like Warrenton and definitely too much excitement for this pastoral setting, miles away.

She walked back over to her desk where she had been working for a little over an hour. Caroline had transformed what had been intended as a walk-in closet into her work area. With the door closed, no one would ever suspect that she had set up a complete high-tech investigation workshop.

Taped on the walls were old clippings from newspaper articles detailing her father's murder. She recreated the crime scene where several hikers found his body in the woods, only a few miles from Caroline's cabin. She had ventured to the spot in one of her first days in the area and found the trail overgrown and abandoned. She never went back. Once was more than sufficient for her.

She kept a second laptop to store all of her investigative data. If someone suspected she was up to no good and she found herself in a dicey situation, Caroline would simply hide it, leaving only her daily computer to be searched or confiscated. She would dump the second laptop in a box and drop it through a hole in the closet floor that opened to the cabin's crawl space,

Caroline also kept a combination safe in one corner of the closet that doubled as a tabletop for her work.

Inside the safe, she stored all of her old photos and her true identity. In fact, inside the safe were more than seven sets of documents for false aliases.

On evenings like this, she would cozy up in the closet and squeeze her beanbag chair into a space two times too small for it. With the closet door closed, she was in her own world attempting to solve the murder of her father.

Max would sit at the front door while she worked. If anyone came within three hundred yards of the cabin, his howl would sound the alarm. He didn't miss a thing. Thankfully, she'd never had to heed Max's warning howl in her brief time on the property. People knew her as the new girl in town who worked as a farm assistant to Mr. McAllister, looking for a break from the big city life. That perception was exactly what Caroline wanted. She was safer that way.

It would be hours before she would finally go to sleep. Max was already tucked in under the covers at the foot of the bed, having been scared away from his guard duties. Caroline watched as the bedding moved up and down with his breathing.

She closed up shop for the night, turned out the lights, and walked over to the window. As she peeped through the closed blinds, she worried that the explosion had come from the direction of the McAllister estate. Was John okay?

She briefly thought about hopping in the Jeep and driving over to check on things. However, this didn't seem like a night to be tooling around. An unannounced visit at this hour might be unwelcome or worse, dangerous.

Her thoughts turned to Jackson. He had been in town to visit with the victim of yesterday's murder. Was he okay? She pulled out his business card but quickly slipped it back into her purse. She decided not to call.

Maybe she'd never see him again, but she hoped she would.

She walked over to her bed and pulled out the top drawer of her nightstand. In the darkness, she felt the cold metal of her pistol. That was all the comfort she needed as she climbed into bed.

Exhaustion finally got the better of her and she fell fast asleep.

She was awakened by her cell phone buzzing on the nightstand. The odd text message from Jimmy read, "Stay home tomorrow. Don't come to work."

X   X   X

Agent Stewart trailed Jimmy and Caroline from about a quarter mile behind their pick-up. With no traffic, it was the safest distance. Surely he wouldn't be spotted. Stewart recognized Jimmy from prior encounters at the McAllister home. He thought it was odd that Jimmy had been sent to give a ride to Caroline. Suspicious enough that it was worth checking out.

Stewart had no idea that Jimmy had recognized him, too.

Parked behind a clump of trees at the edge of the property, Stewart observed Caroline get out of the truck. Jimmy quickly drove away, down the winding gravel driveway, and back onto the two-lane highway. He was gone for the night.

Stewart was preparing to get out of the car and sneak over to the cabin to investigate Caroline's residence when the fireball rolled up into the black sky. He estimated it to be about five miles away, from direction of the McAllister distillery.

Stewart immediately aborted his mission and sped toward the scene.

His suspicions were confirmed when he passed the estate and noticed the smoldering frame of what had been, just a few minutes earlier, a luxury sedan. From the distant highway, he couldn't confirm if the flames had also hit the house, and he wasn't getting any closer.

Nobody needed to know he was around. It would raise too many questions. Factions within the distillery operation had already formed, and he did not need to become involved in assisting the elder McAllister. It was nothing personal. It was merely survival.

Stewart raced through the country roads he knew well. Many years of participating in the distribution of the bootleg whiskey had imprinted the back roads on his memory. It had been good for his career, too. His local knowledge had helped him catch more than one fugitive over the years.

He sped back toward the nation's capital. He would be interrogated first thing in he morning. Stewart had his own questions he wanted answered.

As he navigated I-66 to DC, his thoughts turned to the cash he had stashed away from all the years of running whiskey and keeping the Feds' attention elsewhere while the group engaged in all sorts of illegal pursuits.

He had a nice little nest egg. Recent power shifts and divided loyalties within the group now had him questioning if he would ever be able to enjoy it.

How would the agent's life come to an end? Would it be murder at the hand of another bootlegger? Incarceration? Or would he be able to live the rest of his years on a tropical island?

14

The sun had just risen over the horizon. An early morning glare reflected off the Chesapeake Bay into the bayside mansion perched on the outskirts of Annapolis, Maryland.

The Chief Justice sat at his kitchen table, sipping black coffee as the sun warmed the room. He had been there an hour and a half already. He was showered, clean-shaven, and already dressed in a fine pinstriped Italian suit. His light green paisley tie was loose around his neck. The aroma of aftershave blended with a strong coffee scent. The Chief Justice always wore his coal black hair slicked straight back. Not a scintilla of gray, just like his published opinions.

Some of the older justices sported a messy-hair look—mad professor style. However, the Chief Justice always dressed to impress. And he succeeded.

Only in his late forties, Michael Abramson had already been Chief Justice for four years. He won the support of all of his naysayers within his first year in office and now commanded respect from everyone. Known to approach the older, more experienced justices for judicial wisdom, Chief Justice Abramson was grooming himself to be the finest legal mind ever to sit on the Court.

Abramson had also proven his brilliance in another, more sinister way. He had helped concoct a scheme to ensure that John McAllister's bootleg distillery would be handed over to *his* folks. The folks who would keep the operation alive and well, long after McAllister had passed. The folks who would, once again, broaden the group's initiatives to prostitution, drugs, weapons, and more.

But his plan was much more malicious than his comrades could ever imagine.

A tanned, well-dressed man sat across from the Chief Justice at the breakfast table. He was about the same age, but his hair was mostly gray. His face had weathered from years on the run. A rough beard now covered the face of Abramson's old ally.

He had arrived at the residence under the cover of night, careful not to have been followed.

"Have you spoken with your father?" Abramson asked.

"We spoke last night. I told him that I don't approve of his new hire. He just let her come aboard without the slightest background check. I thought she had really worked on Wall Street, but I can't find record of her at any of the banks in New York. This all seems strange. My old man's getting careless in his old age. We have to end this. Now."

"That's very interesting. What else do we know about this Caroline?"

"Not much. She rents a tiny farm cabin from my father that's about five miles from the house. She doesn't have much of a social life, so I doubt anyone in town can tell us anything about her. My dad loves her like a daughter. He told me they spend hours each afternoons talking about life. He thinks he's turned into some wise old life coach."

"Poor old man. It almost sounds like he wants to give up the business."

"I don't know. That distillery has been in the family for quite some time. I don't think he'd just give it up like that—and certainly not with a chance that the authorities may catch him. There are some major repercussions if that happens."

"Don't act like I don't know that. If anything happens and my name is linked to it, this scandal will rock the nation to its core. That's why we must take control. I let him play me like a fool once before when we were almost exposed. I won't let it happen again. If it weren't for us, there's no telling what could have resulted from that incident."

"We should've been running this operation a long time ago."

"It's in the works," Abramson responded. "I'm waiting to hear back from Stewart."

"Good 'ole Agent Willie? I always liked him."

The Chief Justice stood up from the table and walked over to the counter for another cup of coffee.

"Now that you're here, what do you plan on doing while we wait for everything to fall in place?" Abramson asked.

The other man also stood up from the table and walked over to the coffee pot for his own warm up. He patted the Chief Justice on the back.

"I need to pay a visit to our old source, the man who knows everything about the little town."

The Chief Justice smiled.

"Paul is always reliable. He's privy to the best information around, and he's a decent bartender, too."

"He'd be the one to know something about our mystery girl. I'll wait for him after closing time tonight. But first, I need some sleep."

The man picked up his travel bag off the kitchen counter and went down to Abramson's basement. Ron McAllister was back in town.

Abramson glanced down at his quiet cell phone. There was still no word from Agent Stewart. This was very uncharacteristic of his long-time FBI mole. Abramson was on edge. He needed confirmation that everything was going as planned.

He tried to turn his attention to the day ahead. A morning of meetings with the clerk staff awaited him at the office. There were no pressing oral arguments for which to prepare, so he focused his efforts on penning a scathing dissent directed at the traditional and outdated views of a few select senior brethren. It would be much later that night before he had the chance to circle back with Stewart.

Chief Justice Abramson's cell phone chirped. The caller ID showed an unsaved phone number. But he knew the digits well. It was his other hired help—a dirty, former black ops soldier without a trace of a conscience.

"Mission unsuccessful," the man offered, before the judge had a chance to even say hello.

The irate judge slammed his fist onto the kitchen counter. That could only mean that the Senator Windgate was still alive.

"Hello," said Abramson trying to mask his anger.

"Sir," said the hired assassin. "There wasn't a clear window for the blast last night. I destroyed the car as the target was trying to leave.

Unfortunately, I wasn't able to take a shot at the target either. We underestimated McAllister's security."

"Were there any other victims?" Abramson wondered aloud.

"I can't confirm. I didn't have the opportunity to check for a body. The place was crawling with guards. I can tell you that the car was completely destroyed."

"Thank you for the update. Stand by for additional assignments."

"Yes, sir," replied the assassin, ending the call.

Abramson dialed Agent Stewart again. Still no answer.

15

Jackson woke to tapping on the backseat window early the next morning. He could barely make out the police officer backlit in the sunrise haze. His gritty eyes from the night before didn't help.

"Young man, it's time to get moving. We've had some calls about a possible dead body in this car. Glad you were only sleeping," the officer said through the slightly opened window.

"Sorry," Jackson muttered. "I'm on my way."

The officer nodded and walked back to his cruiser parked behind Jackson's old Bimmer.

Jackson got out of the car to stretch his back and legs. He had slept in the fetal position all night. He was a bit too tall to be sleeping in the back of cars.

Settling into the driver's seat, he collected his cell phone from the center console. Three messages. Why were these people up so early? The first was from his roommate in Charlottesville asking that he forward any mail out to the West Coast for the summer. The second was from his former business partner and caddie, Jeff Barber, advising on the betting lines for that day's games. The third missed call was from Caroline.

She said she was checking to make sure he had made it home safely. There was a weird, random explosion late last night, she continued, and she was worried that it may have had something to do with Philip Waters. Recent happenings in the small town were becoming really strange.

Thrilled that Caroline had already called, Jackson started his car and began the drive back to Charlottesville. Whether it was genuine concern or merely a reason to say hello once more, it encouraged him. He dialed her number and waited while the phone rang.

"Hello," Caroline answered.

"Hi there. I just saw that I missed your call."

"Thank goodness you're okay. I got worried last night after I heard a big explosion. I thought it might've had something to do with the murder."

"I'm fine. I slept in my car last night, so I'm just now heading back to Charlottesville."

"Seriously, you slept in your car?"

That wasn't the response she expected.

"Yep. I've done it many times before. Better than a wreck or going to jail."

"I guess. Hold on a sec. Someone is calling on the other line."

Caroline clicked over. "Hello?"

"Caroline, I just wanted to make sure you got the message that you don't need to come to work today," said John McAllister.

"I got the message from Jimmy when I woke up. Is everything okay over there? I don't want to overstep my bounds, but what was that terrible boom last night?"

"Everything is fine. We just got a little careless with the fireworks," he lied. "We'll clean it up today and you'll never know anything happened when you come in tomorrow."

"Are you sure? I can come over and help."

"That's not necessary. We've got it covered," McAllister insisted.

"Okay, call if you need me."

"Have a great day, Caroline."

Caroline switched back over to see if Jackson was still there.

"Are you there?" she asked.

"I'm here. What's up?"

"That was my boss. Apparently, the explosion came from his house. They told me not to come to work today while they cleaned it up. Weird—I thought that's why they hired me."

"Yeah, isn't cleaning up in the job description for a farm assistant?

Oh wait, I guess they think a girl can't do it. Can't do the heavy lifting," he teased.

Caroline didn't respond. She just let him hang for a few seconds in silence.

Jackson quickly changed his direction.

"So what's on the docket today? You want to grab lunch back at Molly O's?"

Caroline hesitated. She really needed the extra time off to catch up with her work on her father's murder. But a brief lunch outing wouldn't take away from her time. It would be a nice break in the middle of the day.

"Okay. I can do that. What are you going to do in the meantime?"

"I need to find a place to shower. I smell terrible."

Without thinking, and before she could take it back, Caroline responded, "You're more than welcome to clean up here."

"Thanks. I'll take you up on that."

Caroline regretted her offer to Jackson as soon as it left her lips. She had no idea who she was bringing into her home. She knew nothing about this guy. No one else had ever been invited into her little cabin, not even John McAllister or Jimmy. Her mother had never even been out to visit.

She reluctantly gave Jackson directions, estimating he'd arrive in fifteen minutes.

It was still pretty early in the morning. What would they do until lunch? What if they didn't get along, despite their chemistry from the night before? She needed to read a few articles about the murder again. Would she have time?

She started scrambling to make sure her office was in order. Had she been careless? Were there clues to her true identity and project left out in the open?

Caroline scanned the small living quarters; everything looked to be in order. She went outside to play fetch with Max. It would help expend some of her anxiety while she awaited Jackson's arrival.

Jackson easily found the farm entrance, and turned down the gravel drive toward the stand of trees that shaded Caroline's rustic house. Caroline was swaying in the hanging swing when he got out of the car.

"You look awful," she said.

"Thanks," he quipped. "I told you I needed a shower."

Max greeted Jackson warmly, balancing on his hind legs and extending his front paws outward, as if to embrace him. Jackson side-stepped the dog's gesture, sending Max scrambling. He recovered, and his slobbery tongue quickly found Jackson's left hand.

"So this is the lovely abode. It's not much, but I'm happy here," Caroline said.

"You weren't lying. It's a lot smaller than I expected. But you have a lot of land. Is this all yours?"

"No, it's John McAllister's. But all this land does belong to this little shack."

She led Jackson around the corner to show him the expansive vista behind the house.

"Follow me," she said, leading him to the door. "I'll show you were you can clean up."

She steered him through the living room toward the only bathroom. The ancient wooden floors creaked with each step they took. Max followed closely behind wagging his tail, happy to have someone new around.

Jackson was almost through the living room when he spotted the football poster.

"Notre Dame, huh?"

"Yeah, I'm a Domer, through and through. I spent four amazing years there. Wish I could go back and visit more than I'm able to."

"That's funny. I was just there a couple of days ago."

"Really? Why?"

"Oh, I was dating a girl in law school there."

"*Was*, as in past tense?" she asked.

Jackson wanted to move past the subject and take a shower. He immediately regretted ever mentioning anything about visiting Notre Dame. But so did Caroline. Had this little detail of her personal history open the door to more questions about her past?

"It's over," he sighed. "No big deal."

But, it was a big deal. Jackson was surprised at how much he already missed Samantha.

Changing the subject, he asked, "Does this place have hot water?"

"It has very hot water, but be quick. It turns icy cold in about three minutes."

Jackson closed the bathroom door behind him. Caroline prepared a pot of coffee, then ushered Max outside.

She was drawn to Jackson, even though she barely knew him. There was a warmth about him, a kindness. He tried to hide it, but it was evident that he was a good guy. It was too early to tell what kind of feelings she could develop for the handsome law student, but her instincts told her he was harmless to her plan.

16

The smoke and flames from the car bomb had blackened the magnificent white façade of the McAllister mansion. Luckily, there was no structural damage. With a few coats of white paint no one would be able to tell the difference.

The charred spot on the driveway needed only a power wash and new blacktop coating. The destroyed shrubs could be easily and quickly replaced. Still, poor Jimmy had his work cut out for him—he was under strict orders to complete the cleanup in twenty-four hours.

Inside the mansion, Senator Windgate hung up with his wife after giving her a recap of the events from the previous night. She was relieved he was alive, but also alarmed that someone would want her husband dead. He had done so much for his community and country.

Mrs. Windgate was aware of the growing tensions among the members of the McAllister ring. She was one of the few wives who was privy to the illegal activity. She worried that it was coming back to haunt them sooner than she had expected.

"John, what's next?" asked the senator.

"We'll have the house repaired and fixed up shortly. Nobody will be able to tell what happened. The fire inspector is sending a team of investigators to check out the cause of the explosion later this morning."

"That's not necessary. The cause is pretty obvious to me."

"Yeah, but we have to appease the authorities. Besides, your car, or what was left of it, has already been taken away by my workers. It will never be found. There will never be any evidence of a car bomb. By the time they get here, the front of the house will have a new coat of paint on it."

"Nothing says tampering with physical evidence like the smell of fresh paint," the senator chuckled.

McAllister responded, "The fire chief is a close friend of mine. He installed the anti-fire system downstairs in the caverns. He'll report whatever we tell him to report."

"That's a relief. Do you think this is related to my official duties as a senator, or as a member of the McAllister distillery?"

"Did anyone else know you were visiting last night?"

Senator Windgate thought for a moment, and then responded, "I remember having the feeling that someone was following me yesterday, but I don't know who."

"Other than your wife, does anyone else know you're here right now? The last thing we need is for news vans to start showing up reporting an explosion, or an attempted assassination of a senator."

"Nobody else—just whoever tried to kill me."

Senator Windgate was in unsurprisingly good humor. He always was. From what those two old men had accomplished in life, they couldn't help but scoff at death. They had defied the odds for a long, long time.

"I think we should be fine for now. My security staff is on high alert. They have the property covered, and nobody is coming through that front gate without my approval. Whoever did this probably doesn't want a lot of publicity either. If they wanted your life, they had plenty of other opportunities. I'm not convinced that they weren't after the both of us."

McAllister pondered this while taking a peak out the front window from the formal dining room. Jimmy was already painting and several members of the security team were positioned along the front gate.

McAllister continued, "That suspicion makes me fear that it may be a threat from the inside of our little operation."

The senator didn't respond. He was thinking, too, trying to determine what enemies he had made throughout his career. Both men knew their enemies were numerous, but most had been dealt with over the years.

The fire chief came and went without incident. Although Senator

Windgate could not hear the intricacies of the conversation, the chief routinely nodded, agreeing with almost every word McAllister spoke. The small investigation team left as quickly as they appeared, having just barely glanced at the front of the house. Warrenton was full of allies for John McAllister and his cohorts.

The bootlegger walked back into the mansion, smiling.

"There won't even be an incident report filed. The good thing about being this far out in the country is that the fire department received only one phone call. Nobody even noticed."

"Excellent."

"Now we have to figure out how to get you back home," McAllister said with a sly grin. Let's take the old Aston Martin."

He chauffeured the senator home to his Georgetown row house. He kept his home in Richmond, but he and his wife spent most of their time in the thick of the political landscape.

Mrs. Windgate greeted the two gentlemen at the door as they pulled up. She had rushed home early that morning after hearing about the events from her husband.

"Scooter, I'll give you a call real soon. The twenty-year release party must still go on as planned. But first, we need to sit down and comb through the guest list to see if we've missed anything. Any *enemies*," McAllister added with emphasis.

"Have a safe drive back," replied Senator Windgate.

"You be safe, too. Let me know if you see anything out of the ordinary."

He had the top down on the antique convertible Aston Martin. The perfectly waxed white car glinted in the sun. His grey hair flew back in the wind as he accelerated down M Street past the shops and offices in the District.

He was headed downtown with one thing on his mind.

McAllister drove down the long, wide stretch of Constitution Avenue, passing the Natural History Museum and National Gallery of Art. He was headed toward the United States Capitol, where many of his customers spent their days name-calling and jockeying for status in high school popularity games. He knew it was a sad state of affairs, but his clientele kept the cash coming in and he sent the whiskey straight back to them. The exchange was fun and harmless, and encouraged his constituents to keep authorities off the trail of their other secrets.

He knew his wasn't the best whiskey ever, but it was better than most, especially from the small batch selection. More so than the taste, the customers reveled in the thrill of participating in the old tradition and visiting the speakeasy under the mansion.

McAllister continued down Constitution Avenue until he had passed the Capitol on his right. Security guards waved him on, gesturing to him to move along, as he slowed to get a good look at the building behind the Capitol—The United States Supreme Court.

Inside that building, the hallowed halls of American justice, presided one of the most cruel and evil men he had ever encountered. Fortunately, the American people had only seen remarkable judicial equanimity from the Chief Justice Abramson, not the evil side shown to those who knew him well.

Security and Capitol Police approached the Aston Martin, but before they could sternly move him along, McAllister waved and drove on. He needed to get back to the farm.

A shipment of corn for the new mash was due to arrive after dark from a local supplier one county away. Preparations must be made for storage space in the cavern still room. Rye and wheat had been inconspicuously delivered in the middle of the night the week before, so no one would happen upon the farm during unloading.

During his drive back to Warrenton, Chief Justice Abramson was still on the old man's mind. He was now a senior member of the group, brought into the ring at an early age. A cocky college student at Yale, he had finagled his way into the bootleg operation through his friendship with Ron. The other members of the group were hesitant to allow the young student on board at first, but they soon welcomed him with open arms as he demonstrated the reach of his network of young judicial clerks and Capitol Hill insiders.

Could it be that this evil man, who had worked his way into arguably the most influential position in American jurisprudence, was now more than a disliked member of the operation? Was he looking to sabotage McAllister's place? Did he want control of the operation? Had he involved other members in his coup?

Friction between him and Abramson had been obvious within the dealings of the distillery over the past few years. However, most issues focused around minor disagreements, such as how much hush money to pay their suppliers. But McAllister always called the shots.

Occasionally, small skirmishes ensued, but why would someone want to kill him? Or Senator Windgate? No matter how much he wanted to find another reason, each scenario led back to Michael Abramson.

17

A much cleaner, fresher Jackson emerged onto the porch. His wet, wavy hair was combed nicely to one side. He walked barefoot and shirtless to the trunk of his car, where he scavenged around a set of old golf clubs for his duffle bag. He always kept a fresh change of clothes in the trunk in case of emergency—usually a hot date.

He had a much more muscular torso than could be discerned through his clothing. His broad shoulders led to sculpted, athletic arms. His abs were tanned and carved into a six pack. Caroline blushed as she tried not to stare at Jackson.

"I was wondering if I would be looking at you all day in your wrinkled suit," she said.

"These *are* pretty rough looking aren't they? Thankfully, I've got some extra clothes. I just hope I still have a stick of deodorant in the bag."

"Me too," she teased.

He pulled out a neatly folded white polo, khaki shorts, and flip flops. Max followed him as he headed inside to change.

"Is that your Jeep?" he asked when he returned.

"Yeah. I bought it a few weeks ago from some farmer a couple miles away. Unfortunately, there's no top, so I have no idea what I'll do if it rains," she laughed.

"Can we take it in to town for lunch? I'm starving, and I don't think it's supposed to rain anytime soon."

"Sure. I'll take you for a ride in it."

She locked up the house and the two drove into downtown.

To their surprise, Molly O's was much quieter than the previous day. They found their way to the bar where, sure enough, Paul was tending again. They took the first two stools.

"Where'd everybody go?" asked Jackson.

"Well, look who's back for another day," Paul replied. "Everybody has returned to business as usual. Excitement dies down pretty quickly around this town. A few cops were in here just before you got here. Not too many of them still hanging around town. They're wrapping up their murder investigation pretty quickly, but who knows if they'll ever find out who did it."

Caroline thought Paul would mention the big explosion from the night before. Surprisingly, no one seemed to know anything about it.

Paul brought a couple of waters and lunch menus.

"Jimmy stopped by first thing in the morning today. He said we'd probably see you again—told us you had the day off."

"Word travels fast around here," she replied. "I'm glad to see the town is keeping tabs on my life."

"Sounds like you're missing out on some hard labor. He stocked the back of his truck full of paint canisters across the street at the hardware store."

"Really? That's strange. I hadn't heard any plans about painting this week," Caroline said, puzzled. "I talked to Mr. McAllister early this morning, and he said they got a little careless with fireworks last night. They must've done some damage."

Jimmy had disclosed the car bomb story to Paul when he dropped in that morning. Paul had been instructed to see if Caroline had any suspicions about the explosion, or if she had settled for the firework story.

"You know those old guys. They have too much fun sometimes," he said, trying to entice her feedback.

When she didn't bite, Paul walked back into the kitchen to collect the food order for another customer.

Caroline turned her attention to Jackson.

"So, tell me about Jackson Cole. I know that you go to UVA for law school, but where did you go for college?"

"I went to Tulane in New Orleans, before the hurricane hit. I played golf there before they dropped the program."

"Do you still play?"

"I try to play as much as I can, but it's tough to find the time during the school year."

"My dad used to golf all the time."

"Did he teach you how to play?"

"He never had the chance." Caroline paused and thought long and hard about her words before she continued. "He passed away when I was very young."

There was no need to bring anybody into her investigation of his murder. She had already decided not to pursue speaking with the local law enforcement agencies and their cold case squads in the area.

"I'm sorry to hear that."

"It's okay. It was a long time ago," she deflected.

She was still torn up inside. She lived with the pain like it happened yesterday. But that's what motivated her.

"What about your parents? I'm sure they're very proud of you for attending one of the top law schools in the country," Caroline said.

"Actually, they both passed away as well. Cancer took my mother. It was tough watching her pain and suffering as she withered away to nothing. It was not a merciful death."

"I'm so sorry. That must have been horrible," she offered.

"It was a very difficult time. I went away to college and left my dad by himself back home. I guess it was too much for him to handle. He overdosed on sleeping pills one night."

Caroline gasped and grabbed his arm, displaying her genuine sympathy.

Jackson continued, "I don't know if it was accidental or intentional. I don't even know if that's something I want to know. Losing both parents in less than two years was brutal."

"Okay. Let's change the subject and talk about something cheerful. Enough about pain and death."

"I agree."

They exchanged warm, if awkward smiles.

Back in the kitchen, Paul was tucked into a quiet corner making a call on his cell phone.

He whispered in a low voice, "She's clean. She hasn't said anything to make me think she was involved with the explosion."

"That's a relief. John has really taken a liking to her," Jimmy said on the other end.

McAllister had ordered Jimmy to have Paul check out Caroline. Even though he thought very highly of the young woman, he was on high alert about his safety and any threats to his operation. He prayed that he had not been blinded by her kindness and beauty, allowing her to infiltrate his operation.

"I don't think she had anything to do with the car bomb."

"Thanks, Paul. Let us know if you hear anything suspicious."

"Yes, sir. But there hasn't been anything said about it today. Nobody heard anything. You guys live too far out in the boonies."

"Keep us updated with any developments. Thanks again."

Paul hung up the phone and returned to the bar, now crowded with several other patrons.

Caroline asked Jackson, "So now what's your plan for summer?"

"I just talked to an old buddy of mine who lives in Kentucky. I think I'll go visit him, bet on the horses, and play a little golf," he responded. "He used to caddie for me back when I tried my hand at professional golf."

"That sounds fun. I've never been to a horse race before."

"You should come with us. Come for the weekend. You'll be back in time for work next Monday. Besides, how can you work on a horse farm and never have been to the races?"

"I don't think you realize what kind of horses we have. They aren't young, agile thoroughbreds. They're all retired steeplechasers. For most of them, a slow amble is the most they can muster these days. Oh, and maybe kicking at the farm dogs."

"Either way, you should come."

Paul delivered two sandwiches to Jackson and Caroline.

"What's your plan for the afternoon?" Paul asked the pair as he topped off their waters.

Jackson responded first.

"I'm heading back home. I need to clean the apartment and pack a few things for a trip this weekend."

Caroline then chimed in.

"I think I'll go for a hike with my dog in the woods around my house."

"You kids have fun," Paul said as he placed separate bills in front of them. They paid separately.

They walked out of Molly O's into the hot afternoon sun and hopped in the old CJ7. Any bare skin stuck to the sunbaked leather seats, but the breeze through the open top would soon provide a nice relief from the heat.

Max greeted them exuberantly, his leash already in his mouth, when Caroline pulled the Jeep into her driveway.

"He must have heard you from the restaurant," said Jackson.

"He's got good ears," she joked patting the black lab on the head.

"You don't need your leash out here on the farm," she said to Max.

Jackson extended his hand. "It was a pleasure getting to know you these last two days. Let me know if you want to come along to the horse races this weekend. You have my number now."

"Don't get your hopes up. I'm looking forward to getting some work done on my project."

"Oh yeah, you never told me what you're working on," he said, trying to pry it out of her again.

"Just a little research." She smiled as she shook his hand.

X   X   X

Jackson steered the Bimmer down the windy, gravel driveway back toward the country highway. When he hit the pavement, he cranked up the radio and headed home to his apartment in Charlottesville.

After Jackson left, Caroline suddenly felt like she was being watched. It was eerie and disconcerting. Before going inside, she called Max to her side and walked the perimeter of the cabin, looking out into the surrounding fields and woods for anything unusual. The feeling passed, and she went inside to change into her hiking clothes before venturing into the woods.

Agent Stewart peered through his binoculars from a concealed spot in the woods. Early that morning, he had decided to investigate the girl and her connection with John McAllister. Especially after hearing the mysterious explosion. He was beginning to question whether he was the only person being coerced into helping Justice Abramson's cause.

Stewart felt a compelling need to uncover the story behind Caroline Mills. It would help him understand the situation in which he found himself. Things didn't add up with her. And Agent Stewart knew a con artist when he saw one.

There were too many unanswered questions. And the truth would be too difficult for him to find hiding in the trees.

18

Jimmy enlisted the assistance of several members of the McAllister security detail. They power washed the driveway and coated it with a fresh layer of tar and blacktop. The charred, ruined shrubs had already been dug out and loaded into the back of a truck to be mulched. The repair work to the house finally got underway in the afternoon.

The day had been uneventful from a security standpoint. The inspectors from the fire department came and went without incident. Only a few familiar cars had passed by the front gates on the old country road.

John McAllister found Jimmy in the distillery's main ballroom, typically reserved for entertaining. The raised stage was a permanent fixture at the end of the room, as was the wet bar along the front wall. The velvet curtains had been taken down from behind the barrel racks, exposing the cave's bare rock walls.

The empty room was much colder now that it was not bustling with activity. No need for air conditioning in the caves. The distillery maintained a comfortable temperature year round, providing a nice cool relief in the smoldering summers and a warm retreat in the winters—not to mention a perfect temperature for aging whiskey.

Jimmy noticed his boss in the dark hallway, emerging from the wooded entrance.

"What time is the corn scheduled to arrive?"

"It should get here just after dark. Thanks for your help today getting the house back in shape," McAllister responded.

"No problem. How 'bout a little pay raise for my efforts?" he joked.

Jimmy knew he would be taken care of financially. In his five years with the McAllister distillery he had netted nearly a million dollars in under-the-table cash payments. And no one would suspect anything, given his one bedroom apartment and old pickup truck.

"You're always vying for extra cash," John chuckled. "If you really want to get paid, figure out who did this."

"I'm guessing you and the senator didn't make any progress on that front?"

"No. But I have a strong suspicion that it was a job from within the distillery group."

"I talked to Paul earlier. He said Caroline checks out. She's clean as far as he's concerned," Jimmy gladly reported.

He knew this would cheer up McAllister and ease any concerns the old man may have developed about Caroline.

"I knew she was fine. I had Paul feel out her story to make the others happy. You'd be surprised at the backlash I received from some of the members about hiring Caroline. They don't trust her."

It was true. She would be the first one investigated for having anything to do with this. And rightfully so. She was obviously the most recent addition to the farm, if not the actual distillery operation.

McAllister pulled over a stool and rested his old legs. He ordered Jimmy to stop working.

"Jimmy, you know I had a son. People think we've been estranged for years, and while that's a not a bad description of our relationship, I actually speak to him regularly." He paused before continuing, "We spoke just a couple of days ago."

"I'm listening." Jimmy removed his beat up ball cap and took a seat on an emptied out whiskey barrel.

"The funny thing is—he seemed different last time. He questioned my hiring Caroline and seemed furious that someone new had been brought on to work so close to the operation. I emphasized that she didn't have access to any information and knew nothing about the distillery, or any business dealings for that matter."

"Maybe he's just trying to watch out for you—and the group. He probably thinks he'll be taking over the business one day."

"No way. His best friend is Michael Abramson. You know, the Chief Justice. Those two work up some nasty plans sometimes, and without seeking approval from any of us."

"Well, that sounds like a problem. You and Senator Windgate need to rein them in. It's not their business."

"Yes, I know," McAllister wearily conceded.

He reached over and grabbed the extra broom propped in the nearest corner.

"I've been working a couple of hours to prepare a spot for the corn. I figure we can put the bins here before we cart it into the other rooms," said Jimmy.

"Good idea. But I'm thinking about having the group over this weekend. If last night's incident was due to our infighting, we have to get to the bottom of that soon. Can we have the corn cleared out by then?"

"Sure thing, boss."

McAllister had rested enough. Although slowing down in recent years, he loved to work. He and Jimmy finished sweeping the floor and clearing space in the large room to receive the shipment.

This shipment was coming from the distillery's regular supplier. The owner of a farm one county west and his three young adult sons always delivered the shipments of corn when it was their turn in the rotation. They were a vital part of the operation.

It seemed like everyone within a twenty-mile radius, and three generations, was in on the secret. Hopefully, future generations would be able to take part in it as well. While the operation was a longstanding tradition now, and in little danger from local law enforcement, the members still took precautions and played the roles as if they were in the midst of Prohibition.

They finished sweeping clear a spot for the corn, then ventured into one of the back chambers of the cavern, well behind the still room.

Jimmy flipped the light switch to reveal three immense, 400-gallon stainless steel vats positioned against the long, narrow chamber wall. One of the vats was filled to capacity with sour mash, ultimately to be used in the distillation process.

McAllister stuck his finger in the middle vat and tasted the sour mash.

"Almost ready," he commented. "See the bubbling?"

"You're spot on, as usual," replied Jimmy as he sampled a finger full as well.

McAllister had been the master distiller since he had taken over the business from his father. He was as seasoned as any commercial distiller in the industry. Frankly, he was probably better than most.

"The mill is primed and ready to roll once the grains come in," Jimmy said as he walked toward the entrance into another room.

"Everything seems to be falling into place to produce the next batch."

Two of the operation's maintenance staff were performing some last minute maintenance on the enormous open cooker where the ground grains were cooked into sour mash. It had been out of commission since the last batch was cooked. The crew was working diligently to get it back into working order.

"Will we be ready by week's end?" John asked.

One of the maintenance workers responded, "Mr. McAllister, this will be ready in fifteen minutes."

A broad smile lit up McAllister's face. Whiskey making was his passion and his tools were back up. The distilling process, from grain delivery to bottling, created a frenzy around the farm, and the old man fed off of the energy. It was one of the only things in life that still made him feel youthful.

A sharp buzz on the speaker system preceded a male voice announcing the arrival of the corn. The McAllister distillery was gearing up, drowning out any worries resulting from the previous night's events—to the group's detriment.

19

Before heading out onto the vast property for her hike, Caroline retrieved her most valuable possession from the safe in her closet. She placed the black leather-bound mini portfolio into the back waistline of her running shorts. After a quick check to make sure it was secured, she locked up the old cabin and set off on her adventure.

Any traces of fear of being watched or stalked escaped her mind.

Max eagerly set the pace for the two as he sprinted into the fields and ran circles around Caroline. It wouldn't be long before Max would wear down and walk steadily by her side.

They reached the outer property line about twenty minutes after leaving the cabin. It was another wooded area with a small stream running through. Caroline pushed back the brush and followed a narrow path a few yards down to the stream.

Max made a beeline for the cool water. After quenching his thirst he splashed into a shallow pool to cool himself. He then made his way to a sunny, grassy spot close to where Caroline was sitting.

The only sounds were natural: the burbling water, and the rustling of leaves as little forest animals played among the underbrush.

This was her favorite spot, the far reaches of her rented property, away from any distractions. No cell phones, no computers, no visitors. She meditated and analyzed fact after fact of her father's murder. She replayed every possible scenario more times than she could remember, and yet she continued to come up short.

Clues to the murder had brought her to the area—to the outermost suburbs of the nation's capital—but she didn't have enough. The case went cold at the location where the bullet-riddled body of her father had been found with eleven holes in what was left of his chest.

Just as she had done for the past few weeks, she pulled out her portfolio and stared blankly at her notes. Today she began crying.

Caroline was defeated. The move to Virginia was not as fruitful as she had hoped, at least in solving her father's murder.

A couple days earlier, she considered broaching the subject with her boss. He was the ultimate source of knowledge about any and all events in the area, past and present. Surely, he would remember something about the crime, or be able to at least point her in the right direction.

Of course, that would force her to reveal her true identity to John McAllister. It would destroy the trust she had already built with him. She would probably lose her job. And how would she conceal the other secrets from her past life? Even worse, what if he had been involved somehow?

Two photographs dropped from the portfolio onto the ground. One picture was her father's headshot. The other was an old family photo of her, her mother, and her father, taken when she was about four years old.

Caroline reached for the fallen pictures. The flush of exercise in her cheeks paled as she noticed a pile of cigarette butts next to the rock where she sat.

Her gaze followed the trail of cigarette butts and large boot prints that ran adjacent to the stream.

Her heart raced and nausea quickly set in. An unspent .308 cartridge lay just beyond the stream. From her experience, she knew this was undoubtedly from a sniper rifle.

Someone had been here. And not that long ago. Someone was probably watching her work the cold murder case, realizing she was the daughter of the slain man. Someone with ties to the crime, motivation to keep the true story covered.

Her breathing became shallow. Beads of sweat were forming on her brow and her palms were getting clammy. Her knees grew weak as she fought the urge to pass out. A drop of sweat fell from her forehead and onto the photo.

The sound of sudden movement and crackling of twigs in the brush behind her stopped her heart. Her stomach dropped. It was over. She was about to meet the same fate as her father.

She slowly turned her head, swallowing hard the lump in her throat.

He was staring into her eyes, not more than a foot from her sweat drenched brow, tail wagging, chewing on an empty pack of cigarettes.

Tears once again poured down her cheeks as she realized it had only been Max behind her. She hugged his hot, furry neck and took a couple of minutes to compose herself. She needed to collect her thoughts and digest what she had just discovered.

Two thoughts raced through her mind. First: she was completely isolated from civilization. She had forgotten to bring her phone, and she was at least twenty minutes from the cabin. Fifteen, if she sprinted. On the other hand, she desperately wanted—needed—to find out where the tracks led and to whom they belonged.

"I don't know what to do," she said to Max.

He was already thirty feet or so down the stream, tracking the boot prints as the led away from the cabin.

"Max, come back here! Stop," she commanded.

A quick pause to look back to his master and his nose hit the dirt once again. Max was on a mission.

Caroline regrouped, took in several deep breaths, and rose from the rock. She glanced around her surroundings to get her bearings. It did not seem like anyone was nearby. Surely Max would have sniffed them out by now.

She tucked her small portfolio back into her waistband.

Caroline had made it this far. There was no way she was turning back now. Her confidence was slowly coming back.

She tried to convince herself it could have been some random hiker traveling through the back of her property. But deep down, she was fully aware that it was more sinister than that. She could feel it in her bones. Someone had been watching her, and she had more than one secret to hide.

Caroline decided to take the fight to them. She was not backing down, not now.

"This might be the end, but there's no better way to go out," she reassured herself confidently as she followed Max down the tracks.

After walking nearly a half-mile, she had traced the outskirts of her property. She followed the trail along the stream and then cut across a small open meadow before entering into another wooded area.

Luckily, the tracks were still evident to Max, if not visible to Caroline. When they disappeared earlier in the trek, Max was able to keep the trail. He was a good sleuth.

She found herself only a few yards from the country road when the tracks stopped. She was now in the front corner of her property, a few hundred yards from the entry to her gravel driveway. She found tire marks beneath her feet. Someone must have parked a car in the bushes, under cover, and hiked to the back of the property line. The chances of that person being a random hiker were dwindling rapidly. The tires were those of a car, smaller than anything that would be on an SUV.

She kneeled next to the panting dog and surveyed the scene. Other than the tracks, everything seemed to be normal. There was no physical evidence except for the cigarettes.

She was more alert than ever as she hiked back to the cabin. It was untouched. If someone had watched her leave earlier, they failed to take advantage of her absence to search the cabin. Per her plan, she had left nothing of value in plain sight, other than her generic laptop. Everything related to the case was securely locked away inside the safe inside her locked closet. Even if the safe had been discovered, nobody would ever be able to break in to it, let alone move it. It was anchored into the earth beneath the cabin. Her secrets should be safe.

It was late in the afternoon, nearly dinnertime, when she slumped into the couch. She picked up her cell phone to dial the only friend she could trust, even though she'd known him for less than a week.

"Hello," Jackson answered.

"I was just checking to make sure you made it back safely."

"It's an easy trip. I've been home a few hours. Just packing up some things to take to Kentucky for the weekend. You're still welcome to join us."

"It's still unlikely, but when are you leaving?"

"Sometime tomorrow afternoon," he said. "Are you going back to work tomorrow?"

"I am. It will get me busy again. For some reason, I've been kind of paranoid today."

"How so?" Jackson asked.

Caroline hesitated at first, but then divulged a little of her story.

"I don't know whether it's the recent murder or what, but I keep feeling like someone is watching me."

"It's probably just nerves. It's not every day that someone is murdered in a small town. At least you weren't connected to the victim, like me."

"That's true. It's probably nothing." She decided it wasn't important to discuss finding the cigarettes and tire tracks, so she changed the subject. "Have fun this weekend."

"Thanks. Take care."

With her mind racing through all the possibilities, she locked herself in her work closet for the remainder of the night, sifting through the facts, trying to identify any leads whatsoever—about her father and the unknown smoker.

X X X

Agent Will Stewart reclined in a plush leather chair in his home office, puffing on a cigar, thinking about the photographs of her cabin laid out on his desk.

His instincts screamed to him that something was amiss about Caroline. Stewart trusted his keen instincts, which had guided him up the federal ranks rapidly. It was that same awareness and critical thinking that had guarded the distillery from potential threats over the years.

All he had was her first name, and that bothered him. He had no clues and no trace of anything outside of her few months in Warrenton. She was a mystery girl. And she was toying with the wrong organization, knowingly or unknowingly.

On the other hand, Stewart had every piece of information he could ever want about Jackson Cole: former collegiate golfer, entrepreneur, law student, past residences, former girlfriends, family history, arrest record. Literally, everything Stewart could ever want was at his fingertips. Unfortunately for Jackson, Stewart had no way of knowing if the murdered Philip Waters had disclosed any of his findings to him.

Stewart's suspicions were further aroused when he hacked into Waters's computer and found an email draft addressed to his supervisor outlining his findings on the case. Names had been named, including Stewart himself. The agent feared that the whistle had already been blown.

With the infighting and turmoil among members of the distillery group, internal controls had become too tenuous, prompting Stewart to take inventory of his own illegal actions. He had fixed things temporarily when he silenced Waters with a bullet to the back of the head. It had been a tough call, especially against a fellow federal agent, but it meant Stewart's, and the rest of the operation's, freedom from the law—freedom from being discovered—at least for now.

The weathered federal agent now turned his attention back to the two new players. It was time to enlighten the other members to the recent developments. Tactful delivery was a necessity considering allegiances constantly in flux.

20

The sun rose early above the Chesapeake, just behind the Abramson household. Ron McAllister was finally allowed to come out of hiding from his guest room in the basement. Chief Justice Abramson and his wife had hosted the Supreme Court clerks for dinner the night before. The domestic setting, and unlimited libations, provided the opportunity for the Chief Justice catch up on the Court's gossip. The atmosphere had been very light—a nice break from the daily grind for everyone.

"What's the plan today? Did you ever get a chance to catch up with Paul?" Abramson asked Ron.

"You wouldn't let me leave the basement last night. So, no."

"It was too risky. I didn't want any of the clerks to start asking questions. Willie Stewart called late last night," Abramson said. "He said he has some very interesting news to share with everyone. He mentioned that he thinks someone is trying to expose the distillery."

"That's interesting. Any idea who it might be?"

"He didn't elaborate. He said it could wait until we all get together. Speaking of which, your father has summoned everyone to meet this weekend. Are you going to make an appearance? He may fall over dead with a heart attack if you show up," Abramson laughed.

"He's an old man. His time is limited," Ron responded.

They both knew that the elder McAllister's time as the distillery's leader was drawing to an end. If he would not step down peacefully on his own, his son would force him out by any means necessary.

Ron continued, "I'll go see him this afternoon. Can I use your car?"

"Sure thing. Take the silver Audi."

"I want to catch him when we can talk candidly, just the two of us.

Father and son. I'll let him know that you and I don't like the direction the distillery is going. The growth is too slow and too guarded. There are opportunities to make substantially more money. And quickly. We need to get back to the heyday. That generation is winding down. Hell, they've been winding down for years. The current opportunities are too ripe to waste anymore time."

"I just don't see him buying into that," Abramson said, trying to dampen Ron's growing excitement. "But he's your father, so do what you need to do."

Ron raised his mug of coffee, the Supreme Court seal sparkling in the early morning sunlight.

"To a new start for the gang. To more profits and more customers. To the next generation," exclaimed Ron.

The two men tapped their coffee mugs together.

"I have a lot of writing to do. I will be out of pocket for most of the day, so I won't be able to respond to anything until late this afternoon. Don't do anything stupid."

"Like kill the old man?"

They both laughed. Abramson collected his briefcase and suit coat and headed off on his commute to the District.

Ron, clean-shaven now, pulled together some of his finer clothing. It had been years since he'd worn anything other than old t-shirts and beach shorts. It felt good to slip on a pair of expensive loafers and a crisp, freshly pressed button down.

He had lived, for quite some time, like a nomad along the Florida panhandle and the rest of the Gulf Coast, traveling up and down the coastline, hiding from authorities, gaining connections and motivations for his comeback.

He bided his time by frequenting all of the major casinos and even some of the lesser-known underground venues. An average player, he never won much money on the tables. In fact, he lost more often than not. But frequenting those venues gave him access to the best drug connections in the country.

Abramson had visited Ron once when he was migrating along the Gulf Coast. Of course, both men had been under cover. A former CIA operative, who was also a close confidant of the Chief Justice, assisted with their disguises.

It was during that trip that Ron pitched his plan for the distillery operation to Abramson. McAllister whiskey carried some weight. Although not the best, the lore behind the operation made it a top seller. And it was a fun game for the old timers. However, there was more money to be made.

Much like the mafia expanded their empires to include multiple illegal activities, the two men were about to take a local bootleg whiskey operation to a new level—to a level bigger and better than it had been two decades earlier when McAllister and Senator Windgate ran a small empire in the region. Any vice a man could want could be satiated by a simple ask and a reasonable price from the McAllister gang. Money rolled in hand over fist.

The current network of customers and connections included political titans, businessmen, and otherwise elite members of society. They would jump at the opportunity to spice up their profit shares, and their excitement, with a sure-shot moneymaker like whiskey.

Ron would reinvigorate the distillery and add a dimension that it was missing. He could bring in any variety of narcotics through his Caribbean network. The District's drug demand would send profits soaring.

John McAllister must be convinced that this new direction was viable—even more viable than it was years before. Ron was tasked with doing the necessary influencing. As the rightful heir to the estate, the distillery was his to take. There was nothing that was going to get in his way.

Ron understood the consequences if his father had to be forcefully removed or eliminated. The distillery and all of its relationships were his father's life, and only Ron understood quite how important it was to retain his services. It was crucial to do what was necessary to keep his father associated with the operation. He held the power over the customers, and he led the organization well over his tenure.

Ron climbed into the late model Audi. He closed his eyes and relished the feel of the plush leather seats. The new car smell still permeated the interior. How far he had come to feel the touch of luxury once again. The engine roared as he accelerated out of the Abramsons' gated estate overlooking the Chesapeake Bay. He turned southwest toward his very own estate.

x x x

Senator Scooter Windgate spent the morning combing the halls of the Senate offices located adjacent to the Capitol, confirming the guest list for the release of the twenty-year whiskey batch. Rumor of the release had already spread throughout the Senate ranks, albeit only through a secure network of trusted clientele. The hype was building. Not many could remember the last McAllister special batch. In several weeks, a number of the country's lawmakers would attend the bash at the McAllister farm—the "unofficial" retirement party for the esteemed Senator Windgate.

Many of his close allies knew his resignation was imminent. But only a tiny handful, including his wife and John McAllister, knew it was actually in the works.

Since his near brush with death earlier in the week, Senator Windgate had been buzzing on the adrenaline. He had a bounce in his step and a permanent smirk on his weathered face that showcased an air of cockiness not seen since his early years in office. Nobody would keep Scooter down.

He had also announced the name of the to-be-released whiskey to a couple of close allies. He couldn't keep it under wraps from all of his excitement. Senate Proof. McAllister had approved the bottle and label design the night before. The tall, narrow bottle would glow a darkened auburn when filled with whiskey. The creamy, off-white label would feature a sketch of the Capitol building overlaid with the batch name in a beautiful scripted print. Underneath it, a nod to the producer: Courtesy of the McAllister Distillery.

Most special batches were targeted to a segment of the customer list. Some batches included military themes in honor of retiring officers. Others featured symbols of jurisprudence for accomplished legal professionals and members of the judiciary.

This batch, however, was specifically for to the Senate—in honor of the renowned political career of the retiring senator. John McAllister had insisted this be Senator Windgate's celebration. Such a long-time close friend and ally deserved a special send off. Scooter planned to toast whomever had tried to kill him.

21

Caroline had arrived early on her first day back after the explosion and, to her surprise, she saw no signs that anything out of the ordinary had happened at the mansion. Everything looked like business as usual.

She had only been at the farm for a few hours, but she sought refuge from the already sweltering heat in a barn towards the back of the McAllister estate. Jimmy had mentioned that this hot, early summer was out of character for Virginia. The heat had forced her to cut her jeans into shorts. It would be autumn before she needed another pair of jeans.

Caroline was wiping the sweat from her eyes and adjusting her long, blonde ponytail when the silver Audi pulled into the driveway. From where she sat just inside the barn door, she could make out that the driver was a well-dressed man. Another odd visitor to the estate, she noted.

John McAllister was sitting at the kitchen table with Ms. Ruby when he heard three knocks on the door. Senator Windgate was scheduled to swing by the house just after lunch, but that was still a few hours away. He wasn't expecting anyone else.

McAllister was feeling his age today. The excitement, stress, and anxiety of the last few days were taking a toll. Ms. Ruby helped him to the door to answer. When he pulled open the front door, he stood amazed as he looked into the face of his son—a face he had not seen in years.

He reached out to embrace his son, but Ron didn't accept the gesture. He pushed past his father and walked directly to the main floor office. The elder McAllister gave Ms. Ruby a puzzled look.

Ms. Ruby helped her charge settle into his desk in his office before turning to leave the two men alone.

"It's good to see you, Ron," she said as she left the room.

He offered no response. Ron stood, arms crossed, gazing out the back window over the pastures and horse barns. Where was the girl?

X   X   X

Caroline decided to stay out of the heat and clean stalls. She fetched a pitchfork and muscled a half-full wheelbarrow into a dirty stall to begin the tedious task of sifting manure from the hay and shavings.

She noticed her biceps and shoulders were much more sculpted than when she first began working at the farm. Although she had always been athletic in the past, she was amazed at how drastically her fitness level and muscle tone had increased from the daily physical labor.

Working in the dark barn, she was hidden in plain sight. She was quite a distance from the mansion and no one would venture that far to find her. She dedicated herself to a thorough cleaning of the stalls as the afternoon heat intensified.

X   X   X

Ron turned away from the window and looked at his aged father. A man he once looked up to, he now couldn't wait until the elder McAllister passed away. In his mind, the changing of the guard could not come soon enough.

"You look terrible," Ron said to his father, trying to provoke a response.

His father did not respond. He studied the cold face of his son.

"Look, I don't want to waste a lot of time making small talk, so let me cut to the chase."

McAllister interrupted, "You have no idea what you're doing, do you? There's no need to cut to the chase. I can see right through you. Do you think I'm so out of touch that I don't know that you've been keeping company with Michael Abramson?"

Ron was speechless, stunned by his father's accuracy.

McAllister continued, "I am old, but I'm not blind. I'm not deaf, and I'm not dumb. I am more connected in this community than you will ever know. In fact, I know exactly when you came back to the region and crashed at the Abramson's. I have eyes and ears everywhere."

He stood tall behind his desk. The old man was surprised at how quickly his temper boiled.

Ron regrouped and charged the desk, determined to get his message across, "Things are not being run properly around here. The time has come."

"I've always given you the benefit of the doubt," McAllister interrupted again. "If you remember, I was the one who organized and financed your run from the law after the murder. I made sure you and your pathetic buddy Abramson didn't spend the remainder of your years in prison."

"This is about the distillery. You're not fit to run it anymore. Look at you—you barely have any life left," Ron barked, finally able to finish a complete thought.

This was not quite the friendly reunion John McAllister had long hoped for.

To McAllister's surprise and discomfort, Ron walked around behind the mahogany desk and opened a drawer and pulled out a half-full bottle of whiskey. The elder McAllister stood firm, reluctant to give up his position of power to his son.

The whiskey label indicated that it was from a two-year-old batch, and the dust on the bottle was evidence that it had not been opened for some time. Indeed, McAllister drank at a much slower pace than he had in Ron's youth, when it caused friction between them in Ron's formative years. The friction was still present, indicating its deep roots beyond alcohol.

"I've run this business for a long, long time. Please tell me why, all of a sudden, I am not fit to run it any longer," he demanded, standing just inches from his son's face.

Changing tactics, Ron attempted to soften his tone and took a seat on the other side of the desk. He began, "Admittedly, you have done a great job over the past few decades. There's no doubt in my mind that you're a major reason we've all enjoyed so much money.

"But with any business, there's comes a time when a new direction is needed. New leadership and new perspectives should be put in place to propel the business forward in continued success."

"I'm curious to know how you plan on growing the operation," the father replied. "You remember that what we do is illegal. We've spent hundreds of thousands—no, millions of dollars—dodging authorities. We'll always wear a target on our backs for what we did in the past. They know we're here. But they also know who our clients are, and that helps keep them at arm's length. If you give the feds so much as the tiniest chance to come in, they will storm the place and expose all of us."

"I've decided that I want to expand the service offering to our customers."

"How so?"

"Black market gaming, bookmaking, drugs, piracy." Ron paused to let the idea sink in. He continued, "You know that I've seen the inside of every casino in the country, legitimate and not. I've traveled around with some of our most loyal customers, and more importantly, their kids. Listen, I know exactly what I'm doing. I've been laying the groundwork for the last several years now."

"It's not that easy," McAllister said as he rose from his chair, shaking his head.

He turned slowly to the window. A storm was brewing in the horizon to the west, heading for the estate.

"Sure it is," Ron barked back.

"And Abramson? He knows about this?"

"He knows everything," Ron lied.

His father just shook his head back and forth.

"This will never happen under my watch. Expansion opens up too many opportunities for outsiders to pry into our business. Plus, I'm not in the business of ruining lives anymore. Times are different."

"Indeed, times are different. Think about it for a few days," Ron replied. He moved closer to his father, his face inches from the old man's.

"Michael Abramson and I are prepared to do whatever is necessary to change the course of this operation," he whispered, "including eliminating current leadership."

The attempt at intimidation didn't phase the old man one bit.

Ron continued, "You're leaving money on the table, and it's unacceptable to some major stakeholders. I suggest doing a little soul searching."

"Why would you ever want to jeopardize what we've had going for more than three quarters of a century. And you wonder why I never named you as my successor? This is your family business, too. I'd think you would take more care in dealing with it."

Ms. Ruby's footsteps sounded down the hall, approaching the office. There were another set of footsteps with hers.

"The senator is here to see you," Ms. Ruby announced.

"Thank you, dear," McAllister said.

Ron again completely ignored Ms. Ruby.

"Did I interrupt something," Senator Windgate asked.

"No, we're finished here," replied McAllister.

The senator sensed that he just missed a good fight and one look at his old friend told him it had been an emotional one.

"Things will be different around here. And soon," Ron said to no one in particular as he abruptly exited the office.

He headed directly for the front door, hopped into the Audi, and sped down the driveway as the storm moved in. The meeting had not gone exactly as he wished, but his father was now on notice. A power struggle was imminent.

"What was that about?" asked Senator Windgate.

As calmly as possible, McAllister shared the news.

"Michael Abramson and my son want control of the distillery. It looks like we have a fight brewing from within."

The men were silent as they contemplated what was happening.

"I wonder who else they have in their camp."

"There's no telling. But it makes me very suspicious about the explosion the other night."

"If they're willing to go that far, this is very serious," said the senator.

"I'll beef up security starting tonight, and there will be several unsuspecting people on the watch list."

"What about the quorum of distillery members this weekend?"

"Send out the notices. Make sure each and every person is invited. We won't back down to anyone. We can take precautions, but we will never back down."

x   x   x

Caroline prayed for her life as she held tightly onto the back of the ATV Jimmy was racing through the fields.

Jimmy went out to fetch Caroline as soon as the afternoon storm began stirring the air.

"The fields need the rain," Jimmy yelled over the engine and noise from the speeding ATV. "Hopefully it will cool things down a bit as well."

"Just when I was finally getting used to the heat," joked Caroline.

"Mr. McAllister wants you to meet Senator Windgate. He just showed up a few minutes ago."

"Okay."

"It won't take long," he yelled. "He doesn't want you driving your Jeep in the storm."

Jimmy pulled up next to the gazebo in the back yard. Caroline hopped off the back and found Ms. Ruby waiting for her at the back door with a towel.

"I guessed you would want to towel off," Ms. Ruby said.

"Thank you," Caroline replied warmly.

"I also left a washcloth in the bathroom down the hall if you need it."

"You are so thoughtful. Thank you very much."

Caroline never imagined she'd be meeting any of the nation's top lawmakers at the farm. Especially when dressed in cut-off denim shorts and no makeup. Not to mention covered in the aroma of horse. Oh well, she thought, just smile and act like everything is normal.

When she entered McAllister's office, she was startled by how small and frail Senator Windgate looked. She had seen him on the farm several times before, but always from a distance. But the senator surprised her again with a firm handshake to go along with his welcoming smile.

They sat around a table at one end of the office exchanging pleasantries. Caroline shared a few war stories from her time on Wall Street. With financial regulatory reform in the works, the senator considered himself lucky to hear firsthand stories from an insider.

Senator Windgate shared his own story, his rise from schoolteacher to senator, with his old friend interjecting humorous anecdotes every few minutes. There were no clues to the father-son rift from earlier in the day.

Ms. Ruby delivered a fresh pitcher of sweet tea and tall glasses of ice, which they drained quickly.

Caroline's attention was suddenly drawn to her boss's huge mahogany desk. A tall, slender bottle with an interesting label sitting on the corner piqued her interest—whiskey. She smiled and half-cocked her head, curiosity getting the best of her.

"That whiskey label says "McAllister." Is that brand affiliated with your family?"

The two men were turned away from the desk. Senator Windgate's heart skipped a beat when Caroline asked the question.

Ron left the whiskey on the desk. His father would be forced to clean up his mess, again. Some things never changed.

"Yes. As a matter of fact, it is," McAllister replied, trying not to make it a big deal.

"I had no idea you were in the spirits business."

"Not many people do."

Caroline breezed over his open-ended answer, having no reason to dig deeper—yet.

"I've never seen this brand in any liquor store. Where is your major distribution?"

"It's a very local and limited customer base," he said, playing a balancing act of not divulging too much information but not lying to the young woman. "It's all sold by special order."

"Ha, if I didn't know any better, it almost sounds like you're running an illegal still."

"Do you want to see it?" asked John.

"See what?" she replied.

Senator Windgate gave McAllister a quizzical stare. What was he doing?

"Do you want to see the distillery?" John clarified.

Windgate was speechless. Was he was really witnessing this.

"Sure! Where is it?" asked Caroline.

"Right beneath your feet," he responded. "Go ask Ms. Ruby for a sweater to cover your shoulders. It can get quite cool down in the caves."

"Caves?"

"Believe it or not, there is an extensive network of caves beneath this house. I think you'll enjoy the tour."

"I can't wait," she said, not masking her excitement.

After she exited the office, the senator confronted McAllister.

"What the hell are you doing," he demanded.

"Relax," replied John. "She's harmless. I don't want to put her in harm's way, Scooter. I just want to give her a little insight as to what we do around here."

"This is a bad idea, John. I don't like it."

"She'll be fine. Anyway, we're only going to let her in on the distillery tour, and maybe share a few stories about the parties we throw. She'll have no idea about the breadth, or the demographics, of our customer base. She won't be able to grasp the magnitude of the operation. In case you've forgotten, we're pretty clean now.

"I'll go through the story of how my father and grandfather started the distillery at the height of Prohibition, and so on. We'll keep it innocent, and say it's just a hobby to supply some friends with whiskey."

"Hopefully she doesn't ask why we have millions of dollars in equipment down there. That's a large investment for just a few friends. I don't like this at all," Windgate repeated.

Of course, the senator hadn't been completely honest with his friend over the last few years, and he had several serious concerns about letting the new girl into the inner circle.

The two men met Caroline at the front door. They led her to the edge of the driveway, where a pathway led into the forest.

"I've never noticed this path before," she said.

"Follow us," John said leading the way, "it's just a little stroll through the woods."

The threesome navigated the sloping trail. It widened at the end, forming a circular patch of dirt and gravel. The wooden door was locked, and watched by a security guard dressed in all black, gun holstered at his hip, perched above the entryway.

Caroline began to feel a hint of apprehension. She had never noticed, let alone encountered, any security guards on the grounds before.

McAllister unlocked the door and flipped a light switch, illuminating the long hallway.

Sweat was forming on the back of Caroline's neck. Something was off. She suddenly became overwhelmed with a feeling of entrapment.

"Follow me," McAllister said, leading the way through the door.

Senator Windgate fell in line behind her.

Caroline slipped on the sweater and reluctantly followed her boss down the cold hallway. She found herself admiring the many pictures lining the hallway—prominent figures from the political and military ranks. Some were from recent years; others were from decades before.

A United States president was flanked by a much younger John McAllister and Scooter Windgate. Had these dignitaries been involved with the distillery? Were they clients? Or were the pictures merely mementos from another life?

Caroline stopped dead in her tracks. The man in one of the photographs was familiar. He had the same blue eyes that looked back at her in the mirror every day.

It was undoubtedly her father.

She repressed a sudden wave of nausea and braced herself against the wall.

"Are you okay?" asked a concerned Senator Windgate.

"I'm sorry. I suddenly feel sick," Caroline managed to say.

"Do we need to call for help?" McAllister asked.

Caroline leaned against the wall, struggling to figure out what to do next. How would she get out alive? Did they know her father? Had she been duped?

She glanced back at the photograph, confirming that it was, in fact, her father. She couldn't hold it in anymore. She heaved and vomited all over the floor.

"Let me help you to the ladies room," McAllister offered as he gently took her arm.

He led her down the remainder of the hallway and into the main ballroom. He directed her to the ladies room at the front of the large cavern.

"Do you need us to call Ms. Ruby?"

Caroline didn't notice the large piles of corn and rye that almost reached the ceiling of the ballroom. She barely mustered a headshake, indicating that she didn't need any extra attention.

Inside the bathroom, she cleaned her face and waited for her color to return. She did her best to regain her composure before going back to face two men she was certain had information about her father. She was on high alert.

"I think I should call it a day. It must've been something I ate," she said as she emerged from the ladies room. "Can I take a rain check on the tour?"

"Certainly," McAllister said. "The storm is picking up, so we should get you on your way home before it really comes down."

The threesome walked hurriedly back down the hall, Caroline focusing straight ahead to avoid another glimpse of her father's face. They passed another security guard cleaning up the mess she had made. A familiar refrain played in her mind: things were getting stranger every day.

Outside the cave, the two men escorted Caroline to her Jeep.

She carefully pulled out of the driveway. And as soon as she was out of sight, she hit the gas and sped away as quickly as possible. There was no way she was hanging around any longer.

X   X   X

"That went a little different than I anticipated," McAllister said.

"Well, now she knows we run a distillery," replied the senator. "But her sudden illness was a good thing. There's really no reason for her to know too much too soon."

"I was thinking the same thing. We can slowly ease her into the full story."

"Wait until I tell Mr. Michael Abramson about our little girl," McAllister boasted.

"He will flip when he finds out the potential exposure." The senator himself was panicking, on the inside.

"She'll never talk," McAllister said confidently. "I have complete faith in her."

"I hope you're right."

X   X   X

Caroline struggled to see through her tears as she powered down the country road back to her cabin. She never wanted to go back to the farm ever again. She suspected she would meet the same fate as her father.

22

Downtown Charlottesville was vibrant when Jackson returned from a quick round of golf. Stragglers from graduation and the rest of the UVA student body populated the sidewalk cafes on the Mall. For many of them, this week marked their last hurrah before heading home or off to work for the summer. By dinnertime, the libations would be flowing freely across town.

Two pieces of mail awaited Jackson at his mailbox just inside the front door. One was a letter with a Chicago return address in Samantha Crockett's handwriting. The other was a utility bill.

He noticed something strange when he reached the top of the stairs. His apartment door was unlocked. Unfortunately, this was a common occurrence. Stumbling home after a late night of binge drinking, and then forgetting to lock the door behind him—sometimes forgetting to close the door altogether.

He dismissed it as forgetfulness and preceded inside.

While he waited for the shower to get warm he opened the letter.

Before even finishing the second sentence, Jackson ripped the letter down the middle. He shredded it into tiny pieces and tossed it in the trash before jumping in the shower.

The first two lines summed it up: "I met another guy at school . . . we'd grown apart."

He was over her. A blonde had caught his eye. Caroline seemed like she would be good company—light and fun.

Jackson took no notice of the tiny, blinking light in the corner of the living room. Agent Will Stewart had been in his apartment to install the surveillance device in his ventilation system. There was another in the bedroom, both providing a live feed to Stewart's laptop.

The young law student was not of much importance to Stewart, but he would be a useful asset for ascertaining clues about Caroline.

The rain began to pour, scattering the college crowd on the streets below Jackson's apartment. He opened his windows to let in the calming sound of rain, sprawled out on his sofa, and drifted off.

x x x

A dark sedan barreled down the drive connecting Caroline's cabin to the country road, tossing gravel as it swerved around her Jeep.

She jerked the Jeep to a stop on the grass shoulder to avoid the sedan. The sedan fishtailed out of the gravel driveway and headed the opposite direction down the country road.

Even through the rain, her tears, and wet hair plastered to her face, she could clearly see that the front door to her cabin was ajar. Whoever was in that sedan had just been in her house.

Drenched in rainwater, Caroline fought through her emotional fatigue. She put the Jeep in gear and raced onto her property. She was weak from throwing up, but her adrenaline was propelling her forward.

Max was nowhere to be seen. She put the Jeep in park and called his name.

No response. No movement or sounds from anywhere.

An eerie feeling came over her as she approached the front door. It was three quarters of the way open. The rain was falling harder now. Inside the open door, a puddle was forming where the rainwater was splashing onto the old hardwood floor.

A bolt of lightning struck so close to the cabin that the blinding flash and immediate boom of thunder dazed Caroline for a moment. The power to the cabin flickered and shut down. She was in near-complete darkness.

"Max," she called out.

Still no response.

Frightened, she hurried back out to her Jeep and found a flashlight on the floorboard. The batteries worked and it gave off light, though just a little.

Guided by the flashlight, she slowly worked her way into the cabin once again. The living room was trashed. Sofa cushions were cut open and thrown across the room. The sofa itself had been flipped over. The kitchen cabinets were flung open. Her tiny abode had been canvassed from front to back.

There was still no sign of Max. She worried what had happened when tried to protect the cabin against an intruder.

She peered down the hall toward her bedroom. Several of the floorboards had been destroyed in search of anything hidden under the floor. It hit her that if someone went so far as to look under the floor, they must have found the safe in her bedroom closet.

She rushed down the hall, dodging the holes in the floor, and turned the corner into her bedroom.

Max's body lay in a pool of blood in front of the open closet door. The flashlight was quickly dying, so she opened the shades to let in what daylight was outside.

There were two bullet holes in Max's chest. He had been shot guarding her most important possessions.

She looked up to find her entire safe missing. Her cover was broken.

She screamed and threw the flashlight. It shattered into a hundred pieces when it crashed against the wall. She then picked up a heavy crystal flower vase from her nightstand, which had somehow survived the invasion, and slammed it against the wall. The vase left a large hole in the aged drywall.

Caroline kneeled, returning to Max's body, listening for any sign of life.

A slight noise came from Max. She kneeled further down and put her ear next to his bloody mouth. He was barely alive, struggling to breathe.

She picked up his heavy body and carried him to the Jeep, placing him in the passenger seat with a towel over his body to keep him as dry and warm as possible.

She ran back into the house and packed a small bag of anything she may need—a few articles of clothing and her toothbrush.

She looked in the rearview mirror at the cabin as she sped away toward the country road, hopefully for the last time. She never wanted to return. Her life was too important to risk anything else. The discovery of her identity had serious implications.

x   x   x

Jackson's cell phone woke him from his nap. His grogginess quickly vanished when he heard a panicked voice on the other end.

"I don't know what to do," Caroline cried. "Max is dying right here in my Jeep. Someone is trying to kill me."

"Slow down," Jackson replied, trying to calm the situation.

"They're going to find me and kill me."

"What are you talking about?"

"I didn't have anyone else to call, so I called you."

"Okay, okay, but you're going to have to start over. I have no idea what's going on."

"I'm on my way to Charlottesville. I don't have anywhere else to go," she explained hysterically. "I'll explain everything when I get there."

"What about the dog?"

"I have to take him to the emergency vet. He's been shot, twice. He's lost a lot of blood, and he's barely breathing. I have to do something for him. I have to take him somewhere. I can't leave him to die."

"Okay, find a place for Max, then head my way," Jackson instructed, now concerned for both Max and Caroline. What was he getting himself into?

"Okay, I'll call you when I get close to town," she yelled above the road noise. "I'm sorry for getting you into this mess, but I didn't know what else to do."

"It's fine. Drive carefully."

"I'll explain everything later when I get there."

"I hope Max is okay."

Caroline hung up her cell phone and accelerated down the road. It would be impossible to find an animal hospital from the highway, so she pulled off at the next turn.

Luckily, she found a service station and stopped in for directions. The attendant directed her to an animal hospital only two miles away.

"Hold on, Max," she consoled the wounded animal. "We're almost there. Hold on, buddy."

She wheeled into the hospital's parking lot at full speed.

Caroline lugged Max's limp body into the hospital. She was soaked and looked like a wreck, but she didn't care.

He was immediately taken in by the veterinarian on duty.

Caroline didn't have much time to explain the circumstances. She needed to get back on the road soon to get as far away from the area as possible. The guilt of leaving him there alone tore at her conscience. How could she leave her most loyal friend near death?

Not knowing whether she would ever see Max alive again, she left instructions for the vet, and shared a tearful goodbye with the dog, praying that he would be all right.

Caroline got back on the road as quickly as possible trying her best not to dwell on Max's deteriorating condition. If anything happened to Max, she instructed the vet to call her. Until she received a phone call, she couldn't spend her energy worrying about him. She had to get to safety. She needed to focus on survival.

She found herself routinely checking the rearview mirror, searching for any sign that she was being followed.

Paranoia was setting in, controlling her thoughts. Every driver she encountered was surely watching her every move, reporting her location to the killers who were after her.

Emotionally torn up, she tried reconciling her feelings about John McAllister. The old man won her loyalty and trust from the first week she worked on the farm. However, just a few hours earlier, she had discovered him in a picture with her slain father. Strangers don't just pose together in photographs.

The connection between the two men would weigh on her for the remainder of the drive.

23

A threat to his well being, and specifically the threat of exposure of his connection with the McAllister operation, was the only thing that could get the Chief Justice away from his duties at the Court on this busy afternoon.

Michael Abramson jogged down King Street, the main drag in Old Town Alexandria, just outside Washington, DC. The lunch crowd had already returned to their offices, leaving few folks on the sidewalks to notice the nation's top judicial official running frantically down the street.

Abramson wore sunglasses and a faded baseball cap in an attempt to disguise his appearance. The fine Italian suit would easily draw attention, but by the time someone tried to identify the man, he would be long gone down the sidewalk. And he'd left his security escort behind for obvious reasons.

Ron and Agent Stewart waited impatiently for Abramson in a mostly unfurnished studio apartment two blocks off of King Street. A wooden table and four chairs were the only furniture in the apartment, placed right in the center of the living area.

Stewart had taken advantage of his pull with a federal snitch who happened to be the landlord for the building.

"This location will be a perfect command center for us," said Ron, already planning where to put the surveillance equipment in the bare space.

"Glad I remembered our snitch. He owes me big time for saving his ass a few times. I just hope he doesn't start asking any questions."

"If he does, throw him to the wolves. I'm sure the dealers would love to know who snitches on them. That'll keep him honest."

Agent Stewart pulled his laptop out of its case and placed it on the table.

"While this powers up," Agent Stewart said, "help me bring something else up from downstairs."

"What else do you have?"

"I'm not quite sure, but we need to crack it open."

"Crack it open?"

"Yeah, just give me a hand."

The two men almost collided with Abramson at the front door. The Chief Justice bent over panting, catching his breath.

"Where are you going?" demanded Abramson.

"Go upstairs," replied Stewart. "Second floor. Third door on the right. You don't need to be hanging outside for the whole world to see."

"We'll be back up in a minute."

The Chief Justice caught his breath and walked into the building. He waited until he was inside the studio apartment before he removed his cap and sunglasses.

Agent Stewart opened the trunk of his federal issue sedan. Positioned sideways was what looked to be a file cabinet.

"What is that?" asked Ron.

"I have no idea. I thought it was just a file cabinet or storage unit. But it's got a lock system that's more secure than anything you'll ever find at the CIA," replied Stewart.

"Hmm," Ron thought aloud. "Let's take it upstairs and have a look."

"It's pretty heavy. You take that end."

The two men labored as they negotiated the acute turns in the stairwell. The awkwardly distributed weight didn't make things any easier, especially with the projecting bolts that had secured it in the ground under Caroline's cabin.

Once they finally managed to get the unit positioned upright, it became obvious that it was some sort of safe.

"What do you make of this?" asked Abramson, pacing around the safe.

Ron and Agent Stewart sat at the table, sipping cold water, staring at the metal unit.

"Are we secure in here? I mean, are we sure there are no bugs or anything recording our conversations?" Ron asked.

Agent Stewart responded, "If you're asking if I've combed the place for bugs, I haven't yet. But I have no reason to suspect that anybody would know we're here. You were with me thirty minutes ago when we paid my snitch for access to the place."

"Alright," Ron said with some hesitation

"Please, Stewart, tell us why you called us here for this mysterious metal package?" demanded the Chief Justice.

"I couldn't mention it during our call," responded Agent Stewart. "I canvassed Blondie's cabin out on the McAllister property earlier today. I found this locked up tight in her closet. Pretty suspicious if you ask me."

"We're listening," said Chief Justice Abramson, nodding for Stewart to continue.

"Here's what we know. Her first name is Caroline. I have no knowledge of a last name at this time, but I'm hoping this unit holds some valuable information."

"Mills is her last name," said Ron, searching the file directories on Caroline's stolen laptop.

"That laptop also came from her house," said Agent Stewart. "If she winds up being clean, we can keep the laptop, I'll return the metal unit, and she can chalk up her destroyed house to being robbed."

"What if she's already been home?" asked a concerned Abramson.

"I'll dump the unit at the back of her property. She'll think someone tried to make off with it, but couldn't carry it very far."

"Okay, I can live with that."

"Oh, and I had to shoot her dog."

"Pet killer," chuckled Ron, showing no remorse for the innocent animal.

"The stupid dog was guarding the locked closet with his life. He didn't care about anything else in the house, so I knew there must be something important in there. I guessed jewelry, or old keepsakes, but when I got rid of the damn dog and opened the door, I found this thing."

"Let's hope this *thing* doesn't merely have jewelry or old keepsakes."

"I also made a trip to Charlottesville and installed a few cameras in our young man's apartment. If she makes any contact with him, or if he was more involved with Philip Waters than we thought, he'll be easy for us to track."

"About Waters . . . you did the right thing," Ron said.

"You ordered it. I did it," responded Stewart. "Only time will tell if it was right."

Abramson didn't say anything about Waters. He didn't like anything that was happening with the group—the murder, the car bomb, the potential exposure. He definitely had his concerns about Ron running the operation and making orders like that.

The three men huddled over the metal safe. After a few minutes of playing with the security system, they ascertained that it required fingerprints and a pass code.

"I didn't think to bring the electronic code breaker with me," said Stewart.

"Does anyone live underneath us?" asked Ron.

"I don't know. Why?"

"Let's check for neighbors, because if nobody else lives here, or nobody else is home this afternoon, there are a few explosives in the trunk."

"Why do you have explosives in the trunk of my Audi?" demanded Abramson.

"Depending on how things went this morning with my father, I was going to plant a few explosives around the house," said Ron. "Nothing like a little intimidation factor."

"Nothing like begging for attention," retorted Abramson. "You have to be more careful than this."

Chief Justice Abramson remained seated at the table in the studio apartment while the other two men combed the neighboring units for occupants. When he got the all clear that no one else was around the building, Ron retrieved the explosives from the car.

"Do you know what you're doing?" asked Abramson, eyeing Ron as he maneuvered the explosives around the safe's door.

"Kind of," Ron replied, securing the last pieces of what looked to be small sticks of dynamite.

The three men flipped the table on its side and hunkered down behind it.

"On three," said Ron. "One, two, three."

Fortunately, the men had opened the exterior windows before the blast. However, the glass cabinets in the kitchen shattered from the force. Undoubtedly, other units in the building suffered some damage, too.

"Whoa! That was bigger than expected. Let's get out of here," yelled Agent Stewart. "I don't think we'll be welcomed back at this location."

"Quick, grab all the paperwork," ordered Abramson as he scrambled around trying to corral all of the papers that had been blown out of the safe.

With Abramson carrying a bundle of papers and the other men carrying the remains of the destroyed safe, they quickly exited the building and jumped in the two cars.

"Follow me," Stewart directed.

He stopped on the street at a park bordering the Potomac River, about five blocks away from the apartment. Ron and Abramson parked behind Stewart and quickly climbed into the back seat of the sedan. Once inside, they hastily sorted the contents of the safe.

The contents revealed everything, and after scanning over numerous false identities, they finally found the one that revealed Caroline's true identity. After all these years, how could it not be her?

Ron and Abramson sat silently in the back seat of the sedan as they mulled over what they were witnessing, trying to grasp the situation. It was much worse than they'd feared.

Abramson finally broke the silence.

"Good work, Stewart," he said.

"I knew something was odd about her," said Stewart. "It looks like we have a bit of a problem on our hands."

"You have to find her immediately," barked Abramson. "Do whatever is necessary to bring her back. Find out what she knows and who she's told. This girl will not ruin us."

"Don't worry, I'll find her."

"John wants everybody to meet this weekend at the distillery. Don't come back until you have the girl. I'll explain why you're not there. Good 'ole John really screwed up this time—he hires the one girl who can ruin us as his farm assistant."

"This is just great," said Ron.

"I can't believe this is happening," said Abramson. "I have to get back to my office. People will start wondering where I've been."

"You guys go on. I'll hit the road as soon as I get a good lead on the girl," replied Stewart. "I'll take care of her."

"We'll be in touch," responded Abramson. "Call me when you're on the road."

Ron and Abramson climbed back into the Audi.

Stewart opened his laptop, hoping the feed from Jackson's apartment was operating correctly. Everything appeared normal, except that Jackson was packing a suitcase.

24

The cool temperature inside the caverns provided much needed relief for John McAllister and Jimmy. They began the whiskey making process from the newly arrived materials.

Cartons of corn and rye had been rolled into a back room in the cavern that contained the mill. The corn and rye would be ground up and then taken to the open cooker where the ingredients would be converted into sour mash. Yeast from the strain that was perfected decades ago would be added to begin the fermenting process. The sour mash fermented, popped, and bubbled for seventy-two hours before being sent through the still, resulting in "white dog," the newly distilled, un-aged whiskey, straight from the still.

Several locals labored away inside the caverns. They were seasoned professionals. It was obvious that they had been part of the whiskey making operation for many years.

McAllister eagerly began taking the necessary steps to make the new batch. He stood attentive in the room with the mill, watching as the ingredients were ground into tiny pieces.

Jimmy entered carrying two small glasses of clear liquid.

"Who wants some white dog?" he asked with a smile.

"All right," John said as he took one of the glasses from Jimmy.

"This is the first sample from this batch."

"Let's see how we did. Cheers!"

Jimmy took a sip and immediately spit it out.

"Ah, disgusting," he said.

John then took a sip and squirmed, although he grudgingly swallowed the mouthful. He smiled.

"Ah, yes, terrible," he said smiling.

"I'll give you the benefit of the doubt. You *are* the master distiller."

"You see, the worse it tastes from the start, the better it tastes after aging. This will be a top quality batch."

"You must be wrong," quipped Jimmy. "I've never heard that before."

They toasted each other, John downed the remainder of his glass, and Jimmy poured his on the rocky floor.

"Can't say I'm much into moonshine," chuckled Jimmy.

Satisfied with the work, McAllister left the caverns in the early evening and walked alone back up the wooded path toward the mansion. Ms. Ruby was preparing a nice dinner tonight. He didn't notice the small red dot of light on his chest, but he was aware that something was amiss.

With a steady finger on the trigger, the sniper dialed in on the old man's heart, his rifle prepared to unleash a deadly round, ending his reign as leader of the McAllister operation. Before he could fire, the sniper slumped forward as pink mist sprayed out from his back. He never had a chance to pull the trigger. The rifle fell two stories from the top of the barn window and crashed, spooking the gelding in the paddock below.

McAllister's own sniper had followed the assassin's every move for nearly four hours. His fatal mistake had come when his lens glinted in the sunlight hours earlier, catching the watchful eye of the operation's security detail peering out from a hidden tree stand adjacent to the mansion.

"All clear, sir," said a voice into McAllister's hidden earpiece.

McAllister spoke into his left sleeve, "ID the guy and comb the rest of the farm for anything suspicious."

A couple of hours earlier, the sniper's presence had been brought to John's attention. Convinced that he was the target, he proposed the plan to walk alone, isolating himself and leaving himself vulnerable to the sniper's shot. The brave old man's instincts had been correct once again.

He was too old to worry about his own life. With the confidence of a newly commissioned Marine, McAllister knew he would never really be in danger. He had the best security force money could buy. Most members of the team were former black ops, and he offered cash pay that no private employer could dream of matching.

Jimmy found his boss sitting at his dining room table, waiting for Ms. Ruby to serve the scrumptious dinner.

"I need you to go check on Caroline," he said to Jimmy.

"Sure thing, boss. When do you want me to go?"

"Now," ordered the old man.

"Is something wrong?"

"I don't have a good feeling. If they sent someone after me, they surely sent someone after her," he said. "I hope she's safe."

"I'm on my way now," Jimmy said as he exited the dining room.

"Jimmy," he called out after him. "Make sure you're sufficiently armed. Take whoever you need."

"I'll be fine," replied Jimmy.

McAllister knew Jimmy would be fine. Jimmy had served in Special Forces units during the first raids of Afghanistan after September 11. He had the best training one could ever receive. The young man would be just fine.

Ms. Ruby came in to serve the first course of the meal. He could barely touch it he was so overwhelmed with concern for Caroline. He placed his spoon back on the table.

"Ruby," he called out.

"Yes, Mr. McAllister," came her reply as she entered the dining room.

"I need a driver. I'm going to Molly O's. Don't take offense, your meal is wonderful. I have just some important business that needs attention."

"I understand," she replied, smiling.

Ms. Ruby wasn't fazed. When McAllister ran out on a meal—at least three times a week—she never let the food go to waste. The estate's security staff fought over her cooking. She took very good care of them. She would even go so far as to solicit requests from the team for their favorite meals when she suspected her boss wouldn't stick around for an entire meal.

McAllister didn't mind at all. He was happy the men who protected him were well fed. Ruby was a great cook and he was happy to share.

A frantic Jimmy called as he was on his way to Molly O's.

"Caroline's gone," exclaimed Jimmy.

"What?"

"She's gone. Her place has been destroyed. Turned upside down and torn apart," he said exasperated. "There's a puddle of blood on the bedroom floor."

"I'll meet you there. I'm already on my way," McAllister said, enraged.

The driver accelerated toward Caroline's cabin, disregarding all traffic laws in the pursuit.

He arrived at the cabin minutes later, as the sun was beginning to drop low behind the trees in the evening sky. Jimmy waited outside.

"The storm must've knocked the power out," said Jimmy.

"I've got some flashlights. Let's take a quick look around," McAllister said.

The two men canvassed the house looking for any clues as to where Caroline might be.

Had she been kidnapped? Did she run away? Was she alive?

Finally, McAllister said, "Let's pay a visit to Paul at Molly O's. She talked to him. Maybe he knows something."

"You don't think Abramson has something to do with this, do you?"

"I'm sure that evil bastard has everything to do with this," he screamed, his anger boiling. "Him and Ron! If she's been harmed in any way, I will kill him. I don't care what type of office he holds. I'll gladly spend the rest of my days in prison."

Jimmy couldn't respond.

McAllister's driver left the scene of Caroline's disappearance and Jimmy drove the two of them to Molly O's.

The crowd was sparse in the pub. They made their way to the reserved corner booth. As always, Paul was behind the bar.

When he spotted the two men, he moved quickly in their direction.

"Paul, we have some serious trouble," McAllister said.

"I know. I was going to stop by later tonight when I got off work," he responded.

"What do you know?"

"Ron was here earlier this afternoon."

"What?" McAllister replied, acting surprised.

"He was in here, digging for information about the group."

"Did he mention anything about Caroline?"

"He asked a few questions about her, but he mostly wanted to know about the distillery operations," Paul offered, leaning over the booth to hide the conversation. "It's been forever since I'd seen him. He's looking a little old."

"Life hasn't been kind to him in recent years. Running from authorities for years will take a toll on you," McAllister said, intentionally circling the obvious and putting up a calm front. He was old, and he was growing tired. Tired of everything.

"Caroline is missing. Her cabin was ransacked," interjected Jimmy.

Paul was stunned by the news.

"Do you think Ron had anything to do with it?" he asked the two men.

"Probably. Ron and Abramson," McAllister responded. "Keep your eyes and ears open and let us know if you find out anything."

"I most certainly will," responded Paul.

"Paul, she's a good girl. She doesn't deserve to get caught up in this," McAllister lamented.

The two men left Molly O's without eating or drinking. They made their way back to the McAllister estate.

After they left, Paul retreated to the back corner of the kitchen. The kitchen was slow and other than a single cook, he was the only person there. He dialed his cell phone.

"He's alive," Paul whispered into the phone, covering his mouth so the lone cook couldn't possibly hear or read his lips.

"I figured as much," responded the voice on the other end. "I never received confirmation of a kill shot. In fact, I haven't heard anything from our gunman. If they found him, we'll have to change plans. They'll know we're after them."

"Did you do anything to the girl?"

"Not yet. Why?"

"She's missing."

"Thanks for the info," replied the voice. He slammed the phone shut, ending the call.

X   X   X

Abramson paced along his back porch overlooking the Chesapeake Bay, his phone in one hand, cocktail in the other. He took a sip and placed the highball on the deck's railing. After unbuttoning the top two buttons on his shirt, he took a deep breath and peered out over the bay, deep in thought.

He was preparing to ask for a favor that would change the course of everything. If he made the call, there was no turning back.

Where was Caroline? Did Agent Stewart already find her? If so, why hadn't he reported back yet?

From a sailboat drifting down the Chesapeake in the dusk, a member of McAllister's hit team put the Chief Justice in his crosshairs. But the sniper would not fire tonight—not until Caroline was found. He was watching and waiting, ready for the order to come through.

John McAllister knew exactly how to play the game.

25

Agent Stewart finished off his burger and fries while keeping his eyes glued to the laptop screen. The live feed from Jackson's apartment in Charlottesville was streaming to his computer. Pistol on his hip, and a full tank of gas in the sedan, Stewart watched from his front row vantage point, seated at the Old Town Alexandria bar, with his computer angled ever so slightly to block any potential onlookers.

Stewart tried to anticipate Jackson's next move, especially after hearing him give Caroline directions to his apartment.

She was likely already be en route to Charlottesville. But before Stewart could pursue the chase, he wanted to see if they'd provide any inkling as to what their plans would be.

x   x   x

The high-pitched buzz signaled to Jackson that someone was waiting at the front door to his apartment.

Jackson released the lock. Caroline took two steps at a time to his third floor apartment, where he waited in the open doorway.

"You look terrible," he said, "Come in."

"Thanks," she replied, still soaked to the bone from driving through the rainstorm. "I'm a mess."

"Yeah, I'd say so."

"Where can I change out of these wet clothes?"

Her frantic pacing and refusal to look him in the eye made him realize how serious this situation had become.

Jackson pointed her toward the bathroom in the back of the apartment. He'd never seen someone so panicked.

She was not the same person he'd met a couple of days earlier. Caroline was in fear for her life. She was traumatized, distant.

When she emerged from the bathroom, the rich aroma of spaghetti overcame her. Her blonde hair was completely dry and pulled back in a ponytail. She wore a pair of khaki shorts and a plain blue t-shirt that highlighted her bright blue eyes.

"Something smells wonderful," she said, smiling for the first time since she arrived.

"Well, since you took the liberty of taking a shower, I got bored and decided to fix dinner. I hope you're hungry."

"Thanks. That's nice," she replied again, color returning to her face.

They spooned up some spaghetti and sat around an old kitchen table. A phone book propped up one of the legs, while a baseball bat served as another leg. Definitely a bachelor pad.

"Thanks again for letting me come."

"Sure thing," said Jackson.

Just as he had suspected, she'd be going with him to Kentucky for the weekend. The circumstances were a little different than he originally anticipated.

"So, let me fill you in on the details," began Caroline.

"I'm listening, whenever you're ready."

"Well, you know that I moved to Virginia not too long ago to work on the McAllister farm. I also told you I was working on a personal project. And you know that my father passed away when I was a young kid."

"Yeah," said Jackson, following along.

"Well, my father was murdered."

"Oh."

That wasn't the insight he was expecting. It suddenly hit him that this was a very serious matter. He was nervous as to what he might learn next.

"His body was found in the Warrenton backwoods. He had been shot too many times to count. The case went cold just after his body was discovered. Nobody in the area seemed interested in trying to solve the murder. My mother lobbied the local politicians and law enforcement to pursue the case harder, but everyone gave her the cold shoulder. I was too young to know much of what was going on, other than the fact I lost my dad. Looking back, I think my mother could've done a lot more."

"I'm guessing that since he was an outsider, nobody really cared too much. Kind of like the recent homicide. Things quieted down pretty quickly after that first day of investigating. According to Paul, of course."

"The second day I moved to town, I stopped by the county police department and requested some information."

Her pace of speech was picking up as she got more into the story and began to relay some of the trickier facts.

She continued, "The weird part was that they just handed me the file, like they didn't even want it anymore."

"They just gave you the file?"

"They just handed it over. I haven't been back, so I have no idea if they made copies or what."

"Had they worked on the case recently?"

"Not at all. The last note in the file was from 1998."

"So what do you know?"

"Unfortunately, I don't know anything more than I did when I moved here. And what I do know is more from my personal investigation than from what was in the case file."

They finished their dinners and threw the dirty dishes in the sink. Caroline followed Jackson into the living room where they sat on opposite ends of an old faded blue sofa. Caroline sunk much deeper into the sofa than she anticipated. But it was nice to be still for a moment, to be nestled securely into something far away from danger, even if it was a lousy old couch in a bachelor pad.

It was getting late into the evening, and the crowds were returning after the rain cleared. The early summer air was refreshing as it circulated through the open apartment windows bringing with it the sound of the nightlife three stories below.

"I think we should head downstairs for a drink. What do you say?" Jackson asked.

"That sounds great. I could definitely use a drink, or ten," she responded.

Jackson pointed Caroline to his roommate's bedroom to get ready. Changing into jeans in his own room, he was still oblivious to the blinking red light from the ceiling corner.

When he exited his bedroom, Caroline was waiting for him on the couch.

She looked beautiful. She had brushed out her ponytail and let her blonde hair fall over her exposed shoulders. Blue was obviously her color. And her tanned legs were much more athletic than Jackson would have guessed.

Jackson wore his usual sloppy bar attire.

Caroline didn't mind. She was happy to have a friend who wasn't out to kill her.

X   X   X

Caroline grabbed a vacant table on the sidewalk of a newly opened wine bar while Jackson went inside to order two glasses of wine. It took nearly ten minutes for him to navigate the crowd, which was fine with Caroline. She enjoyed being invisible in plain sight. It was much safer than being on the run in the middle of nowhere.

They fit right in with the young adult crowd.

Across the Mall, a local band began their set. The crowds filling the outdoor tables at the surrounding restaurants, including the wine bar, turned their attention to the band and listened as they ran through their repertoire of popular cover songs.

Jackson encountered a few of his classmates and introduced Caroline. Over the course of the evening, people joined and left the table frequently. Jackson knew that rumors about a new girl would circulate the next day, especially since nobody knew about his breakup with Samantha. But by then they'd be long gone, on their way to Kentucky. He couldn't care less.

Two hours and five drinks later, they were trading stories, laughing hysterically at their escapades. Caroline tried to impress Jackson with her very own Bourbon Street and Mardi Gras stories. But, not to be outdone, Jackson always had another tale of debauchery up his sleeve.

"If the offer is still open, I'd like to go to Kentucky with you and your friend for the weekend," said Caroline. "I really need to get as far away from this place as possible."

"I figured you'd be along for the ride," he said with a charming smile.

We should head back, then. We've got an early start ahead of us and a long drive to Kentucky."

"How early?"

"Probably 6 a.m. or so."

"Seriously? You should've cut me off an hour ago," she laughed. "I hope you don't expect me to drive!"

"I'll handle the driving, but we do need to get going."

Caroline didn't want the night to end. For a few short hours, she had forgotten everything else. She felt safe and secure in the friendly Charlottesville atmosphere, enjoying Jackson's company.

As they made the short walk back to his apartment, the effects of the wine and conversation were wearing off. Caroline was running for her life.

Jackson only knew the basics of the situation. She was certain that he understood the danger she, and now both of them, faced. But she knew she would have to divulge more information during the long drive the following day. She wanted him to be aware of the imminent danger—for the safety of them both. And she didn't want him to do anything that would tip off their location.

X   X   X

Agent Stewart placed his hand on the laptop screen, ready to close it down, when the live feed showed Caroline and Jackson entering the apartment. From his corner stool at the Old Town bar, he watched Caroline tuck herself in on the couch and Jackson flop into his bed. They were fast asleep in less than two minutes.

Stewart would make the drive to Charlottesville first thing in the morning. He was eager to ask Caroline a few questions before turning her over to Abramson and company.

He closed down his laptop and paid his tab. As he climbed into the sedan, he pulled out his cell phone and dialed John McAllister's phone number. He hadn't contacted him since the fiasco with the girl began.

McAllister had no way of knowing her true identity, or did he? He always lived up to his reputation of being one step ahead of the game. Maybe he had been duped this time?

There was no answer.

26

John McAllister's cell phone lit up on the corner of his desk, displaying Agent Stewart's name. It was the second missed call from him in less than thirty minutes. It was the only time Agent Stewart urgently needed to speak with McAllister, and he was unavailable.

With one leg crossed over the other, and a glass filled with his own distilled whiskey, McAllister sat at a tiny round table in the middle of the cavernous ballroom.

Senator Windgate sat across the table. The old policymaker puffed on his cigar as the two men sat in silence down in the coolness of the caves. They had been in the room for a few hours.

A foiled assassination attempt earlier in the evening, and the detonation of a car bomb in front of the McAllister house earlier in the week had the two men scrambling to come up with a plan.

McAllister spoke first. "According to the report from our team, Abramson was at home on his back deck."

"Who do you have out there?"

"I have someone tracking Abramson, that's all that matters."

"Good. So where do we stand?"

"We don't have any confirmation that Abramson is behind this. But everything points to him."

"What about Ron?" Windgate asked.

"I try not to think about it, but I know he's in with Abramson. How can I call my own son an enemy?"

"He'll come to his senses. Just give him time."

"We don't have time to give. But I hope he does, before anybody gets hurt. Or killed."

"Or before the distillery is taken over by people who will expose it, ruining all of the hard work we put in over the years to keep this network thriving. We'll all go down if that happens. The press out there loves this stuff. It will destroy us . . . our legacies."

"Let's not let any of that happen. We need a plan. And we need to find Caroline."

Senator Windgate had watched his friend's admiration of Caroline grow over the last two months. It was quite strange the way he had taken her in and mentored her. McAllister usually kept his distance from complete strangers, yet he let Caroline in close to his personal matters. He trusted her very much, and he had no reason to think otherwise. Or so he thought.

"John, she seems like a very bright young girl," said the senator. "I don't see her getting into trouble without a fight. She may be on the run somewhere."

"There's probably something you should know about her," said John. "I'm listening."

"I know Caroline better than you think I do. I even know her better than she thinks I do."

He paused to consider how he wanted to tell the senator. The two men sat alone in the cavern with only one illuminated chandelier shining down on the table. The darkness hid the walls of the large room, and he gazed out into the vast darkness.

He continued, "Scooter, Caroline isn't who she says she is. Her first name is Caroline, but her last name is not Mills."

"I'm still listening, but I'm a bit confused now." The senator stiffened in his seat.

"She has no idea that I know, but I've known all along. Everyone accused me of not performing my due diligence before bringing her to the farm. That's foolish. It's downright scary how much I know about her."

Windgate was becoming a little nervous now. The long-time confidants told each other everything regarding the distillery—to an extent. There was no other way to operate, to ensure their success. Senator Windgate was McAllister's right-hand man. But the aging senator was just learning that his confidant, business partner, and best friend had kept something from him, information that could have serious consequences for the group.

"John, who is she?" asked the senator in a demanding tone.

"Scooter, she got sick in the hallway the other day because she saw her father in a photograph on the wall."

Before the enraged senator could respond, a sudden flashlight beam appeared down the long hallway, approaching the two men. As the sprinting footsteps drew closer, Jimmy's face began to emerge in the darkness. He was running as fast as he could toward the old men.

"Where is your phone? I've been trying to call you for hours," said Jimmy, breathing heavily from his long sprint.

"I left it up in the house," said John. "Scooter and I needed some time to get our heads straight and come up with a plan."

"Tell somebody you're down here next time," said Jimmy. "We just found out that Paul has turned. He was spotted on Abramson's deck after he got off work last night."

"That bastard," Senator Windgate said as he slammed his fist on the table.

McAllister remained silent, keeping his distant gaze.

"That puts us at square one with Caroline and Ron," said Jimmy. "We don't know if there was truth to anything he told us at Molly O's."

The senator was enraged. He whirled his chair into the darkness of the room, out of sight. The only sounds were the echoes of the chair crashing against the cave wall.

While Jimmy stood amazed at what he'd just witnessed, he also felt relieved, and slightly reassured, to see the amount of fight the old senator had left in him.

McAllister finally stood from the table.

"This changes things," he said with an uneasy calmness. "The lines have been clearly drawn. The war has begun."

Jimmy stood back and waited for the master distiller to continue.

"I never thought we would have to do this, but some members must be cut out completely," continued the old don.

The message was clear to Scooter and Jimmy, as they knew exactly what "cut out completely" meant.

"I will have Paul killed," screamed Senator Windgate. "Consider it done!"

His words echoed against the cavern's walls.

Jimmy had heard about the old man's reputation for a quick temper in his younger years. However, he had never seen such a display by the old man.

McAllister stepped away from the senator, eyeing him suspiciously.

Why the sudden outburst? Was this anger merely a front? Was Senator Windgate conspiring with the others? Or was he genuinely on board? More importantly, did he just take the bait?

A few worried looks were passed between Jimmy and his boss, as they tried to determine what was motivating the old senator. It was not like him to demand another's life. It had been decades since that spark left the senator.

Had Windgate forgotten about the pact that no lives would be taken ever again? The criminal activity of the past would no longer be tolerated within the organization.

"Nobody is going to die," McAllister announced in a stern, but calm voice. "At least nobody is going to die by our hands. We've dealt with murder before, and it nearly destroyed everything."

Senator Windgate retrieved a handkerchief from his pocket and wiped the sweat from his brow. He sat down in another chair. He took long, deep breaths, calming his excited nerves.

"I'm sorry," he finally said. "I don't want anyone to die by my actions. I'm too old to have to deal with that on my conscience."

"So that's all that's stopping you," Jimmy teased. He smiled and patted the old man on the shoulder trying to lighten the mood and relax his nerves.

"Funny," he replied. "I could still take you down in two seconds, youngster. Don't push it."

McAllister desperately tried to hide his concern from the other two men.

"I trust both of you," he said, looking each of the two men in the eyes. "I don't know who else I can trust, so don't speak a word about the distillery, Caroline, or any of our whereabouts to anyone."

"Yes, sir," responded Jimmy.

Senator Windgate nodded in agreement.

"Let's hope they haven't reached anyone on our security detail," McAllister said. "Jimmy, comb the men on our team very carefully. Look for anything that might indicate they've turned. Let me know immediately if anything comes up. And I will keep my phone with me from now on."

"I think I've had enough for tonight," said the senator. "I'll call my wife and let her know that I'm staying here."

"Sounds good," replied John. "We'll get an early start in the morning."

They followed Jimmy's flashlight beam down the long hallway to the cave's entry. Two members of the security detail, clad in head-to-toe black and brandishing automatic weapons, greeted them at the door to escort them safely back to the house. Security measures had definitely been heightened since the last incident and McAllister wasn't taking any chances.

"How many men do you have?" asked the senator as they walked up the wooded pathway towards the mansion.

"I won't divulge that number. Let's just say I have eyes and ears everywhere. Not just on the property either."

That statement struck a nerve with the senator. McAllister was withholding information from his longtime partner—information that Scooter desperately wanted to know.

After the senator said goodnight and showed himself upstairs to a guest bedroom, McAllister slipped into his office to retrieve his phone.

Everything looked to be in place. He took his cell phone into the bedroom in case anything urgent came about during the night.

As he was walking down the hall he checked his missed calls. Three missed calls from Agent Stewart.

In McAllister's mind, there could be only one reason for Stewart to call—for information. He would never reveal anything to Agent Stewart. Without thinking twice, he erased the missed calls from the phone's history.

His trusted inner circle was shrinking drastically. No one could be trusted. In fact, for some reason, he had a hunch there was an enemy inside his estate.

27

Agent Stewart woke early the next morning to get a head start to Charlottesville. It would be an easy trip. Knock on the door, flex a little muscle, and bring the girl back for questioning.

His heart skipped a beat when his computer screen showed an empty bedroom and unoccupied sofa.

He was already out the door on the early Northern Virginia morning before he homed in on the GPS device he had attached to Caroline's car. From his smartphone, he discovered her Jeep was still parked outside Jackson's apartment building. However, it didn't take a genius to figure out that she wasn't still there. He had no luck tracking her location through her cell phone either.

Caroline had been smart enough the night before to turn her phone completely off. In fact, she almost threw it into a dumpster behind Jackson's apartment right before they left town. But she thought better of it and decided to keep it powered off, and not before forwarding Jackson's phone number to the animal hospital where Max was recovering.

Jackson was up before dawn, ready to hit the road. While he'd had as much to drink as Caroline, his tolerance was much higher. He didn't suffer any effects from the night before.

Caroline's stories weighed heavily on Jackson's mind throughout the night, making it difficult for him to rest. The events she described from the few days before, and his own connection to the murdered man in Warrenton, motivated him to leave in the dark early hours of morning. He was eager to escape town and any threats that may still be in Virginia.

His only hope was that everything would be back to normal when they returned a few days later.

x   x   x

Agent Stewart did not dare call Chief Justice Abramson to inform him that he had missed his opportunity to catch the girl. He pressed down harder on the accelerator and arrived in Charlottesville in record time.

His collar loose, with sweat already soaking through his light blue button down, Stewart plowed through the front door of the apartment building, oblivious to any onlookers.

At the top of the stairs on the third floor, he burst through Jackson's apartment door. He didn't mess around. He began canvassing the place looking for clues as to where the couple may have gone.

Jackson stopped just before the Kentucky state line to fill up the car. The sun was now burning the morning dew from the grass at the service station.

"Good morning," Jackson said through the slightly cracked passenger window as he filled up the tank.

Caroline had slept through the entire drive so far. Her blonde hair was a wreck, and the seat belt had left imprint lines across the side of her face. She wiggled out from under a Tulane sweatshirt he had let her borrow.

"Good morning," she mustered, stretching her legs and arms as far as she could reach in the cramped car.

"I'm going to run in and pay. Do you want any coffee?"

"Yes, please. Let me get my purse out of the trunk."

"Don't worry about it. It's on me."

"Thanks," she replied, rubbing her eyes to wake up. She was still feeling the effects of last night's wine. She barely remembered him dragging her off the couch and into the car.

Jackson returned and the aroma of freshly brewed, gas station coffee filled the car.

Agent Stewart never had a chance to tag Jackson's car with a tracker.

But he was able to leverage his connections within the Bureau to gain access to Jackson's credit card activity.

"Bingo," the aging agent whispered, scanning through the young man's recent transactions. The purchase of gas at a truck stop in Huntington, West Virginia, was all Stewart needed. The pair was heading west on Interstate 64, although the destination was still unknown.

Agent Stewart barreled down the highway at top speed. In his government sedan, no state trooper would harass him. He kept his laptop open and connected as he sped down the interstate. He would know within seconds of any future transactions on Jackson Cole's credit card.

It was still early in morning for most folks, and the roads were clear. At the rate he was going, Stewart hoped to catch up to them by early afternoon.

The brisk morning air and the smell of freshly cut highway grass replaced the smell of coffee as Jackson and Caroline cruised down the interstate with the windows open.

The coffee was a bit strong for Caroline's liking, but it was exactly what she needed to power through her mild hangover.

Jackson, one hand on the wheel, the other catching air out of his window, gazed into the distance as he steered the car through the eastern Kentucky hillside. His wavy, light brown hair was blown straight back by the wind.

He couldn't help but think about what a great time he had the night before. It was a genuine good time. No pressure. Just two friends taking in the night. For a couple of hours, they enjoyed a reprieve from recent dire events. Their shared sense of escape, real or imagined, allowed them to form a bond, a quick friendship that already carried a massive amount of trust.

Caroline reached into her purse and pulled out a pair of aviators to shield her eyes from the bright morning sun. With her eyes hidden, she could sneak a few peaks at the handsome young man sitting next to her.

She barely knew him, but there was something about Jackson that attracted her. Maybe it was the circumstances. She felt secure, like she had someone to watch out for her. She didn't know if it was real, but it didn't matter. She liked him.

For so long, she had been living a lie. She quickly gained the trust of John McAllister, but it was the result of false pretense. She wondered how long she could keep her secret past, and true identity, hidden from Jackson. Was it really even necessary to try?

Just before she could open up—to share the truth—she lost her nerve and thoughts of trust quickly subsided.

"So tell me about the track," she said, intentionally bringing up a different subject.

"What do you want to know?"

"I've never been to a horse race," she replied. "What's it like?"

Caroline lobbed the softball to Jackson. She wanted a distraction from her inner turmoil. He replied as if he had rehearsed the perfect answer a thousand times.

With a crooked grin he began, "You see, it's the purest form of sport."

"Here we go," she sighed, dipping her aviators so Jackson could see her eye roll.

"Beautiful creatures thundering down the track with the force of a freight train and the grace of swans. When the field passes you by, you feel the thunder of hooves pounding in your chest. There's no rush like it."

"Ok, so how do you pick a winner?"

"The best horse always wins. Not from an odds standpoint, because the books don't always tell the truth. But the best horse always wins. Don't ever get caught up in placing bets on pedigree, distance, track condition, jockey, and trainer. Just look at the hind legs. The strength of their gallop comes from their butts—just like a woman," he laughed.

"You had me until that last bit," she laughed.

"I couldn't let it pass."

"I guess it could've been a lot worse than that," she said.

Jackson pulled into a rest area along the highway.

"I need to make a pit stop," he said. "I'll be back in a minute."

Caroline nodded and remained in the car. Once Jackson was out of sight, she pulled out her cell phone and turned it on. There was a voicemail, and for the first time in a few hours, she found herself feeling desperately lonely.

The message didn't do much to improve her outlook. She grew faint as she listened to the concerned old man warn her of the danger she faced.

John McAllister pleaded in his message for her to come back to the farm under his protection. He said that he had no idea why she was hiding, but that he'd protect her from whatever or whoever was after her.

She wondered how much of the truth he already knew. Could she trust him? Was this merely a ploy to get her back so she could be silenced forever?

Caroline powered off her phone again and placed it back in her purse as Jackson returned to the car. Her cheerful demeanor had long vanished.

"I just talked to Jeff," said Jackson as he climbed back into the car. "He said his girlfriend just kicked him out—we can't stay there anymore. So I booked us two rooms downtown. He always has some sort of girl drama going on."

Caroline didn't respond. She continued to stare out the passenger window. Selfishly focusing on her life-endangering predicament, and forgetting about bringing Jackson into harm's way, she failed to realize the terrible mistake she had just committed.

Agent Stewart's laptop pinged with a new message indicating that Caroline's phone had been located. From the pair's location, Stewart realized he was gaining ground. They probably had no idea that they were being tracked. His job would be easier than expected.

Adrenaline pumping from the excitement of the hunt, he hit top speed in the sedan. Weaving through the mountains of West Virginia, he was closing in on Caroline faster than he expected.

Agent Stewart's cell phone rang with an unknown number.

"Get the girl and bring her to the old mine," said the male voice, purposefully disguised with technology to hide the caller's identity.

"Who is this?" demanded Agent Stewart.

"Just bring the girl to the old mine. You know exactly where I'm talking about," said the voice followed by a click, ending the call.

The startled agent pulled onto the emergency lane and brought the sedan to an abrupt halt.

He had been trained in his earlier days with the Bureau to identify callers using voice-disguising technologies. He would listen to fluctuations and flex patterns to identify criminals. He was one of the best, but this caller was good. The slow, methodical tone, with no emotion, proved it very difficult to solve.

And the old mine? Agent Stewart knew of only one old mine, where he witnessed the aftermath of the most horrific crime he had ever encountered. Every inch of the scene was covered in red. He never knew a man's body could hold so much blood.

Agent Stewart knew what this was about—silencing an old demon forever.

As his car idled on the side of the highway, he looked at himself in the rearview mirror, reflecting upon his life, as he had done frequently of late.

There were many things he regretted from his dual life as a criminal and as a federal agent. Given the chance to go back, he would do many things differently.

The guilt had been getting much worse over the past few months. He was losing sleep, not eating right, gaining weight, and chain smoking again. It was a deadly combination.

But he had to find Caroline. One more criminal act and he would call it a career. He would walk away from the distillery operation and its cronies forever.

Sitting there on the side of the highway, his phone rang again. This time it was Chief Justice Abramson.

28

Senator Windgate had already left the house when John McAllister got up that morning. Jimmy informed him that the old senator had declined any additional security detail. Old and stubborn, he dared anyone to come after his life. He would "give 'em hell," or at least that's what he claimed. Even after his car had been bombed and a sniper had been killed aiming at McAllister, Windgate would never back down.

McAllister admired the old senator's courage, but he worried about his close friend and business partner. If the Abramson camp nearly infiltrated them while within the safe confines of the McAllister estate, it was only a matter of time until they hit Senator Windgate while he was alone and unprotected.

While lying awake in bed the night before, he had an interesting realization. It seemed as though Senator Windgate and John McAllister were only targeted when they were in each other's company.

But more importantly, the assassination of the senator would mean the end of the road for everyone involved. The distillery would be exposed, and many of the nation's prominent political leaders would undoubtedly bow out in shame. The most powerful of the political elite would call for heads upon hearing of the senator's assassination, while at the same time ducking into the shadows and covering their dirty tracks.

The hunt would reach into the depths of the Supreme Court and the United States Senate. It would cause widespread panic and a loss of faith in the system. Or at least what was left of it. It would probably be the final nail in the coffin for the country's economic crisis.

This alone had the potential to change the course of the nation—proven corruptness and illegality in the highest of elected and appointed chairs. Everyone always suspected it to be true. Now, unfortunately, it would be proven.

McAllister needed a break from the stress, so he and Jimmy spent the morning and early afternoon in the caverns. Only two more days until the quorum of the group's members. Abramson, Ron, Senator Windgate, McAllister, and a few others, gathered in one room, face to face.

Jimmy swept the floors until they were spotless. McAllister spent most of his time testing samples from a newly mature batch of whiskey that would become Senate Proof.

He planned to bring the group to its senses by focusing their attention on Windgate's pending retirement and the unveiling of Senate Proof. That, he would urge the other members to remember, was the reason for the group's existence—to promote the finest whiskey around. It was an old bootleg game for old men. Nothing more—at least in recent years.

He kept testing more samples until he could feel the warmth of the whiskey's effects in his cheeks. He didn't care. If anyone deserved a few drinks, he did. He'd paid his dues over the years in more ways than he could count.

Thoughts of Caroline soon preoccupied the old distiller's mind.

He walked into the grand ballroom in the cavern and headed directly down the long hallway towards the cave's entrance.

Jimmy stopped cleaning for a moment and watched the old man pause halfway down the hall and turn to one of the pictures.

McAllister admired his much younger physique and then quickly turned his attention to another man. He knew for a fact it was the last picture ever taken of the Caroline's father before his death. The events of what actually happened would always remain a mystery to him.

Caroline's father had attended a late night event at the distillery. It was the unveiling of that year's batch of whiskey. The members of the distillery hadn't taken any precautionary steps to cloak the event in secrecy. Looking back, they were rather lax about even keeping it private.

At first, McAllister had been stunned that an unknown outsider had penetrated the distillery's walls and wandered into the party.

Who was this stranger who bypassed his security? How did he even find out about the event?

To avoid creating an awkward scene in the middle of the party, McAllister approached the stranger, extending a hand and welcoming the man to his estate. Caroline's father introduced himself to John McAllister about halfway through the night. He was a very handsome and well-mannered man, possessing the same blue eyes that the old man admired every day in Caroline. The stranger disarmed his suspicions with his warm smile and polite manner. The two men found themselves engaged in conversation for the next thirty minutes.

The story went something like this—the young man was in Washington, DC, for a business conference. Late one night, he found himself at the Hay-Adams Hotel rubbing shoulders with some older gentlemen who were not part of the conference. Later into the night, conversation turned to a secret distillery in a quaint little town not too far from the District. Caroline's father, Robert, gathered just enough information that night to find his way to the party the following evening.

Robert made the drive to Warrenton in just over an hour as the sun was setting. He spotted a caravan of official-looking vehicles heading down a winding country road, so he decided to follow. As the caravan was waved into the driveway of the massive McAllister Estate, he was waved right in as part of the entourage. The security detail must have thought he was one of them.

Without acting too surprised, Robert slipped on his sports coat as he got out of his vehicle and was escorted by an imposing security guard down through the woods to the distillery doors.

No name check. No invitee list. Nothing. The guards must not have detected anything suspicious about him. He looked like he belonged, and consequently, he was let in without a second look.

Robert made himself at home and joined the group of men he had met the night before at the Hay-Adams Hotel. They welcomed him into the distillery and made introductions. Soon, Robert was wheeling and dealing like never before. Until he met the legendary master distiller and host, John McAllister.

The now older John McAllister focused intently on the photograph hanging in the hallway. He desperately tried to recollect the events that had followed that evening. He never expected that the mysterious man and his subsequent murder would haunt him for so many years. The group did everything in their power to brush the event under the rug. There was never any convincing evidence that the group was involved. None of the elder leaders could honestly state for certain that the murder was connected to their organization.

However, the damning evidence was coming back in John's memory.

After Robert had moved on to meet some other groups of people that evening, McAllister went by himself into the back cavern room containing the then large, wooden vats of sour mash. His anger brewed as he mulled over the possibilities of his illegal whiskey operation being infiltrated by outsiders.

What if Robert wasn't who he said he was? What if he was about to expose the distillery? The drugs? The weapons? The corruption?

Many times through the years he had questioned his rage. Had it been necessary?

So many catastrophic possibilities had run through his head that he stormed back into the party and pulled Ron and Michael Abramson aside. He ripped them apart. They had been given specific orders to monitor the security staff and its procedures. McAllister let them know how badly they had failed. He came as close as he had ever come to striking Ron with a closed fist. This had been the youngsters' first opportunity to prove themselves worthy of having some limited control of the distillery. And they blew it. Miserably.

Less than five minutes later, there was a commotion in one corner of the ballroom. McAllister's emotions had settled considerably. He was casually listening to the jazz band when the antics occurred.

Ron, Michael Abramson, and Will Stewart rather conspicuously escorted Robert from the cavern. Nobody knows what happened after the three men tossed him out. Rumors circulated that they took him into the woods and gave him a nasty beating. But not much else was known about the events that followed. The three of them would never speak to authorities, or anyone else for that matter.

Luckily for them, there was not enough evidence to charge them when Robert's bullet-riddled body was found two days later in the woods.

McAllister banned his son from the operation, exiling him to some remote location on the Florida Panhandle. Michael Abramson absolved himself of the events and went on to a rather successful legal career, always maintaining some involvement in the distillery operations.

Because he was Ron's best friend and probably knew the truth behind the murder, the elder McAllister had no choice but to keep him as part of the team. Keep your enemies closest, as the old saying goes.

Agent Stewart wasn't going anywhere. His stake in the operation was vested, and he could be trusted to get things accomplished. But it was very odd that he never came forward with an account of the events.

Maybe the three men had nothing to do with Robert's murder. That was quite possible—it could have been a random act of violence. Maybe Robert stumbled across some backwoods landowner who took offense to him trespassing on his property. And after a time, McAllister bought into that theory. In fact, he was almost ready to allow Ron back into the equation until Caroline showed up on the radar. All of those haunting memories had returned to the forefront of his mind.

Caroline possessed the same disarming, warm demeanor as her father. She could light up any room. Soon after McAllister realized that she had no idea of the connection between her father's murder and the distillery, he brought her in close to his inner circle. He loved talking to her about life and her dreams. He really enjoyed having someone with whom to talk, especially someone who was intelligent and beautiful.

But he had let his guard down. If anyone failed the distillery, it had been him. Miserably. He walked her through the same hallway where he had last seen her father. Caroline saw the picture. And things would never be the same.

McAllister had kept that picture on the wall as a reminder—never ever let your guard down. And that's exactly what he did.

Jimmy came trotting down the hallway.

"Mr. McAllister, we have a visitor arriving."

"And who is it?" asked John, still halfway in his dream, desperately trying to avoid reality.

"The Supreme Court."

Jimmy always referred to the Chief Justice as the entire Supreme Court. It was half mocking, and half ignorance.

"Great. Things seem to get more and more exciting around here," said the old man as Jimmy caught up to his brisk walk down the hall.

Chief Justice Abramson climbed out of his convertible as Jimmy and his boss emerged from the wooded path. The esteemed judge appeared to be arriving straight from the Court.

The look on his face indicated that this would not be a pleasant meeting.

29

When Caroline saw Jeff Barber waiting for them at the hotel, she was shocked by his appearance. He was not the smooth sophisticated millionaire she had imagined. Looking at his scruffy beard, the tobacco dip in his teeth, and the sweat stains on his ratty t-shirt, she immediately regretted coming along.

Jackson had booked rooms at the historic Seelbach Hotel. From the elegant marble columns and Native American murals in the lobby, Caroline realized she would be spending the next few days in luxury. Despite the trashy appearance of his friend, Jackson earned some credit for his choice of accommodations.

To the right of the lobby was the hotel bar, a popular spot for live jazz according to the front desk clerk. Jeff came out of the bar carrying three drinks, one for each member of the trio.

Great, she thought to herself, realizing this would be a binge-filled reunion between Jackson and Jeff.

I'm sure glad I came along for this ride. At least I'm safe, for now.

She reluctantly accepted the drink from Jeff and took a sip, almost choking because it was so strong. Caroline was still reeling from the effects of the night before, and the last thing she wanted to taste was hard liquor.

"I'll take this up to my room and finish it later," she lied.

"Fair enough," replied Jeff.

Jackson and Caroline found their adjacent rooms on the sixth floor of the hotel. Looking out her window, she could see the downtown entertainment district, highlighted by several restaurants, clubs, and bars.

She hoped she wouldn't have to spend too much time down there.

She wanted to stay away from public space, fearing that she would be vulnerable and easily taken by her enemies.

She also hoped Jackson wouldn't be in any kind of danger here. She couldn't hide the guilt she felt for bringing Jackson into her mess. She did, however, feel a little safer this far away from Warrenton.

The luxurious bathroom quickly caught her attention and before long, she was running the hot water for a relaxing afternoon bath.

After a call for room service, she slipped into the complimentary robe and ordered bottle of champagne on ice. She poured the rest of the drink Jeff gave her down the bathroom sink. It was terrible. If she was going to drink, it would be champagne today. One bottle and she would be good for the rest of the night. No worries in Louisville.

X   X   X

Jeff and Jackson sat opposite one another in the wing chairs in their hotel room. Since Jeff's girlfriend had told him not to come back, he would be staying in the room with Jackson.

They had done it plenty of times before. On the road, playing golf on the mini tours, they would pile into the cheapest hotel room they could find, often sharing a double bed. It made for some epic stories, usually involving escapades with local women—all night on the town before the tournament the next day. That's the primary reason Jackson never made it big playing pro golf. He had the talent—just not the drive and determination.

When the twosome weren't out carousing, they were building their business and programming web content they would later sell for millions. What a lucrative partnership they had created.

Sitting in the hotel room, they opened the curtains revealing the city's modest skyline.

"You look terrible," Jackson began. "I talked you up so much, and you have to embarrass me like this. You could've at least showered. You look homeless."

"You didn't tell me she is so damn hot," Jeff responded.

"She's definitely got the look," Jackson grinned.

"You're not—"

"No, no," Jackson interrupted. "We just met a few days ago," cutting off any hint that the two might be into each other. A lie on his part, of course.

Jeff laughed at his friend while he downed his second drink. Jackson still had a little bit left of his first.

"So what's the deal at the track?" Jackson asked, changing the subject. "Do you have any hot tips for tomorrow?"

"Of course I do. Have you forgotten that I'm the best handicapper ever? Bet on the jockeys tomorrow. I've got an inkling about the little Frenchman."

"So are you up for the year?"

"Not a chance," he answered truthfully.

The two old friends shared a laugh at Jeff's misfortunes in the gambling arena. Some people just shouldn't come into large sums of money at an early age. There was no telling how much Jeff had remaining in the bank. Frugality was not his calling card.

"Well, I guess I'll clean up a little," said Jeff. "You guys up for anything fun tonight?"

"You know me. I can rally the troops anytime."

"Perfect. We'll show Caroline a little of Lexington's Irish heritage," he said, referring to a strip of pubs in the Highlands neighborhood.

Jeff poured another slug while Jackson finished off his first. The afternoon had the makings of turning into a crazy night.

x   x   x

Caroline had just finished her bath when she heard the knock on her door. As soon as she opened the door, she could smell the bourbon on Jackson's breath. In the three hours or so since she had last seen him, he and Jeff had obviously done some damage to the liquor cabinet.

"I hope you're up for a good night," he said, already glassy-eyed.

"Didn't we just do this last night?" she grumbled, trying to show her disinterest.

She'd already had half her bottle of champagne and was feeling just fine. She wanted nothing more than to slip on some comfortable clothes and lay around her room all night. At least she would be safe there.

"Oh, come on," Jackson responded. "When's the next time you'll ever get to take a spontaneous road trip like this? You can't bail on us tonight."

"I'll think about it," she conceded after a long pause.

A much cleaner Jeff came around the corner and presented her with another drink. If it wasn't clear by now, Caroline had a firsthand understanding of Jeff's vices—alcohol and gambling. Just what she wanted to deal with for an evening on the town.

His beard was gone and he looked well groomed. She might even find him attractive at some point now. Or maybe it was the champagne speaking. Her only complaint was that he had overdone it with the aftershave.

"Now that it won't look like I'm out with a mountain man, I'll come out for a little while," she said.

She immediately regretted it as images of being caught flashed in her mind.

"I'll see you in an hour down in the lobby," Jeff said. He then left them alone, his overwhelming aftershave lingering.

Caroline invited Jackson into her room. She wanted to confirm that he understood that they were in danger. She was concerned that he didn't understand the magnitude of the situation.

Upon entering, Jackson noticed the half empty bottle of champagne still on ice. Fair enough. She could go about this her own way.

"You do realize that someone is after me, and they'll probably catch up to us sometime in the next few days."

"I know. I'm trying not to think about it," he responded. "We're a long way from Virginia. I think we've bought ourselves plenty of time."

"I hope so," she said, looking for reassurance.

"Jeff and I won't let anything happen to you. He knows this city like the back of his hand. If things get ugly, you'll have plenty of places to hide for a while."

"Thanks," she smiled. "I hope we'll be okay."

"We'll be fine."

Caroline did feel a little better. The combination of the champagne and Jackson's comforting words lifted her spirits. Something about him seemed to calm her. She was now ready for some fun—another night in a row. Jackson left her to get dressed.

The two young men couldn't help but stare as Caroline stepped off the elevator. Her blonde hair was flowing and she was as beautiful as Jackson had ever seen her.

Caroline realized the two guys hadn't slowed down with the alcohol as she approached. Each had a full Julep cup and reeked of bourbon and cologne.

She knew they were gawking at her. And although she enjoyed it, she brushed it off. She was used to the attention.

They hailed a cab in front of the historic hotel and off they went to the Highlands.

Seconds after the cab left the Seelbach, Agent Stewart drove by the hotel. Fortunately for him, Caroline had neglected to turn off her cell phone when she checked into her room.

Fortunately for her, at least for now, she had left it in the hotel room.

Agent Stewart parked in the garage behind the hotel and flashed his credentials to the front desk clerk. Without a warrant, his request to search the premises was denied. And the hotel also did not have any record of a guest named Caroline.

In no hurry whatsoever, Agent Stewart saddled up to the Seelbach Hotel bar and waited for Caroline's return.

It would give him plenty of time to come to grips with his conversation with Chief Justice Abramson.

30

John McAllister sat across from the man he was certain had ruined his son's life, the same man who had made the old man's recent life a living hell. He was glad he could remain calm.

The master distiller and the Chief Justice were the only two in the office. The doors had been closed, shutting everyone else out of this important meeting. But because trust was lacking among the members, help was very near. Jimmy stood alert just outside the closed door. Other members of the security team were positioned to enter through the office windows in the event of an emergency.

If it had not been the Chief Justice, McAllister surely would have made a statement with the visitor. But there would be no violence today.

John respected the position, but not the man.

The two men sat in silence for several minutes. The only sound was the ticking of the oak grandfather clock in the corner of the ornate office.

Michael Abramson seemed agitated. He acted put off. He looked disturbed. McAllister sensed that the Chief Justice had shown up at his estate out of desperation. Why would the most powerful legal mind in the country leave his post in the middle of the afternoon to visit a foe? Was this some sort of a ploy? Was the Chief Justice seeking information?

All of these scenarios ran through John's mind as he sat behind his desk, studying his visitor's every move.

Abramson broke the silence with a terrible screeching sound—his chair sliding back over the hardwood floors. He stood up and walked over to the window. The horse barns out back were just as he remembered them. He had spent many summers in college working the fields with Ron.

"Look, I don't have too much time," he said crisply. "People will start asking questions if I'm gone from the office for too long."

"First of all, you try to have me killed," McAllister began. "You try to kill me. You try to kill Scooter."

"You don't have a clue as to what I've tried to do."

"You invaded my property—the very property where I welcomed you like a son. I let you into my personal business—gave you responsibility. I trusted you. I thought you could lead this operation one day. Not my own son, but you."

The disappointment was evident as the old man spoke. McAllister was genuinely appalled by the manner in which Ron and Abramson had acted over the recent years. They were trying to steal his prized distillery out from under him. They were going to ruin everything and disgrace the legacies of everyone involved.

If McAllister wouldn't fork it over, he knew he would be eliminated. He was an old man who had lived a long, full life. Nobody would care if something happened to him. People would honor his achievements in politics and business and mourn his death. But nobody would care if he was gone. New blood had taken over the local political responsibilities. His businesses were run by people whose names he could barely remember.

"John, you're very smart, and I respect that."

"I'm sure you do," retorted the old man.

"All I ask is the same," Abramson continued. "I've sure earned it."

"So because you've been gifted with a legal mind, I should hand over control of the distillery to you."

"I'm not asking for the distillery. I'll take it over in due time. That's not my immediate concern."

McAllister knew exactly what *due time* meant. He'd either be forced to relinquish control to Abramson, or he would be removed by other means, like the sniper in the barn. He glanced out of the window to confirm there was a shooter waiting to pull the trigger on his life.

"Then what do you want from me? Why are you here?" McAllister asked.

"I'll go ahead and cut to the chase."

"It's about time. You're not the only one who has a busy schedule."

Ignoring the old man's remarks, the Chief Justice continued, "I came across some pivotal information last night," he half lied.

"What information?"

"Information that I'm willing to share with you, granted you call off the surveillance. I'm not dumb. I can see them out in the Bay. The boats, the cars passing by—I know you have me covered left and right. I also know you're not dumb enough to harm the Chief Justice of the United States Supreme Court."

"So you did learn something from me after all these years."

"I'm a survivor, too. You don't get to be Chief Justice without knowing how to stay one step ahead of the game. The politicking, stepping on others' necks—it's all just part of the game. At the same time, I've always had to cover my back, watching for the people coming after me. And they do."

"Fair enough. I'll call off the snipers, but I expect the same in return."

"Don't be so sure that they're mine," said Abramson.

"And you were saying about some shocking new information?" asked McAllister, returning to the pressing subject.

Abramson pulled out a manila folder from his briefcase and placed it on the desk in front of McAllister. He returned to his seat to await the old man's reaction. Justice Abramson sat there, stone-faced.

McAllister straightened up and leaned over the folder, hesitant to open its contents. He had no idea what could possibly be inside.

His weathered hand still as steady as a surgeon's, he opened the folder. For a few brief moments, he flipped through the handwritten note from the Chief Justice and then scanned the remainder of the contents.

First, it was confusion. Then McAllister's face reddened with rage. His anger boiled and he looked as if he would attack the visitor.

"What is this?" he demanded, pounding his fist on the desk. "Is this some kind of game? Am I supposed to believe this?"

The Chief Justice remained seated and calmly replied, "Why else would I have come to you, if it wasn't the truth? We both know we each share opposing views of this business. I'm moving beyond the distillery concerns and looking out for our well-being. Let's be honest, the distillery is harmless anyway. You're distilling and distributing spirits without a permit. Big deal."

He paused to let the old man digest what he had just seen.

Abramson continued, "Our operation may not be as tight as we thought it to be. We have severe leaks, or at least I do from my end. You can rest assured that I will do everything in my *limited* power to tighten up those holes."

"This changes everything," said McAllister, his shoulders slumping over in despair.

"I know. It changes everything completely."

Standing outside the office door, Jimmy struggled to hear what was being said. He stood ready to enter with his gun drawn at a second's notice.

From what Jimmy could hear, the conversation seemed to be peaceful. One of the men on his security team, observing through the office window, said the two men were engaged in a serious conversation, conducting serious business.

Jimmy, puzzled by all of this, the out-of-character visit from the Chief Justice and the ensuing discussion, didn't quite know what to do. He softly knocked on the door.

There was no response. He radioed to his security team, and the curtains had been drawn inside the office. He unholstered his handgun, and slowly turned the knob to the door. It wasn't locked.

He cracked the door open ever so slightly, and to his relief, the old man called out.

"We're fine, just finishing up."

"I do have to get going now. I've been gone from the Court too long. I'm sure I'll go back to a thousand questions regarding my whereabouts," added Abramson.

Jimmy took liberty and opened the door completely. John McAllister stood with his back to the doorway, placing the folder in his file cabinet. Abramson was milling around, collecting his briefcase before heading back to the city.

When McAllister turned around, Jimmy immediately sensed an uneasy tension in the room. It wasn't anger. It wasn't sadness. It was concern and confusion.

Chief Justice Abramson pushed past Jimmy and exited the office without acknowledging the young man. Whatever had just happened, there was still bad blood brewing among the members of the distillery. And Jimmy knew that Abramson was still as dangerous as ever.

He followed the visitor out of the mansion and watched him closely until he had driven out of sight down the country road.

McAllister took a seat at his desk. He was all alone in his office. The curtains were still closed, giving him plenty of privacy from the watchful eyes and ears of his security team. He could not believe what Abramson had just shown him.

Sadly, there was no question in his mind that the information was, in fact, truthful.

His office phone rang—it was Senator Windgate. John was in no mood to speak with Scooter, so he ignored the call. The senator would have to wait until tomorrow as McAllister needed some time to wrap his mind around the recent developments.

The entire organization was crashing down around him. There was no way to keep news of all the infighting from being spread around the town gossip circuit. Pretty soon, prestigious clientele in Washington, DC, would catch wind of the rumblings and break from the distillery as well. The fear was that some might even try to turn in the operation in an attempt to cover their own backs, while keeping all of the cash from the years of bootlegging and drug running.

John forced his thoughts to Caroline, deeply worried for her safety.

"Keep running," he said aloud. "And never look back."

31

It was a beautiful evening in Louisville's Highlands neighborhood. People, young and old, flocked to the locally owned restaurants and bars. Old oak trees towered over the eclectic mix of bistros along historic Bardstown Road.

The patio scene buzzed as Jackson, Caroline, and Jeff struggled to find a spot to land. They eventually found some prime real estate on the outside deck of an Irish pub. They could feel the rhythms of the live music inside the bar, and the smell of beer wafted through the outside air.

The sun set beautifully in the western sky. The bright orange fireball disappeared over the historic homes that had been converted into condos and apartments for the yuppie and townie clientele.

Caroline looked stunning. Every man in the bar watched her every move. She could feel their eyes on her and she loved it. She knew exactly how to play the game, and she embraced the genteel southern way in which they played it.

Jackson and Jeff sat back, speechless, as daring young men would come up and speak to her. She'd make quick work of them, sending the boys back to their friends in defeat. She was approachable, but cold as ice to the unworthy.

But only because Caroline had her eye on one guy tonight—Jackson.

Maybe it was the champagne she'd enjoyed earlier in the afternoon. Or maybe his boyish charm was growing on her. Whatever it was, she made sure he saw her in action.

She didn't flip her blond hair or bat her electric blue eyes. She didn't have to. She was in the driver's seat, and the two men watched guy after guy fail.

Jackson and Jeff were going strong with the whiskey. Jeff had reached a different level having had more than twice as much to drink as the other two combined.

He knew everybody in the bar, and everyone knew him. Obviously, he was a regular at this establishment, which helped out when the table needed drinks. Every waitress on shift was at his beck and call.

Jackson was happy that Caroline was settling in and beginning to have a good time. He was too.

"So are you glad you made the trip now?" he asked, raising his voice above the crowd noise and music.

"I think so," she replied. "I had to get out of Virginia."

"I know. You were really starting to freak me out."

"Thanks," she said, rolling her eyes.

"Are you still scared?"

"Yeah," she admitted. "I have this feeling that someone is this close to finding me," she said, holding her two fingers an inch apart.

"What do you think they'll do?"

"Kill me," she said, trying to move past the subject quickly.

"That's a little severe, dontcha think?"

"Well, this is serious business. They think I know something that I don't."

"Hmm. Then let's enjoy our last days of freedom," he said, lifting his glass for a toast.

"Agreed. Let's live it up," she smiled.

Jackson made Caroline promise to forget her worries for the rest of the night. She readily obliged.

Jeff didn't partake in the toast. He was on the make, his back turned, fully engaged in conversation with a relatively attractive brunette.

"She's lovely," Caroline quietly joked, nodding in the brunette's direction.

"She's okay," replied Jackson, joining in on the game. "I've seen better."

"Tell me about it," she said coyly.

"I'm talking to her right now," he volleyed.

She nearly spit out her drink as she burst into laughter. Caroline wasn't impressed with his attempt. Sadly, she expected that kind of childish response from Jackson. But she still found herself attracted to the handsome young man.

Jeff abruptly got up from the table and wandered off with the cute brunette, leaving Jackson and Caroline alone together.

"Don't worry, he'll be back shortly," said Jackson. "His charm wears off quickly."

They shared a laugh at Jeff. He was long gone by now, somewhere inside the bar, probably meeting the poor girl's friends.

"At least he cleaned up before we came out," said Caroline.

"Yeah, he's not known for the best personal hygiene. Just be glad you don't have to share a hotel room with him."

"So you made him shower?"

"Nah, he did that on his own. Probably wanted to impress you."

"Oops, might be a little too late for him," she chuckled.

The band announced they were taking a quick break, and more people poured outside to the deck area. Jackson and Caroline were happy not to have to yell across the table to each other.

"So what's your story? I told you I just got out of a relationship. Any boyfriends? Crazy exes?" asked Jackson.

"We've been running for our lives, and you want to know about my boyfriends?"

"Well, yeah, why not? Plus, I don't want to think about being chased right now. I'm feeling pretty good, and I'm trying to forget about this mess you got me into. *And*, you promised not to bring up that subject for the rest of the night."

"Fair enough," she conceded. "No boyfriends. Not for a long time. You see, I'm very selective."

"I knew it. You're one of those."

"And that's supposed to mean what?"

"You know exactly what that's supposed to mean. You're probably all caught up in your career, or your former career, and demand perfection from any guy who comes your way."

"Why wouldn't I demand perfection? Every girl deserves the absolute best."

Jackson rolled his eyes and threw his arms over his head, also taking it as an opportunity to order another round of drinks from a passing waitress.

"Take me, for example," he said. "I find you mildly attractive," he lied. He found her breathtakingly beautiful.

"Okay, I'm listening," she sighed, reluctantly entertaining his opinion.

He couldn't hide his cocky grin.

"I consider myself a reasonably good catch for any young lady," he began.

"That's debatable," she interjected.

Ignoring her remark, he continued, "But you, your highest of high standards wouldn't even allow you to give me the time of day."

"Hey, I'm here, aren't I?"

"Come on, I think we can both agree that this weekend excursion is a little different. Do you really think you'd be here if you weren't under duress?"

Caroline turned her head slightly and smiled. Maybe she would be here anyway. Either way, she'd never let him know.

"I'd come on to you, and you would start preaching to me," he continued. "You'd tell me I drink too much, or I slack off too much. You'd say that I'm incapable of growing up. And my friends? You've already insulted my one friend. They'd be too dirty. No personal hygiene."

"You don't have me figured out at all."

"That's just my take. I've seen my fair share of girls like you."

"Oh, just stop yourself. You don't even know what you're talking about," she said.

She was surprisingly agitated by Jackson's point of view. Maybe he had had too much to drink.

Jeff appeared out of nowhere. He had lost the lovely brunette. Or had she lost him? He set down three more drinks for the group just as the waitress reappeared with the round Jackson had just ordered.

"Double time!" he exclaimed.

Caroline shook her head in disbelief. She was with a duo like none other. Jackson and Jeff were three sheets to the wind, and she was trying to carry on a semi-genuine conversation with Jackson. It was a lost cause.

She could tell that her own inhibitions were beginning to leave her. She had to be careful, especially with everything that was at stake.

"I think we should dial it down a notch," she said, much to the dismay of the two boys. "I do want to enjoy the day tomorrow."

"Are you serious?" asked Jeff.

The two guys looked at each other.

With a wave towards Caroline, Jackson and Jeff got up from the table and began mingling with the ever-growing crowd.

Caroline eyed the drink Jeff had just brought to the table.

"Why not," she said to herself.

She cringed as she took a rather large gulp of the whiskey. It reminded her of what she had sampled at the McAllister distillery, but it was still too strong for her liking.

Caroline's thoughts immediately focused on the McAllister distillery and the danger she was facing. Her head started spinning and her stomach turned over as she tried hard suppress the adrenaline.

Tears filled her eyes and she had to quickly turn away from the crowd to shield herself from embarrassment. What had happened to her? She used to be tough. Why couldn't she take it anymore?

Jackson and Jeff had gone inside the bar, out of sight. She got up from the table to search for them, leaving several untouched drinks behind.

The band began playing again, this time a cover song from the '80s. In her former life, Caroline would've sprung into song with the band. But she'd had enough for the night. She couldn't wait to get back to the safety of her hotel room.

She was overwhelmed with emotion and feeling claustrophobic of the crowd of strangers around her. She looked both ways and could not find Jackson. And once again, she felt completely alone.

There was no one to watch out for her. Not Jackson. Not John McAllister. Not anyone.

Still no sign of Jackson, and she began to panic. She was lost.

The band's deafening music only made matters worse.

She reached into her purse to grab her cell phone, but it wasn't there. It was sitting on the table back at the hotel room.

She took another lap around the patio area, and still no sign of the boys.

Finally, she spotted Jackson with his arms wrapped around a petite blonde in the corner. He really would go after anything with a skirt.

Frustrated from the recent events of the night, she turned and walked out of the bar.

She fumed at herself for being even remotely attracted to Jackson. Maybe it was the alcohol. But, she had grown to admire him in the short time they'd known each other. But now, it was very obvious he didn't care about her. She was just another girl along for the ride.

Caroline flagged down a cab and hopped in. She ordered the cabbie to take her back to the Seelbach Hotel.

Meanwhile, Jackson and Jeff were drinking the night away, mingling with crowd. Jeff met up with old friends, and Jackson made new ones.

In front of the Seelbach, Caroline jumped out of the cab and stormed up the front steps. She powered through the lobby, hurrying to get to the safety of her room.

She walked right past the watchful eye of Agent Stewart.

The hotel bar had closed about an hour earlier, so he was positioned on the lobby sofa where he could observe all of the guests coming and going.

He sipped what remained of a drink. He knew she would stay in for the remainder of the night. There were no concerns of her leaving. He had plenty of surveillance on her now.

Agent Stewart had already checked into a room two floors above Caroline's. He had thought to request the same floor but didn't want to seem too suspicious to the hotel clerks. He would grab her the next morning, and the ordeal would be over for both of them.

Jackson and Jeff stumbled back into the opulent hotel lobby two hours after Caroline. Agent Stewart was still perched on his lookout spot. He observed the two drunkards laughing and half-wrestling their way up to their hotel room. They were of no concern to him—they posed no threat whatsoever. Hell, they had allowed the vulnerable girl to travel back to the hotel alone.

This was too easy. He dialed the Chief Justice to give a report of the night's events.

The plans had changed.

32

Molly O's was more than a hundred miles in the rearview mirror as Paul sped down the highway. He had his orders. And he had his mark.

Paul had long been privy to information regarding the distillery. He knew the client list well, as most patrons would stop in at Molly O's to chat with the old bartender. And in his former life, he had been the front man for distributing all of the cocaine for the Mid-Atlantic region.

Paul was also the holder of all gossip—he heard everything. And he took full advantage of his position, pitting members against each other when necessary. Some people would say his schemes quickly escalated to the level of extortion; he viewed it as protecting his future.

The moonlight barely illuminated the dense trees lining the highway on the early summer night. Paul was one of the only travelers on the roads this late, occasionally passing a group of tractor-trailers.

Paul was more than a bartender. And the distillery's executive committee definitely knew he was more valuable than just a town gossip. Paul had been called upon several times in the past when circumstances became dire. Only a select few knew about his role, but those who did appreciated his efforts very much.

When nobody else wanted to dirty his hands, Paul was as reliable as ever. He intimidated. He changed minds. He collected debts. And he killed. But not since that time, two decades ago, when he vowed he would never do it again.

He had been called upon once again. This time it was from an unlikely distillery executive who reached out to him—a man who was often at odds with the longtime bartender. The coercive threats made against Paul and his family had been enough to make him carry out his task without thinking twice.

Never before had the executive committee tried to oust a member of the inner circle, at least publicly. There had been plenty of disagreements over the course of time, but nothing that escalated to the level of the recent events. A power struggle was at hand—a microcosm of the power struggle among the nation's elite that had to remain hidden from the public eye.

Paul knew his duty. His adrenaline raced as he sped across the state line. The would-be murder weapon was tightly nestled against his leg as he drove. He clutched the steering wheel until his knuckles were white.

Paul had received the order earlier that afternoon, directly from the senior member of the group. Later that evening, before he hit the road, Paul touched base with every member of the inner circle. He considered there to be six—John McAllister, Scooter Windgate, Ron, Chief Justice Abramson, Agent Stewart, and Jimmy. But then again, what did he really know? Maybe there were more.

After speaking with each member individually, Paul was still unsure about being set up. Had he opened his mouth too many times? Did he know too much? Was he being played?

Now he wasn't convinced that none of the other members knew of this particular hit.

If none of the others were aware, this hit would cement Paul's loyalties to one particular man—a man he secretly despised.

Instead of torturing himself over the whole ordeal, he focused on his mission. He focused on his game plan—on his target. By the next morning, it would all be over.

The cell phone lit up the interior of Paul's car, indicating that a text message had arrived from the mission's originator. The message clearly advised where the target could be found.

Paul acknowledged receipt of the message and heard nothing more the remainder the night.

He arrived at the destination with several hours of darkness remaining. He could not sleep. In fact, he was quite restless.

Paul thought back to the first time he was asked to make a hit. He was told it was a one-time thing. And then, the victims began to pile up. He struggled to put those memories out of his mind forever. But every night as he closed his eyes, he could see his victims' eyes staring back at him.

He questioned whether he could actually go through with this one. But he had no choice. His wife and children would never know his involvement as long as he carried out the hit. If he failed, he would never see his family again.

This hadn't been the modus operandi of the distillery for many, many years. But these threats were so severe, and the recent events were so out of the ordinary, that he didn't dare question the authenticity.

Paul accepted his reality very quickly. And he was prepared to carry out his business as planned. In fact, he already planned a gourmet feast with his wife at Molly O's upon his arrival home. She would never know.

Paul was overly confident in his ability to carry out the hit. Instead of checking into a hotel, he waited out the early morning hours in his car, treating himself to a pre-victory cigar. A twelve-pack sat on ice inside a cooler in the trunk of his car. Undoubtedly, he would need to take the edge off once his mission was complete.

But as he waited idly in his car, he contemplated the backlash from other members of the distillery operation. Paul began questioning the necessity of the hit. He didn't want to pull the trigger; he didn't understand the reasoning behind the act.

This murder would surely attract regional, if not national, news coverage. This could be fatal to the overall distillery operation.

Was this the intent? Paul would never know. He would carry out his mission as planned.

33

Jackson couldn't distinguish between his pounding headache and the pounding at the door. It just wouldn't stop. Jeff was still dead to the world.

Begrudgingly, Jackson opened his eyes and found himself still fully dressed in his clothes from the night before, sitting in one of the wing chairs in the hotel room. He didn't quite make it to his bed before passing out.

Ignoring the knocking at the door momentarily, he took a minute to get his bearings.

The curtains had been left wide open. And the bright morning sun beamed into the room, making it unbearable.

He closed his eyes and grasped at the table next to his chair, praying that his hand happened to grab his sunglasses. Alas, after several seconds of searching, no luck.

"Okay, hold on," Jackson groaned, finally succumbing to the knocks. He squinted to block out the bright light and reluctantly made his way to the door. If it was housekeeping, he would give them a piece of his mind that they would never forget.

He stumbled across open bags that were scattered about the floor, nearly falling directly into the door.

Jackson opened the door. He couldn't see anything other than a dark silhouette against the lights of the hallway.

He heard an agitated sigh coming from what he began to make out as a female figure.

As his eyes slowly adjusted to the light, the voice confirmed her identity.

"So did you have a good time last night?" Caroline asked, not amused.

"Uh, yeah," Jackson muttered. "Did you?"

"Oh, yeah," she quipped, emphasizing her sarcasm.

She charged right past Jackson, uninvited, taking advantage of the slightly open door.

"You *boys* think it's fun to just leave a girl all alone to fend for herself," she charged.

She didn't hesitate to flip on a few lights to enhance the natural light from the morning sun.

Jeff didn't budge an inch. He was still out cold. For a second, Jackson wondered if he was even alive. But then he remembered all those hung over mornings traveling the professional golf mini-tours. This was par for the course.

Caroline was not the least bit pleased with the events the previous night. She had been left high and dry by the cads—forced to return to the hotel alone. She had no problem taking care of herself. It was the principle that she was upset with. Had she known she would be left to her own devices, she wouldn't have left the hotel room, let alone joined Jackson on the road trip.

"I already ordered breakfast up here to the room," she said. "It will be here in about ten minutes, so I suggest you wake up your friend and start cleaning yourselves up."

Caroline positioned herself in the wing chair opposite the snoring Jeff and stared at him, willing him to wake up. Jeff must have felt her steely gaze because he was stirring within seconds.

"Why are you here so early?" whined Jackson.

"Why did you leave me last night?" she answered right back.

"Sorry, the night just got away from us, I guess."

Caroline merely responded with an evil smile, and nothing more.

Jeff finally got up and walked straight to the bathroom, slamming the door behind him. He was not amused by Caroline's antics.

The heaves from the bathroom could be heard through the door, disgusting both Jackson and Caroline.

"Amateur?" asked Caroline.

Jackson couldn't hold back a chuckle, even though it amplified his headache.

"Let's just say he's not currently on top of his game."

Feeling she had proven her point, Caroline couldn't help but lighten up. And Jackson was finally clearing the haze. He excused himself and went into the other room to change out of his filthy clothes. He returned wearing his signature seersucker shorts and white polo.

"You're going to shower, right?" she asked.

"I'm not going anywhere near that bathroom with what's going on in there right now."

On cue, Jeff let loose another heave behind the bathroom's closed door.

Room service arrived and Jackson didn't hesitate to dive in to the food. He was quite impressed by the spread Caroline ordered. The aroma of freshly brewed coffee, fried eggs, and bacon quickly filled the hotel room.

Jeff's self-inflicted miserable condition was an afterthought as Caroline and Jackson downed their breakfasts, and most of his.

Jackson caught himself admiring Caroline as she pranced across the room to refill her coffee mug. Boy, did he ever screw up last night.

Her pale blue sundress skimmed her figure. It was cut lower in front and a bit shorter than he'd seen her wear before. Was he just imagining that she was trying to get his attention? Jackson couldn't hide his crooked grin as he thought about how much he had been admiring her lately. Maybe when they went back to Virginia, he would do something about it. Yes, that would be the plan. *After* they returned home.

Although Samantha Crockett's departure from his life was recent enough to still sting, she was quickly being edged out of his mind. He was moving on. But first, he needed to get through the weekend without ticking off Caroline again. No more shenanigans or leaving her behind.

X   X   X

Agent Stewart started his morning early. He sat in the hotel Starbucks huddled over a newspaper, sipping coffee as he waited for the girl to come out of the hotel.

He knew her exact whereabouts. He knew that she was in Jackson and Jeff's room eating breakfast. He was stalking her every move.

The time had come for him to catch his prey. Agent Stewart would wait out the hunt only a little while longer—long enough for the girl to get outside so he could make a quick snatch and getaway.

The game plan was different now, and he felt much better about his role in taking Caroline. At least she'd be safe under his watch for a short while.

His appearance had changed dramatically from the night before. In case anyone observed the so-called kidnapping, he would never be identified.

He wore a bushy, fake red beard on his face. He covering his eyes with a pair of thick tinted glasses. A ragged baseball cap with a red ponytail protruding from the back covered his head. Stewart left no stone unturned. He had even stuffed his shirt and pants, adding about thirty pounds to his already bulky build.

A trained master of disguise, he didn't even recognize himself when he glanced at his reflection in the window. Well done, captain.

He peered through the eyeglasses, praying that Caroline exited the hotel before the sidewalk became too crowded. It was still early enough on the Saturday morning that not too many people were walking around downtown Louisville.

X   X   X

When the trio exited the building for a waiting taxi, Agent Stewart pushed open the door to the Starbucks prepared to take his target.

He stopped dead in his tracks as he stared into a familiar face. He knew this was the end of the road—the end of everything. In his quick accounting he realized, after everything had been said and done, he was fine with it.

A small group of customers screamed and scrambled for cover as the blood exploded throughout the interior of the small coffee shop.

The lifeless body of Agent Stewart fell backwards halfway through the doorway. His hat and wig were blown several feet from his body. The bright red blood pooled onto the tiled floor.

The taxi transporting the trio had already departed the hotel when the hit occurred. None of the three had any knowledge of what had just happened back at the hotel.

Paul took one last look at the body of Agent Stewart, raised his weapon, and fired one more shot into Stewart's chest for good measure. He quickly climbed back into his running car and sped off.

He had taken no caution to avoid being seen by witnesses. He did, of course, have the backing of a group that included members of the Senate and Supreme Court. There was no doubt in Paul's mind that he would be taken care of.

His sedan picked up speed as he ran red light after red light trying to gain ground on the taxi. He had no clue as to their destination, so catching up was crucial.

When he finally caught up with the taxi, he slowed to avoid detection. He followed them to legendary Churchill Downs where he watched Jeff enter through a entrance on the backside of the track while Jackson and Caroline followed a sidewalk around to the front entrance.

Paul parked his car on a side street and planned his next move.

The first race of the day was still a few hours away.

x x x

Churchill Downs' twin spires weren't as impressive as advertised. At least according to Caroline. Expansion had dwarfed the trademark twin spires over the years. More millionaires demanded more seats on Millionaire's Row. And so did their respective businesses. Lights now towered over the grandstand, trumping the old views of the historic spires. Racing had gone corporate.

There were no special events scheduled for this race card. No concerts. No giveaways. One stakes race. Attendance would be 1,500 people at best. The advent of off-track and online betting meant the serious gamblers no longer had to travel to tracks. They could bet on any race across the country from the comfort of their couch.

Caroline had looked forward to being engulfed by the fashionable Derby hats and genteel atmosphere. But as she stood by the statue of Barbaro, galloping his way to victory, she couldn't help being a little disappointed. There was no excitement in the air. A few people milled around the museum entrance, but nothing more.

Jeff exited through the front entrance and joined the group.

"What was that all about?" asked Jackson.

"I had to settle up a few accounts from my people. You know, my customers."

"I told you he ran his own book," declared Jackson.

"Hey, hey, hey. Let's be a little more quiet about that," he said quietly. "It's not something we want to broadcast around to everyone."

Caroline was annoyed.

"So that's why we had to get here so early? I'm going to the museum," she announced.

Jeff had one more money drop to complete, so he waited outside the front entrance. Jackson kept him company as Caroline dangerously wandered off alone.

"Stop," screamed Jeff as he took off in a dead sprint towards Caroline. He wouldn't get very far.

Jackson, with his back still turned towards the museum and Caroline, ducked when he heard the crack of the gunshot. Shortly after taking cover, he heard the grotesque sound of Jeff's body hitting the sidewalk.

It wasn't until he heard Caroline's terrifying screams that he turned his head to see what was happening.

Just beyond his good friend's lifeless body, an older man wrestled Caroline into the backseat of his car. She kicked and clawed. She landed a few blows that would've stopped many men. Her assailant was stunned by a few of the kicks, but undeterred.

Jackson lay on the sidewalk, still in shock, not realizing what he was seeing. Nothing made sense to him. He couldn't move.

The old man grew impatient with Caroline's struggle, his gun making a sickening thud when it hit her across the head. Her body went limp and he shoved her into the car.

Before the security guards could react, Paul was gone, barreling out of the parking lot with Caroline unconscious in the backseat. The tires screeched as he turned the corner and fled the scene.

Jackson crawled over to Jeff, but it was too late. The bullet had hit him in the chest. Jackson felt for a pulse in Jeff's neck, bur he was gone.

Caroline was gone, too.

He had no idea what he had just witnessed. Panic was starting to set in. Jackson just wanted to disappear. He feared for his life, and he would not be caught talking to investigators.

He scrambled to his feet and took off running down an unfamiliar road adjacent to Churchill Downs.

After a few blocks of running as fast and far as he could, he stopped to catch his breath.

He found himself on a rundown street lined with several boarded up houses, no doubt the site of illegal activity. Locals, alert on their front porches, watched his every move.

Dressed in his fratty seersucker shorts, Jackson did not fit the profile for someone belonging in this neighborhood. Or maybe the blood covering the front of his once white shirt was the reason for their attention.

Jackson was oblivious. It didn't matter though. Not now.

Jackson's adrenaline was coursing in his veins and he took off again in a dead sprint—this time to an idle cab two blocks away.

Jackson was so distracted by the police presence in front of the Seelbach Hotel that he barely thought to thank the cab driver for the free ride—a blood-covered shirt will garner a free ride any day of the week, either from fear or pity.

The local police department *and* the Feds had the entire front entrance roped off.

Jackson figured this was somehow connected to Caroline's kidnapping and Jeff's murder. He didn't realize how correct he was.

Agent Stewart's body had already been removed from the Starbucks, and the investigation was in full force.

Jackson ducked into a back alley and found his way into the hotel through a service entrance. He removed his shirt to hide the bloody mess. He didn't need any unwanted attention.

Surprisingly, he weaved his way through the front lobby and back to his room without attracting any attention whatsoever. The recent murder preoccupied everyone at the hotel.

Inside his room, he stuffed his belongings into his overnight bag as quickly as possible. He then took a brief shower to remove any evidence of the blood and sweat from the earlier attack.

He was back in his old Bimmer within the hour, getting the hell out of Kentucky.

He had lost two friends in a matter of a few seconds. Jeff had been murdered in plain sight. And Caroline had been kidnapped or killed.

Jackson was scared out of his mind.

34

Ron strolled down the National Mall on this late summer evening. Government workers had already departed for home in the suburbs, and young city dwellers jogged up and down the Mall. Tourists, bikers, and walkers crowded the sidewalks. It was here, against the backdrop of the Capitol, the Smithsonian Museum, and the long, grassy mall that Ron did most of his strategizing. This is where he felt at home.

Ron admired the day's final sunlight bouncing off the Capitol. It would soon be dark. Ron thought the monuments and government buildings were even more beautiful illuminated against a dark, starry sky.

He thought about Michael Abramson, and their first run to the Senate offices with a load of McAllister whiskey. It was a night very similar to this one—just after dusk, a perfect temperature, lots of tourists milling around.

It was the summer after their second year in college. Ron and Abramson had been roommates for two years and had quickly become best friends.

Abramson returned to Warrenton from school with Ron each of the first two summers to work on the farm. In the process, he was let in on the family secret. It would be several years before Abramson realized the vast illegitimate empire the McAllisters were running, but for some reason, he trusted John McAllister, and the family trusted him.

After several summers of merely sweeping cavern floors or setting up tables for distillery events, Ron and Abramson took a significant step toward becoming essential to the family business.

They were asked to make an important delivery to Senator Windgate. The catch was that it was to be delivered to his Senate offices.

This was a test. If they were caught, the Senator and John McAllister would merely disown the young men, and they would be left high and dry. Or, at least that's what they had been told. Realistically, the old men weren't that cutthroat.

In fact, the bottles did not even contain whiskey. They were filled with harmless, auburn-colored water.

There was no way John McAllister would have put the future of his business in the hands of two college kids. Not without testing first.

From an early age, Ron felt that he would always live in his father's shadow. The elder McAllister was the town mayor, a very successful businessman, and made a fortune running illegal schemes and sharing profits with the nation's elite. This mission was his chance to cement his place in the long line of successful McAllisters. If successful, this would allow him to garner some control in the operation. Ron was, in his own mind, the rightful heir apparent.

An open bench caught Ron's eye and he wandered over to claim it. The sun had finally set, and the temperature began dropping, making for a lovely summer night.

Ron reached into his backpack full of supplies and found his sweatshirt. Among the supplies were two handguns and two cell phones. He slid the wads of cash totaling $5,000 into an inner pocket to keep it hidden from the rest of the contents.

Ron stretched out his legs, admired the Washington Monument, and drifted back into memories.

He understood the magnitude of the mission and its importance to the distillery. Abramson, on the other hand, had no idea of the significance. He was only along for the ride. And a quick hit of cash.

Ron and Abramson successfully delivered the phony load to the senator's office. They didn't find out about the trickery until some three years later when the old senator spilled the beans after having too much to drink.

Ron was chaffed by the revelation. But Abramson brushed it off. By that time, they both exerted significant influence in the distillery's affairs. Although not quite privy to all the other illegal activities, the young men took pride in controlling the bootleg whiskey business. It was a harmless entry into the world of organized crime.

Ron and the elder McAllister were already bickering constantly when Senator Windgate divulged the secret. It fueled the father-son feud and prompted Ron to create friction among the distillery's younger members and its old guard.

In hindsight, this was clearly the ultimate beginning of the power struggle that was currently coming to a head.

Abramson had no choice in the matter. He sided with Ron. He solicited support for Ron's initiatives even when he disagreed with them. Ron was the reason he was first invited into the inner circle and he was his link to its future.

Abramson hailed from very humble beginnings. He was the first member of his family to attend college, and his natural talent and intelligence put him on the fast track to law school.

Ron, identifying the potential in Abramson, took him under his wing and introduced him to the proper people in the proper places.

Everyone in the McAllister gang was taken in by Abramson's charm. After they realized the kid's tremendous potential, they propelled him well on his way to a spot on the Supreme Court. Senator Windgate was one of his biggest supporters from the very beginning. And he had always been a big supporter through the judge's career. Until now.

The Chief Justice helped Ron hide when necessary, especially after the gruesome murder of Caroline's father. He also passed along inside knowledge of the operations to Ron when John McAllister gave his son the silent treatment. He often found himself running interference between the father and son. He knew how to navigate the political game, and he used it to his advantage with the distillery business.

Ron opened the backpack and pulled out one of the cell phones. He quickly scanned his surroundings for any observers.

He dialed. No answer.

He waited about ten minutes and dialed again. Still no answer.

Just as he was about to pack his things and move on, he received a call from the number he had dialed.

"Why the hell aren't you answering when I call?" answered Ron.

There was nothing but silence on the other end. Not a single sound. After a few seconds, the unidentified caller clicked off of the call.

The unexpected silence shocked Ron. Was the call an accident? Or did he just blow it? Who had he just revealed his identity to?

He pocketed the cell phone and took off down the National Mall at a brisk pace, trying to avoid any attention.

If someone was playing games with him, he would soon find out. There was one place—one person—he had to see.

X X X

The sweat would just not let up. It poured down his face, down his neck. His collar was soaked. Half tears and half sweat, the salty taste trickled over his lips. It made Paul sick to his stomach as he raced down the highway.

He couldn't bring himself to look into the rearview mirror, fearful of seeing a murderer be staring right back at him. But he had completed the job. His family would be safe.

The girl hadn't moved a muscle in hours. This was quite concerning to Paul.

His mission was to bring her back without incident. And without injury. She was not to be harmed in any way. Yet, he had been forced, by necessity, to smash the handle of his handgun into the side of her head, knocking her unconscious.

What repercussions would he face? Who would he be forced to answer to? Was he being trailed by local law enforcement? He had shot and killed a young man in cold blood. The promise of protection from the group's members wasn't comforting anymore. He was terrified.

Agent Stewart had been a valiant and loyal foot soldier for the distillery for more than two decades. And he had been eliminated in the blink of an eye. Surely, the same would happen to Paul upon his return. Especially if the girl had been harmed. Or if the unfortunate murder of the young man exposed the organization.

Paul thought only of his family. They were the reason he had hooked up with the distillery group in the first place. College money for his kids. Extra savings for a comfortable retirement. It wasn't just occasional extra cash. It was life-changing money.

His job was simple. Control the town gossip in Warrenton and serve as a buffer between the operation and any outside interests.

He had been called on several times before to handle dirty work, but those jobs had seemed easier. He was younger and more eager to make an impact. He would've done anything to be invited into the group.

During the lonely car ride back into Virginia, Paul faced reality. With an unconscious girl laid across the backseat of his car, Paul realized that he was being played as the fall person. If anything went down, Paul would be caught with the girl, caught with a murder weapon, and placed at the scene of the crime back in Kentucky.

He was a lowly bartender. Not a single soul would believe that he rubbed shoulders with senators and judges.

He wouldn't stand a chance. Maybe this is how it had always been. Maybe he'd been naïve. He never was one of the insiders.

Paul grabbed the handgun laying on the passenger's seat. He gripped the handle tightly until his fingers turned white. How would he ever defend himself against the scope and power of the McAllisters?

Suddenly Caroline lunged forward and dug her fingernails into Paul's eye socket.

He fired two blind shots towards the backseat struggling to regain control of the car, which jerked violently into the median.

Caroline, still dizzy from the head trauma, bounced around the backseat as the car rumbled through the grassy median and back into the emergency lane.

She steadied herself enough to use her nails again—this time scratching down the side of Paul's face. He screamed out in pain.

With a desperate swing, Paul's gun delivered another sickening blow to Caroline's head. She didn't utter a single sound. She just went limp and collapsed into the back seat.

After narrowly escaping catastrophe, Paul pulled over to the side of the highway.

He pulled to a stop and took several deep breaths, regaining his composure. With a handful of napkins from the glove compartment, he tended to his wounds and wiped the blood from his face.

The girl was still unconscious, and after securing Caroline's hands and feet with some rope, he hit the highway for the remainder of what had been an unfortunate, eventful mission.

35

Even after locking himself inside his apartment, Jackson knew he was still in danger. He was paralyzed on his couch, chin propped up on his hand. He couldn't move. His muscles didn't twitch.

Laid out on the table in front of him were a handful of Caroline's belongings. The purse she had dropped while being apprehended, a change of clothes she had left in his car, and a folder of papers—copies of the same research she had kept hidden in the closet at her old cabin.

Jackson didn't dare to go back to Kentucky to look for Caroline. He wanted to help, but he knew he would be pursued and captured, just like she was. She might have even been killed shortly after he last saw her.

Jackson had been touched by more tragedy than conceivable for one lifetime. After losing both parents, he had no one to lean on for support and guidance. His close friend, Jeff, had been a source of encouragement, first in their years on the golf course, and then during their entrepreneurial ventures, and even afterwards. Jeff was a wild card, but he was there whenever Jackson called.

Now he was gone, too.

Part of him wanted to clear out his checking account and set off across the country to start a new life. The other part, the much bigger part, wanted to help Caroline.

He didn't know her. Hell, there was no way to distinguish the truth from the lies. But he knew she was a genuinely kind person. And he knew he was the only person in the entire world who could help her. He was the only one who knew she was in danger.

So he sat, deep in thought, his body locked up from fear.

The red flash finally caught his attention. For almost two hours, the red light flashed in his peripheral vision, asking to be noticed. The blinking light was trying desperately to save the young man. Subconsciously, he acknowledged it. But finally, he decided it was time to investigate.

Jackson unleashed every ounce of pent-up anger as he violently tore the snaked camera from the corner of his living room.

With the remains of the camera and its cords piled at his feet, he scanned the rest of the apartment. And that's when he saw it—another bug blinking in the corner vent of his bedroom. Who had been watching him? How long had they been tracking him?

With the same vengeance as the first, he destroyed the camera, shattering the electronic device into dozens of tiny pieces.

Sweat now poured down his forehead. He was ready to take action.

Jackson Cole tapped into a purpose like never before in his life. He had never been a hero. He wasn't even a decent human being half the time. He used people, took advantage of them, and never extended a helping hand. He took much more from life than he gave.

Now, everything had changed.

Jackson quickly gathered all of Caroline's belongings and stuffed a few of his own into a duffle bag. Included among them was his roommate's fully loaded hand gun. He was on a mission.

He stormed down his apartment stairs and was gone just before the black SUV screamed to a halt in front of his building. Two men, dressed in all black, were halfway up the stairs before the smoke from the vehicle's tires had cleared.

They burst through Jackson's front door to find Jackson was gone and their surveillance equipment was in shambles on the floor.

The two men tore apart the apartment looking for clues as to where the young man could have gone.

One of the henchmen found Jackson's cell phone on the kitchen countertop. It was clear that the young man intended to leave no leads or clues as to his whereabouts. No cell phone meant no GPS tracking.

For the first time, he was untraceable.

After realizing there was nothing to find—no clues about Jackson and nothing of value regarding Caroline—the two men left the trashed apartment and fled as quickly as they had arrived.

A group of loitering college kids barely noticed the suspicious thugs.

With no way to track where Jackson could have escaped, the SUV hit the highway and hightailed back to DC where they would have to report the unfortunate news.

X   X   X

The Bimmer's tires squealed as Jackson roared through the front gates of the McAllister estate. He sent the guard scrambling for cover from the loose gravel kicked up by his tires.

A loud pop stunned Jackson. He thought, "It's over. This is the end—going out in a blaze of glory."

However, the continuous thumping noise and the rough ride clearly indicated that his two back tires had been blown out.

As the car slowly rolled to a stop, Jackson was greeted by a fully armed guard at his driver side window.

"How can I help you, sir?" Jimmy asked, opening the car door from the outside. The question was cold. No smile.

Jackson hesitated but quickly regrouped and confidently climbed out of the car. He took inventory of his two blown tires and watched the team of snipers approach the vehicle. Jimmy was flanked by four other armed guards, and Jackson was target.

Jackson was poised, standing tall, and staring down Jimmy.

"You'll get a bill from me next week for those tires. Now show me where I can find Mr. McAllister," he ordered, as he began to walk past Jimmy.

"Not so fast," said Jimmy.

The sternness in Jimmy's tone combined with a death grip around Jackson's right arm by one of the guards conveyed the message loud and clear. Jackson stopped.

He looked Jimmy directly in the eye.

"I'm not playing games here. I have questions, and I'm not leaving until I get answers," Jackson demanded, leaning inches away from Jimmy's face.

"Let's go," Jimmy replied, wiping Jackson's spit from his cheek.

183

With Jackson in tow, two guards escorted him into the front door of the house. Jimmy cleared the way and led the entourage back to McAllister's office.

"That's enough," Jimmy said to the guards. "I'll take him from here."

Jackson wrestled his arms loose from their tight grasp. He mockingly brushed off his shoulders and sneered at the guards as they walked down the hall to return to their posts.

Jimmy closed the office door. If he knew he wouldn't be shot on the spot, Jackson would've clubbed Jimmy over the head and made a beeline toward John McAllister. He knew he'd surely be intercepted and dropped in his tracks.

It's crazy how a mind can spin through so many scenarios when adrenaline, anger, rage, and fear are all pumping through the body.

"Sit here," said Jimmy, motioning to a seat across from McAllister's desk.

Jackson didn't say a word. He had nothing to say to Jimmy. He would gladly wait to give McAllister a piece of his mind.

Not knowing whether he would leave the estate dead or alive, Jackson conceded that his fate was not in his hands any longer. He relaxed, as much as the circumstances would allow, sat back in the plush leather chair, and awaited the arrival of John McAllister.

Jimmy paced in front of the door, also waiting for McAllister. He was ready to take down Jackson at the slightest hint of any aggression toward the old man. He eyed the young law student like a hawk.

Two soft knocks on the door and Jimmy slowly turned the doorknob and cracked the door. He confirmed that it was John McAllister and cautiously welcomed the old man into the office.

"Jackson, I've heard so much about you," John began the conversation as he made his way to his desk chair.

It was a rather warm welcome given what Jackson had just encountered from the security team. He was unsure how to take this.

"Thank you, sir," was all he could muster.

"My team tells me you made quite the entrance," he chuckled. "I hope they weren't too rough with you."

"Not at all, sir," replied Jackson, turning his head to give Jimmy a look.

Jimmy didn't budge. His focus remained on Jackson, ready to pounce at any instant.

"Don't worry about him," McAllister said referring to Jimmy. "He's merely doing his job. Wouldn't want any surprises to catch us off guard, would we? Still, I know you're harmless. You don't want to hurt anyone here."

Jackson thought about the handgun. He had left it in the trunk of the car. There was no doubt that it had been confiscated by now.

Yes, he was, in fact, harmless. That explained the old man's unconcerned demeanor.

"Jimmy, give us a couple of minutes," the old man said, motioning for Jimmy to leave the room. "We'll be fine."

"But, Mr. McAllister—"

John cut him off with the raise of his hand. No explanation was necessary. Jimmy gave a slight forward nod and ducked out the door, closing it behind him.

It didn't matter. He would be anxiously standing guard just outside the door.

"Mr. McAllister, I appreciate the respect and trust you are showing me, but I do have some serious questions to ask, and I want to get down to business," Jackson began.

He leaned forward in his chair, eager to learn as many details about the ordeal as possible.

"Please call me John. You are Caroline's friend, aren't you?"

"That's correct."

"Ah, the same handsome guy she was seen with at Molly O's."

"Yes, sir."

"You certainly made quite the impression that night. Jimmy was concerned that he'd never get her to leave you. But that's neither here nor there," he said, his voice trailing off. "I'm guessing the two of you have had some excitement lately."

Despair was outwardly evident in the old man's voice. McAllister was obviously going through a tough time. His slumped body language said it all. It was as if the world had turned on him completely.

"I will probably have a few questions for you as well," he continued.

"Where is she?" asked Jackson, cutting straight to the chase.

"I don't know. I thought you would have that answer."

"Really? That's all you have?" Jackson replied, already becoming agitated. "I saw one of your men kidnap her right in front of me," he continued, raising his voice. "You killed my best friend. In cold blood!"

Jackson stood up, and the door flew open. Jimmy's weapon was pointed at Jackson's temple.

Jackson immediately sat back down. Jimmy lowered his weapon, gave a slight nod to his boss to assure him that he would be out there before he turned to leave the room, closing the door behind him again.

McAllister didn't flinch throughout any of the excitement. He had seen so much worse during his reign as don.

The old man turned to face the window. The curtains were open, exposing the vast beauty of his estate.

Hidden among the fields and barns was a security team second to none. Only, the old man couldn't decide if they were protecting him, or targeting him. Money often changed hands among the underground operations, but in times like these—times when bodies began to pile up—the old man became nervous. Never before had he been in a position like this.

"I'm sorry for your loss," he said to Jackson, still gazing out the window, but fully engaged in the conversation. "When I tell you that I know nothing about Caroline's whereabouts, or what recently transpired with your friend, I'm being completely honest with you. If you can't respect that, and you still don't believe me, then it would be best if you left the premises. You're presence here creates a very large security risk."

"Who took her?" Jackson asked.

"It's news to me that she's missing. But I do have a couple of people in mind," he said turning back to engage Jackson eye-to-eye. "These people are not to be taken lightly, and it's only a matter of time until I'm their target. I've already been the target."

"Who are they?"

"They are the very people we trust to lead our country, protect our freedoms, and ensure that justice is carried out appropriately."

"I've lived in DC before. That criteria covers half of the city's population."

"There's only a handful who actually run the show. Agendas become aligned, money changes hands, legitimately and illegitimately, and naysayers are removed from the game."

"I'm not quite following you," said Jackson.

His patience was running thin and his only care was finding Caroline and who killed his best friend.

"Okay. I've been on both sides of this, and unfortunately, I'm on the side being removed right now. The next generation always thinks they know how to improve things. They won't listen to time-tested wisdom. They want instant results—not willing to lay a solid foundation."

"I apologize, Mr. McAllister," Jackson interrupted, "but I'm still not quite understanding where you're going with this. I'm looking for Caroline. Her life is in imminent danger. Does that make sense to you?"

"I understand that," he replied, exhaling deeply and leaning back in his chair. "I'm getting there. You have to be patient and let me finish my point."

Jackson reluctantly nodded indicating he understood.

"I can't send you to the wolves out there. They will eat you alive. It's bad enough that you came barging in here. I'm sure they'll be waiting for you as soon as you leave."

The old man didn't realize Jackson had evaded his pursuers and left no trail for them to follow. He didn't give Jackson the credit he was due. But he could tell the young man was a survivor.

"I can take care of myself. I just need you to point me in the right direction," Jackson said.

"I'm getting there," McAllister said again. "There are four major players in this operation. Of course, there are more involved," he continued, "but in my eyes, only four of us really matter. My son, Ron. Senator Scooter Windgate. And Chief Justice Michael Abramson."

Jackson was stunned by the names rolling off the old man's tongue. These were, indeed, powerful players. A week never went by without one of those men being mentioned in the headlines, excluding Ron.

McAllister let the information sink in with the young man.

"I don't know what's going on within the group, but some people think Caroline got a little too close to the action for their liking."

"So they killed her?"

"I'm not sure. I pray that isn't the case," he said.

The old man swallowed hard as if he was about to divulge his life's darkest secrets.

"I know more about Caroline than she thought I did," he said. "I know who she is. She doesn't know this, but I brought her here to give her a window into her past. And she deserved better from me. I haven't handled this well at all. But she also kept something from me."

"Is that so?" Jackson blurted, annoyed by the old man's lack of directness.

"Yes."

"Do you know where she is?"

"Like I said before, I don't know anything about her whereabouts. The last I heard was that she skipped town with you."

"And how do you know that?"

"Let's not get into that. Just assume that I know more about you than you think."

The conversation frustrated Jackson. He envisioned coming into the estate with guns blazing making demands on John McAllister. But he'd been shut down so easily—so quickly. McAllister was controlling the conversation, so Jackson decided it was time to give in and play along.

"So you mentioned you knew a lot about Caroline. What exactly do you know—or think you know?"

"Jimmy, give us some space," McAllister called out to get Jimmy off the door.

Two knocks and then the wooden hallway creaked as footsteps faded into the distance. He may have been old and fragile, but he commanded the estate like a decorated general.

The old man leaned forward.

"To start, her name is not Caroline Mills. It's Caroline Peterson."

"Yeah, so I already know this. She told me. She also told me one of your cronies murdered her father."

Jackson realized he may have offered too much too soon. The old man took a few deep breaths and continued.

"Sure. We can go that route."

"I'm listening," Jackson prodded the old man along.

"Robert Peterson happened to finagle his way into one of my events many years ago. He evidently overheard a group of my customers talking about the party. He was an intelligent man, much like his daughter, so he put two and two together and made his way here to the party."

If only Jackson knew how honest the old man was being with him. Unfortunately, he couldn't trust anyone at this point. However, he outwardly displayed nothing but interest. And the old man continued.

"He was a handsome man. He had a friendly smile and an easiness about him. It's no wonder he was able to make his way through our security, though it was not quite as intense back then. There was no need for it. We were kings. If you didn't belong, you didn't dare show up."

"It sounds like you know him a little better than you would from just one party," interjected Jackson. "What happened to Caroline's father?"

"I know about Robert because he introduced himself to me and we talked for a few minutes. He seemed like a fine person. But to answer your question, what happened next was truly tragic."

McAllister took a deep breath, this time preparing to actually divulge the distillery's most damning secret.

He began to speak but caught himself. Instead, he swiveled around in his desk chair and opened a cabinet behind his desk. He placed two empty glasses and a bottle of his homemade whiskey on the desk in front of Jackson.

Without asking, the old man poured two healthy fingers and pushed the glass toward Jackson—no ice, no mixer, just whiskey.

Wrinkled forehead and all, Jackson picked up the glass and shared a quick toast with his host. McAllister immediately downed the entire serving. Jackson cringed as he took the smallest taste.

It was terrible. The hinges in his jaws tightened, and he could feel the nausea before the liquid even hit his stomach. Why would so many people insist on buying this poison? Cheap bottles of much higher quality were available at any liquor store. Jackson could attest.

"Caroline knows most of what I'm about to tell you. I told her just before you two left town," he lied. "But there's more to it, and that's what is important here."

"So you're saying it's not important that you murdered her father?"

"Let's get this straight," McAllister ordered. "I did not murder Caroline's father. There are details of that day I do know, and there are a lot of things that are still a mystery. Some other members of our executive committee—"

"Mafia," Jackson interrupted.

The old man ignored Jackson's rudeness and continued, "Some members thought our security was a bit lacking. Nobody knew where he came from or why he was here."

He paused, and then continued, "Now, what I'm going to tell you can never be repeated. I think it's valuable information so you know who you're dealing with. This is no mom and pop backyard club. These are serious men."

Jackson wanted answers. He wondered if the old man was stalling so his crew could plan a way to eliminate Jackson, never to be seen again.

"Somebody in our group, I don't know who, ordered my son, Ron, and his best friend, Michael Abramson, to take the man out and give him a good ole' beating. Nothing too serious, just enough to convince him to stay out of our business for good."

"Two days later, a hiker found his bloodied, shot-up body in the woods not too far from here. It was a public relations disaster. Authorities combed the property for a month looking for clues. They found nothing. They were told not to find anything. You see, Senator Windgate and I had them in our back pockets. And we spent a lot of money that year. Enough to keep the case unsolved to this day."

"That's just ridiculous!" Jackson shouted, pointing his finger in the old man's face. "I will see to it that you pay for this! All of you!"

"Sit down," John calmly replied. "That won't happen. We're as corrupt as you'll ever see, so I wouldn't advise doing anything to get yourself hurt. Besides, I like you. If you want to help Caroline, you'll have to use some tact.

"Anyway, Ron and Abramson took Robert back into the woods and gave him a pretty good beating, probably worse than they should have. But, according to their story, as they turned to leave him bloodied but stumbling to his feet, shots were fired from the brush. They never saw who fired the shots. To this day, it remains a mystery. However, one of those two boys, if not both, had to have something to do with it. Ron was overstepping his bounds in other areas of the business, so I blame him.

"By that time, it was clear that Abramson had a very bright future ahead of him. Ron, not so much. So we banned Ron from the area for two decades. He was ordered to stay away and never be seen. I didn't want him anywhere close to my operation. He was into stuff that was much worse than harmless bootleg whiskey, and it was only a matter of time before the top would be blown off the operation."

"Do you think it was somebody within the group?" Jackson asked.

"It must have been. No one else knew about the party that night. And furthermore, not many people at the party knew we kicked out Robert Peterson. Not many people even noticed Robert Peterson.

"For the next twenty years, I kept an eye on Caroline and her mother. That incident was the first time I wanted to reach out and help one of our victims. It should've never happened that way. Nobody should've lost a life. Not like that. When I saw that Caroline had applied for my farm job, it was as if some divine force was bringing her close to me. I was going to have a chance to reconcile the wrongs she had suffered, as well as make up for so many other unholy acts we committed over the years."

"And you never told her."

"I never had the chance. I was slowly bringing her along, but she saw a picture of her father on the wall down in the cavern. I always kept it there to remind me of how far we'd fallen.

"Jackson, don't go at this alone. There are some really evil people on my team. You already made the mistake of coming here, don't do anything else to put yourself in danger."

"What about Caroline? I can't just let her disappear," said Jackson. "I've already made up my mind. I don't have any family left, and you killed my best friend."

McAllister let the accusation pass.

"I'm leaving," said Jackson, turning towards the door. "I'll find her with or without you. And I'll bring this whole place down."

"Let me tell you one more time: Don't do anything you'll regret," was all the old man could say before Jackson was out of sight.

Jimmy popped back into the room.

"Follow him, and don't let him out of your sight. He's a smart kid. He'll lead us to Caroline."

Jimmy obliged and quickly left the room.

Once he was alone again, McAllister walked over to his file cabinet and pulled out the folder that Chief Justice Abramson had delivered earlier. He stared into the pages of the file for several minutes, wondering how such a thing could be possible.

John McAllister had no reason to believe anything Abramson said. However, the old man knew deep down that there was no denying this truth.

His concentration was immediately broken by a shot. No silencer. This was a message. John moved as fast as his limbs could carry him to the front of the house. Before he could reach the door, several members of his security team grabbed him and put him under cover.

Out the front window, McAllister saw Jimmy's lifeless body lying on the front lawn, just steps away from his truck.

Jackson was long gone, and no one from McAllister's team was on his trail. Untraceable again.

36

Several law clerks accompanied Chief Justice Abramson for lunch at a popular restaurant. Located on D Street, just a quick stroll from their offices, the group enjoyed the seafood and steaks in a private dining area.

The Chief Justice tried to stay abreast of the current affairs of the clerks, but he never succeeded. Between his official duties on the Court and those relating to the distillery, there was little time to worry about what was happening with fellow Justices or their clerks. He seemed to be in good graces with most of them, so there was no reason to waste any more time preoccupied with their activities.

At the same restaurant, several members of Congress enjoyed their lunches in the main dining room. The place bustled with activity as aides and runners scurried about, keeping their bosses in the know.

Men in fine suits filled the restaurant, but none of the suits were as finely made and tailored as the Chief Justice's. He was still quite attractive, in his professional prime, and his sense for fashion made him a popular target for photo ops. Although contrary to how an organized crime member should act, he loved the attention.

Women often stopped by his table just to say hello and get a peek at the man. He was not only a legal legend, but he was a legend with the ladies. Although rumors floated around there was never any concrete evidence of infidelity in his recent marriage.

Today's was a working lunch. No alcohol was present. That's why the table became silent when a well-dressed man arrived in the private dining area with two cocktails—one obviously for himself, the other for Chief Justice Abramson.

The man was clean-shaven with a perfectly tailored charcoal pin-stripe suit. He flaunted an open collar, exposing the top of his tanned chest. His hair had recently been cut as shown by the crisp tan lines around his ears and neck.

"Good afternoon, Michael," said Ron.

Abramson excused himself from the table, visibly jolted by the awkward visit, and joined Ron in a back corner of the restaurant, far from earshot of any listeners.

"What the hell are you doing here?" asked Abramson.

"Something's going down, and I have no idea what it is," replied Ron.

It was apparent from Ron's breath that he had already enjoyed a few cocktails before intruding on the Chief Justice.

"What are you talking about?" asked Abramson. "You can't just come in here and interrupt official Court business. That's completely uncalled for! And stupid!"

"I can't get in touch with Agent Stewart," said Ron.

That caught Abramson's attention.

"I also saw where some news outlets have identified a murder victim in Kentucky as someone very similar to Stewart," Ron continued. "Somebody with federal credentials. Somebody got to him before he could catch the girl."

"Either that, or they waited until he had the girl and then took her from his possession," said Abramson. "Do we know if it's him for sure?"

"It must be," replied Ron. "That's the only explanation for us not being able to reach him. But more importantly, we have no idea where the girl is."

Ron was Abramson's best friend. The two were inseparable. But Abramson could only think back to what he saw in the manila folder that he handed over to John McAllister.

"You are sure you don't know where the girl is," said Abramson, making no effort to hide the accusation.

"Are you serious? Do you think I'm in on this?"

"I don't know, Ron. You tell me. There's a lot I don't know right now. And I don't like it."

Tension escalated between the two friends. Dishonesty was the root of most falling outs, and there was a lot at stake between these two men.

"Go find the girl," Abramson ordered. "Go find her. Go find her body. Find out who took her. She can't be on the loose. She already knows too much information. She'll take us all down."

Ron understood Abramson's frustrations and concerns. He shared them entirely.

After a brief discussion hidden deep in the recesses of the back of the restaurant, the two men parted ways. Ron left the restaurant to search for Caroline.

The Chief Justice rejoined his lunch party, not a sip taken from his cocktail, and tried to downplay the unsolicited encounter. Before long, he was back to shop talk with his clerks.

After Ron was out of sight, and the Chief Justice was back to work, a nondescript man at the bar picked up the phone. He had been sipping cranberry juice, watching the two men intently behind his aviator sunglasses.

He relayed the message of what he just witnessed to his boss. Then he left the restaurant to trail Ron.

Upon leaving the restaurant, Ron hailed a cab and ordered the driver to take him to an elementary school in Bethesda.

He arrived about fifteen minutes after the program started, and quietly took a seat in the very back, careful to not draw attention to himself.

The children seated in the front of the auditorium were eagerly awaiting a speech from Senator Scooter Windgate.

Ron couldn't hide his smile at the irony of the program. Windgate was a huge proponent of America's War on Drugs, and he was about to deliver a high-spirited message to the school kids about just saying no.

"If only they knew," thought Ron aloud.

Realizing that this was not the place to speak with the senator, Ron exited the school building as quietly as he entered. It was scary how easily he evaded school security at this affluent elementary school.

Everything going on had him scrambling, uncharacteristically taking dumb chances.

He would meet up with the aging senator at a later time. He had a mystery to solve. Where was the girl?

A cab just happened to be waiting in front of the school.

Ron didn't think twice. He climbed into the backseat and the taxi sped off down the road as the driver adjusted his aviators.

37

The throbbing finally began to lighten up. Caroline gently rubbed the lump, crusted with blood, on the side of her head. Tears filled her eyes from the dreadful pain.

She was engulfed by darkness, not even able to see more than two feet in front of her. Other than a few strange, unidentified sounds, Caroline could hear nothing. Utter darkness and deafening silence.

She had no idea how long she had been in the car. For a moment, she couldn't determine whether she was still in the trunk or if she was in an open space. She finally stretched her arms as far as they would go, nothing restraining her limbs, confirming she was no longer in the trunk.

She was slowly regaining her bearings. Although she was lying on a thin blanket, she was on top of a hard, cold surface.

She rolled over and hit the cold, rock-hard floor.

As her senses sharpened, she heard footsteps drawing nearer. They were not coming from the room, but probably a hallway.

A door at the far end of the room cracked open, allowing in a strip of light at the end of the hall.

Because of the darkness, Caroline hadn't noticed that she was blind in her right eye. It was swollen shut. She reached up to touch it, but winced in pain as she grazed the wound. That explained the blood on her mouth. It must have been running down her face for quite some time.

A silhouette briefly appeared against the backdrop of light in the doorway. But the door shut quickly, returning Caroline to darkness.

A watchman just taking inventory, making sure she was still there, Caroline guessed. She couldn't make out whether the figure was male or female, but it was rather small—not too imposing. Even in her current state, she liked her chances if it came down to another physical scrap.

Realizing there was nothing holding her down, she tried to stand up. She lost her balance immediately and fell back to the floor, missing the blanket and smacking the solid ground.

She tried to determine whether her lack of balance was from being drugged or from her head injury. With no way to find out, she assumed the worst. The truth serum she had been given earlier had probably run its course through her veins over the last few hours, undoubtedly forcing her to expose her true identity and all manner of personal secrets.

"Hey," she softly called out.

A soft echo replied. From the sound of it, she gathered she was in a very large space.

On her hands and knees, she gingerly placed one hand out in front of the other, moving slow and steady. She tried to feel her way toward the open door she had seen moments earlier.

There was nothing but cold concrete in front of her. No furniture. No guards. Just nothingness. She had the sensation of being watched—being mocked by her captors as she groped blindly through the darkness.

Caroline guessed that she had crawled about thirty yards when the door flew open. She estimated that she was twice as close to the door as when she started, but only because she had been moving in a diagonal direction from the door.

When the onlooker noticed the girl was not on the blanket, he panicked and nervously felt his way around for the light switch.

As quietly and quickly as possible, Caroline scurried as far as she could.

The man finally found the light switch and flipped it. Caroline was instantly blinded, her eyes unaccustomed to seeing light in what seemed like days.

She barely made out the outline of a large cabinet against the wall just a few feet away. Blindly, she felt her way to it and wedged herself tightly against the side. Luckily, a blue tarp was next to her and she eased her way under it without making much noise.

Her fears that the man had seen her were relieved when she heard him yelling that she had escaped. He slammed the door behind him, leaving the lights turned on.

Caroline remained quiet and didn't move. Hopefully, they wouldn't come back inside what she could now see was a warehouse. She tucked herself under the tarp and planned her escape.

Across the room, beside the blanket where she had awakened, were her shoes. She was so determined to get to the door, she hadn't realized she was barefoot.

After ten minutes or so, vision blurred and balance shaky, Caroline mustered the strength to walk over and put her shoes on, careful not to make a sound.

She still hadn't heard a thing from outside the warehouse room. Large industrial rolls of aluminum were stacked on shelving behind her. Nothing she could see helped her determine her exact geographic location.

Her heart raced and her brain was flooded with adrenaline as she approached the warehouse door, ready to fight for her freedom.

She cringed when sweat stung the open wound above her right eye. But the pain was temporary. She had a bigger battle to fight.

The doorknob didn't make a peep as she turned it and ever so slightly cracked the door. Nobody was out there. She was free.

She opened the door completely, looking both ways up and down the hall, and confirmed that she was alone by.

Her footsteps were the only sound in the hallway as she sprinted toward the exit sign. Freedom was only a few steps away. She would get outside and scream as loud as her lungs would allow. Balance was not an issue anymore. Pure flight instinct had taken over.

Caroline came to a screeching halt when she reached the exit. Through the window in the door she could see a man with his back turned to the building. He was yelling obscenities into his phone.

"Where the hell is she?" he screamed, sweat soaking through the back of his shirt.

He looked very familiar to Caroline, but she couldn't quite remember from where.

She slammed the door open into the man's back, knocking him face first onto the ground. She took off in a sprint while the man reached for the phone that had been knocked out of his hands. As she ran, she could hear the man barking orders into the phone that she was, in fact, on the loose.

It would only be a matter of time until the pack of wolves sniffed her out of hiding. She knew she had to act fast.

Caroline noticed she was in some sort of industrial park. Several jet planes flew overhead very low to the ground, indicating an airport was nearby.

She could hear the man gaining on her. As she looked over her shoulder, she saw him pull a handgun from his waistband.

The sound of the first shot paralyzed Caroline for a brief second but, upon realizing the shot had missed, she ran on, faster than before. There was enough distance between the two that he'd have to be very accurate to hit her with a shot, especially with a handgun. She'd gladly take her chances, especially with an amateur criminal.

A few more errant shots whizzed by Caroline as she continued around the warehouse. She almost completely circled the warehouse when she saw the car. It was the same car from her kidnapping. Then she recognized the man's voice. It was Paul, the old bartender from Molly O's.

Paul had made the critical mistake of leaving the car door open and the keys in the ignition.

In full stride, Caroline leaped into the front seat of the car, turned the key, put it in gear, and stomped on the gas pedal.

Paul's last round shattered the back window of the car, but it missed the her. She was speeding to freedom.

In the rearview mirror, she saw Paul back on the phone. She knew she had to ditch the car fast if she wanted any chance of survival.

At the nearest intersection, there were several highway signs among a large sign for Washington Dulles International Airport.

She followed the signs pointing toward DC and soon she was on the highway. She floored it, praying that she would get pulled over for speeding. She would do anything to get the authorities' attention. She hoped that by going so fast, she'd also be able to easily tell if someone was trailing her. Any chasers would have to drive aggressively to catch and keep up with her.

She turned off the highway when she saw the first Metro sign. Public transportation could get her anywhere and she could disappear among the crowd. But how would she explain her terrible appearance and physical condition? Would they even allow her on the trains?

Caroline ditched the car in the parking lot of the Metro stop. She cautiously walked into the terminal, trying not to attract any attention to her swollen face and ripped clothing.

An abandoned newspaper on the ground caught her attention—a perfect way to hide her battered face.

Using the old quick sneak method she had seen during her days riding the subway in New York, she sneaked right behind a paying customer and through the turnstiles. She was in—closer to safety.

She found an unoccupied bench far down the line from other patrons and waited for the train, acting like an avid newsreader. The Orange Line train would be arriving shortly.

A stranger sat down beside her, not more than a few inches away.

"Don't make any sudden moves. Don't speak. Just listen and do as I say," said the male voice, loud enough so only Caroline could hear.

She dared not lower the newspaper to see who it was. It was not Paul.

"The game's over, Ms. Peterson," said the voice.

Pains shot through her spine. They knew exactly who she was.

A few seconds later, the man spoke again, "Get up slowly and casually walk towards the exit. I will be right behind you, so don't do anything stupid or I'll end it right here. Don't test me. I'm giving you the chance to live, even if just a little longer."

This man was serious.

Who were these people? How did they find her?

The man rudely retrieved a tiny tracking device from the waistband of her jeans. How could she have missed it?

She left the newspaper on the bench, exposing her wounded face for the world to see as she walked across the Metro platform. She received a few double-takes, but no one attempted to offer assistance. The Metro stop wasn't very crowded, severely diminishing her chance of finding any assistance.

In the parking lot, the man led her to a taxi parked next to the car she hijacked from Paul. He opened the back door and she climbed in without a fight.

The man was tall and well built. He wore aviator sunglasses and a navy blue baseball cap. His appearance and demeanor indicated a military background. He matched the description she always envisioned when people talked about mercenaries—evil men who would kill for any amount of money.

His biceps bulged through the sleeves of his tight, long-sleeved t-shirt. His hands dwarfed the steering wheel like a toothpick. If those hands were to wring her neck, she'd be dead in an instant.

Escaping was not an option this time. Just keep surviving, she kept repeating to herself.

Caroline leaned her head against the window as the man drove to their destination in silence. Next to her in the backseat, she noticed a rather large blood stain.

It was fresh. The blood was still wet, and the iron smell hit her like a brick wall.

She closed her eyes and prayed.

"Please, God, let it be quick and merciful."

38

John McAllister took no chances when he arrived at the corner coffee shop in Georgetown. He had not arrived in the Aston Martin, the Porsche, or the limited edition Camaro. With his life in grave danger, he took every precaution.

He sat in the backseat of his armored sedan, flanked by two heavily armed members of his security staff. The driver navigated through traffic with ease, keeping an eye out for anything out of the ordinary. He had multiple emergency routes memorized in the event of an attack.

McAllister gripped the manila folder tightly. And that was the primary reason for the meeting with Senator Windgate so early in the morning—to discuss business.

The old man dreaded the conversation but knew that it was necessary to maintain order—as best as possible given the circumstances.

The armored sedan, like the vehicles used in the president's fleet, pulled up to the curb. McAllister climbed out of the car, not waiting for the driver to open the door, and walked directly into the coffee shop.

Senator Windgate was seated at a table for two beside the window. The other patrons in the shop were not regular customers. McAllister recognized them as part of the senator's security detail. Many of them had also worked for him in the distillery operation.

McAllister and Senator Windgate would be able to speak freely.

The coffee shop was a common meeting place for the two men. The owner of the shop opened his place of business to the distillery to use as a distribution hub. In the back, a large storage area, much too large for a coffee shop, was often used to store cartons of whiskey bottles, among other illegal substances, waiting to be delivered to their customers.

Some folks would come to the coffee shop before or after hours to pick up their order. Others would have one of the distillery's many runners bring the order to their place of work or, if too risky, their home. The operation was a well-oiled, efficient machine.

McAllister sat across from the senator, sliding the folder across the table to him.

"Scooter, we're under investigation," said he, visibly concerned.

"For what, the distillery?" asked Senator Windgate.

"No," John answered. "They're not investigating our distillery. Believe it or not, I don't think anybody really cares that we supply homemade whiskey to our own friends."

"Then what?"

Scooter was caught off guard.

"Heroin. Cocaine. Marijuana. Prostitution."

"John, we got out of that business more than two decades ago. How could they be looking back that long ago?"

"I know that I've been out of that business for more than two decades. That's why I'm here."

McAllister gestured for the senator to open the folder.

Scooter looked through the pictures and files for about five minutes in complete silence. "Where did you get this?" asked Senator Windgate.

"That doesn't matter."

"To hell it doesn't matter," screamed the senator. "This implicates me!"

"You've been using our fun little distillery operation to continue to run drugs behind my back. You used my businesses to pad your pockets," McAllister replied, raising his voice. "And at the expense of all of us! How could you do such a thing?"

Scooter looked away from the old man, avoiding eye contact. Then he turned to face him.

"John, you know this better than anyone. Once you go dirty, you can never come clean again."

"You're out," McAllister screamed. "You're finished. You're out of the group. You will not take us down with you."

A few members of the security teams stood up, not knowing quite what to do about the old men and their shouting match.

"Not so fast, John," Scooter replied, his smirk saying it all.

"Where is she?" John asked.

"You see, that's part of the game, John," said Scooter, finally acknowledging his control. "I have everything you think you have. I have all of the power in this operation. And if someone is going to take the fall for all of my illegal—allegedly illegal—activities, it will be you—either the hard way, or the easy way. It's your choice."

"Where is she?" John asked again.

"She was too much like her father. She got in a little too deep, old pal."

"I'm not your pal."

McAllister stood up, ready to storm out the door. He leaned over to Scooter, inches from his face.

"I'll find her," he whispered. "And I'll take you down. Don't ever underestimate me."

He walked calmly to the exit.

"It's a shame about Jimmy," the senator called out as McAllister reached the door.

He turned immediately and lunged at the senator. He grabbed the senator's neck right before the security teams reached them.

Without much effort, the two elderly men were separated and McAllister was physically escorted to his car.

The senator suffered only a minor scratch on his neck, but the rift left behind a much more permanent scar on their relationship.

Senator Windgate had leverage—he had the political allies for sure, but McAllister could not know if he had Ron or Chief Justice Abramson in his back pocket. And McAllister had no way of knowing if the senator did, in fact, have the girl. But his suspicions indicated yes.

Moments after John's entourage sped away from the coffee shop, Senator Windgate emerged from the front door, polished as ever.

A handful of local residents recognized him on the sidewalk and he eagerly shook their hands and exchanged a few kind words. Nothing was out of the ordinary for the politician.

The ride back to the McAllister estate was painfully long. Traffic around the District was always terrible, but this time was worse than most.

McAllister thought about the senator's remark, "Once you go dirty, you can never come clean again."

There was a lot of truth to that statement. John knew that some details of his past could never be disclosed. And as hard as he tried, he'd never be able to escape some of those decisions. However, in his old age, he was doing his best to come clean and leave a positive legacy on the world—one that didn't involve dark caves, dark activities, and dark cover-ups.

Yes, for years, McAllister had been as dirty as they came. He distributed every illegal substance one could imagine. He controlled the drug lords in Washington, DC. He even controlled the territory wars between gangs, making sure the most efficient and profitable gang won the battle. Because, in the end, all he cared about was his bottom line: Money, and lots of it.

McAllister made a fortune in legitimate businesses. From banking to small-scale industry, the McAllister name was attached to many different companies—legitimate enterprises that were never tarnished with illegal activities.

Yet, he made an even larger fortune in illegal activities. He learned from his father and grandfather during the Prohibition Era how much money could be made by skirting the law—especially when you're in bed with the authorities.

At an early age, he had learned the art of manipulating authorities. Everybody has a price, and it's just a matter of asking what it is. For a natural born salesman, it was too easy. It wasn't even fair.

He had been raised as a privileged kid on his family's dirty money. It was ingrained in him. But he'd become too greedy.

When the distillery began losing more and more money each year, John needed a new cash flow. It was demoted from enterprise to hobby status. McAllister needed something that would get his blood pumping—something that kept alive the thrill of being above the law. No one cared anymore about his small scale, backyard distillery anymore. That was the juice of a previous generation. He needed something significant.

So he turned to narcotics. He turned to prostitution. He ran the show with Scooter as his right hand man. And he groomed Ron for the business throughout his high school and college years, much to the chagrin of the late Mrs. McAllister.

Cash poured into the business. They were almost caught a few times, but they had two men deep inside the FBI. Agent Stewart was a young, up-and-coming agent, and he was indoctrinated into the gang early in his career. He was easy. He coveted the expensive things that he could not afford on a typical agent's salary. McAllister made it happen, and Agent Stewart became a long-standing loyal soldier.

They were also assisted by Stephen Forrester. Forrester led the drug enforcement division in the FBI. He diverted investigators away from the McAllisters whenever necessary. And he was paid handsomely for his services.

On one occasion, Forrester even found a mid-level drug pusher in suburban Northern Virginia to take the fall when investigators had somehow pegged the McAllisters.

But Ron's carelessness almost cost them the entire McAllister empire. That's when the elder McAllister pulled the plug on drug activities, vowing to never sow a rotten oat again. Or so he thought.

At that time, he knew he would eventually pay for his sins. But he never imagined it would be this late in life. He thought it would be when he met his maker face to face.

There was no possible way that McAllister would let the senator's recent transgressions bring down his entire operation, his legacy. Not like this. Not now. But there was no one left in the Bureau to deter the investigators. His only hope was that Scooter could pull some strings. After today, however, McAllister figured Scooter would point the investigators directly to him, implicating him in decades of wrongdoings.

Forrester hadn't been in contact with the McAllister operation for years. He had left the Bureau and taken a partner position at a corporate law firm in the area. He made out quite handsomely, getting out with a new position and a stash of dirty cash.

The ominous black smoke billowed into the sky as McAllister's driver steered closer to the estate. John already knew. He didn't need to get any closer.

His fears were confirmed when they pulled into the front gate. Ms. Ruby was standing in the front lawn, tears streaming. The old mansion was an inferno. Years and years of memories were lost forever.

A member of his security staff informed the old man that while they were investigating an alarm near the back of the property, someone intentionally set fire to the mansion. McAllister realized he had left the team too thin at the home base, in order to keep him safe while traveling to meet the senator. He'd worried that something might happen back at home, but not this.

Thankfully, Ms. Ruby was unharmed.

"Everybody, come with me," McAllister ordered. "I've got a plan. I've been prepared for something like this."

He led the group down the hill beside the smoldering mansion. On his way, he checked the garage housing his antique automobiles. Not a single scratch on anything.

They continued along the path but stopped halfway to the front entrance of the cavern. After a brief pause, the old man pulled back a few low hanging limbs and exposed a concealed trail. He led the team, including Ms. Ruby, down the dirt trail for about forty yards until they reached a tiny wooden door in the side of a rock wall.

John punched a code into the electronic keypad, unlocking it. It opened onto a very primitive hallway, outfitted with rock walls and a muddy, damp floor.

A lantern had been left near the front entrance to light the path.

The team hustled down the dark hallway until they reached another wooden door.

John's old hands fiddled with his keys until he found the correct one. He unlocked the door and pushed it open.

He flipped on the lights revealing an elaborate bunker outfitted with everything from flat screen televisions and laptops to a refrigerator stocked with food and water. This was the new central headquarters.

The room could easily hold twenty people, but that would not be necessary. Only McAllister, Ms. Ruby, and the security team were inside.

The floors were tiled, the walls nicely finished. It would make a comfortable hideout. He turned on the generator to warm the room.

He instructed pointed out the amenities and encouraged everyone to get comfortable. The televisions provided elaborate surveillance footage of the entire estate. From the back boundary line in the woods, through the horse fields and barns, and all the way to the front gate, every inch of the estate could easily be monitored from this room. Jimmy had been the only member of the security team to know of the room's existence.

"This door, right here," John said, pointing to a nondescript door on one of the walls, "opens to a passage that will lead you to the garage. The cabinet will roll to the side when the garage door is unlocked."

Everyone was focused on him.

"This door, over here," John explained, referring to a door on the opposite wall, "will lead you to a room behind the main ballroom— the room containing the stainless steel vats. The opening is tiny, keeping it out of sight. You'll have to duck to get through it, but once through, you can just slide out from behind the vats unnoticed."

The team nodded, and several security members were already on their way to man those posts.

"And, of course, you've seen the main way in and out."

In the corner, John's makeshift office looked too cluttered to be used on more than special occasions. Miss Ruby thought this must be where he hid out when he went missing.

McAllister picked up the phone on his desk and dialed out on the secure line.

"Chief Justice," he said, "we need to talk."

39

The posh, sixth floor office of Schneider Sims & Zelli had a magnificent view overlooking K Street. Lobbyists and corporate lawyers hustled below on the sidewalks, wheeling and dealing their way to fat paychecks—mostly on the average American's tax dollar.

The firm culture at Schneider was very non-traditional. Unless the litigation department was going to trial, neckties were highly frowned upon. Everyone, from paralegal to senior partner, wore jeans on most days of the week.

One of Jackson's draws to the firm was its emphasis on always providing the staff with the latest technology. Smart phones, laptops, and the latest tablet devices filled the briefcases of the workers. The firm should have been a perfect match for him, with a tech-savvy background on his resume.

The receptionist at the front desk of the firm instantly recognized Jackson Cole. Who couldn't? His reputation as a notorious boozing womanizer spread quickly throughout the firm during his one summer of employment, explaining why the firm didn't ask him to return.

However, he remained in close contact with Shaun Martin, the senior attorney assigned to mentor him during that summer.

Jackson could not remember the receptionist's name. But he had a feeling he had hit on her a few times.

"Can you page Shaun Martin for me?" he asked.

"No problem, Mr. Cole," she replied while dialing Shaun's office phone. "Have a seat, please. He should be right out. Can I get you water or something else to drink?"

"No thanks," he lied. He really could've used a stiff drink.

Jackson wandered over to the waiting area and took a seat on one of the red couches. While it was very chic, he soon realized comfort had not been a consideration when designing the furniture. It was terrible.

He gazed out the window, at the street below, at the buildings lining K Street, and at the blue sky. He wondered how many more days he'd be alive to see the bright blue sky.

"Jackson," called Shaun walking past the receptionist.

He was tall, rail thin, and walked with an air of confidence that few could match. Not even Jackson. That was partly the reason Jackson had been drawn to Shaun.

His hair was cropped very short and he wore a pair of invisible frame glasses. His crisply pressed open-collared shirt was perfectly polished casual.

"What's going on with you? You look awful," announced Shaun as he approached closer, half seriously.

Jackson didn't smile this time. He was here strictly for business.

"You would never believe what's been going on," he replied. "Is there somewhere private where we can chat?"

"Yeah, sure," responded Shaun, caught off guard by Jackson's serious request. "Follow me. We'll talk in my office."

Jackson followed Shaun through the network of hallways to his new office. He tried to avoid eye contact with his former coworkers. The last thing he needed was distractions. He was in no mood for small talk.

"It looks like you graduated to a window since I was last in the office," Jackson teased, attempting to loosen up.

"Indeed, I did," boasted Shaun, mockingly showing off his new view. "Furthermore, I have a fabulous panoramic view of the lovely parking garage next door."

Shaun did have a window, but the prime views of K Street were given only to the highest performing partners in the firm.

"Seriously, you look terrible. What's going on?" Shaun asked, changing the subject back to Jackson.

"If I told you that two people I'd talked to in the last few weeks have been murdered, one being my best friend, and a girl I just met had been kidnapped, would you believe me?"

"I guess not," replied the attorney, stiffening up in his chair. "But you have my attention now."

Shaun's expression turned serious as he became legitimately concerned for his friend.

"Okay, start at the beginning," Shaun continued. "Tell me what happened."

Jackson proceeded to tell a very detailed version of his story, from the initial interview with Phillip Waters and his subsequent murder, to meeting Caroline Mills, and her other identity, and the story that followed all the way to her kidnapping.

"What was the old guy's name again?" asked Shaun.

"John McAllister," clarified Jackson.

"That's a crazy story. I want to help you, but I have no idea where to begin. If the operation is in with Scooter Windgate, and God knows who else, going to the authorities will be worthless. First, nobody would believe you. Second, even if they did, I'm sure everything would be covered up, and you would be taken out of the picture. So where does that leave you?"

The two men sat in silence for a few moments contemplating the next steps.

"There's someone here you should talk to," began Shaun.

"Can I trust him?"

"I'd trust him with my life," Shaun stated boldly, adequately masking a lie.

Shaun led Jackson through the network of hallways and back through the lobby to the elevators. They took the elevator to the building's ninth floor. Most of the senior partners, including the firm's managing partner, had elegant, modern offices on nine, away from the chaotic churning of the hungry young attorneys.

This is where multibillion-dollar deals were signed. Just thinking about the money that passed hands on this floor made many young attorneys weak at the knees and hungry for the life.

Jackson had never been invited to this floor during his short tenure at the firm. He never thought he'd make his first visit wearing a wrinkled t-shirt and blood stained shorts and having not showered in three days.

Jackson waited in the sitting area while Shaun had a word with one of the administrative assistants. As he waited, he envisioned the comfortable life he would enjoy as a big time corporate attorney. These offices were as nice as they come.

But Jackson wanted more from life. He didn't need the big paycheck. He already had a nice nest egg—if only he could live to enjoy it.

Shaun returned to the sitting area to collect Jackson and lead the way to the closed door of a corner office.

The attorney gave three knocks, then poked his head in.

A deep baritone voice ordered the men to come inside.

The smell of cigar smoke overwhelmed Jackson as soon as he set foot inside the office. It was the smell of *I don't give a damn*. It was the smell of hard-earned respect. And more importantly, it was the smell of unlimited success.

"Mr. Forrester, I'd like you to meet Jackson Cole," Shaun began. "He was one of our summer associates last year, and I think you may be able to help him with some serious trouble he's facing."

"Very well, Mr. Martin," boomed the deep voice. "I have a few minutes. Please give Jackson and me some time to speak in private."

Shaun shook Jackson's hand and headed back down to his office. He would be waiting when Mr. Forrester was through hearing Jackson's story.

"Please sit," Forrester said, directing Jackson over to a round table and chairs in front of his K Street window.

The man was everything Jackson thought a managing partner should be. Salt and pepper hair neatly combed and parted on the side. Perfectly tailored navy blue suit with a subtle pinstripe over a starched open collar white executive button down. Jackson was sure his shoes had been shined on his way in to the office as he could almost see his ugly reflection in the shoes.

Forrester's face was nicely tan, no doubt from countless rounds of golf at the premier clubs around the District.

When Jackson shook his hand, Forrester's massive paws nearly crushed Jackson's skinny hands.

The man was imposing, yet he offered a disarming smile. Jackson immediately felt comfortable with him. Jackson's immediately trusted, for better or worse.

"Welcome back to the firm," Forrester began, as he took a seat across the table from Jackson. "I don't think we had the pleasure of meeting last summer, but I'm always willing to help out former associates in any way that I can."

"Thank you, sir," Jackson replied. "But I want to make sure you understand the magnitude of the situation. Two people that I've been in contact with in the last couple of weeks, one being my best friend, have been murdered. A girl I recently met was kidnapped on a trip we took together. I feel like I stumbled into something that I had no business walking into."

"I see. Please continue, you definitely have my full attention."

"I've had the wildest past few days that anyone could ever imagine. I'm looking for help. I'm looking for answers. And I can't trust a single soul right now."

"Son, you can trust me," he responded. Forrester leaned forward. "I don't know how I'll be able to help, but I'll do my best to point you in the right direction. But, after hearing what you just told me, I think it's best that we take this conversation away from the office. You know, for the safety of the others at the firm. As you'll remember from your summer here, we steer away from criminal law. We focus on business deals and lobbying around here. Safe things."

"I understand, sir," Jackson responded, "but I don't know how much time I have."

Forrester took out a scrap piece of paper and jotted down a few notes. He handed it across the table to Jackson.

"This is my home address," he explained. "Come by tonight around 8 o'clock. We can talk in more detail there. I may be able to put you in contact with some authorities—authorities that I trust."

Jackson didn't have the patience to wait around all afternoon and evening to speak with someone who may or may not be able to help.

Each minute that passed was another minute Caroline was in danger. He could only hope that she was safe—if she was still alive.

Jackson took the paper and thanked Forrester for his time. Shaun was waiting outside the managing partner's door when the conversation concluded.

The younger attorney escorted Jackson back to the elevators and traveled down to the ground floor lobby with him. The two men walked outside to the sunny, vibrant afternoon sidewalk.

So many secrets had been spilled on this sidewalk. Shaun knew Jackson's would not measure up to some of the dark political gaming that went on.

"Jackson, stay safe this afternoon, and be careful tonight," he advised. "What I'm about to tell you could cost me my job, and even more importantly, could put me and some others in harm's way."

He paused and looked around the urban area, careful that nobody would hear his secret.

"I looked up John McAllister and you'll never believe what I found," he continued. "He's actually listed as one of our clients. Assigned to Stephen Forrester."

Jackson froze. He was well past the point of no return. The coffin was closing quickly on Jackson's life, and surely, once word got back to McAllister and company, Caroline's, too.

Jackson couldn't form any words. He swallowed the lump in his throat and gave his former mentor a man-hug. Then he turned and walked away like a lost child. He wandered down K Street not knowing which direction he was heading.

"Be careful out there," Shaun called out as Jackson walked away.

Jackson didn't respond. Head down, he kept walking.

On the ninth floor, Stephen Forrester sat less-than-poised at his desk. His palms were uncharacteristically clammy. And for the first time in many years, he was gravely concerned that his past would soon be revealed.

He picked up the phone.

"John," Forrester began. "You have a serious problem on your hands."

X X X

Jackson didn't have a choice. He dialed the number.

Samantha Crocket rarely answered the phone when an unknown number appeared on her phone. Luckily for Jackson, this time she did.

"Sam, it's Jackson," he said. "I'm in trouble."

"Where are you? What are you doing?" she answered. "I've tried calling you a couple of times in the past couple of weeks but your apartment number and your cell phone have been terminated. Are you okay?"

"Not really," he answered. "I don't have too much time to talk. I have a prepaid phone that I just bought on the street."

"Okay, what's up? I'm worried about you."

"That's surprising," he retorted, but quickly caught himself before starting an argument. Instead, he cut straight to the chase, "Sam, I've nearly lost my life a couple of times in the past few days, and Jeff's dead."

"What! How?"

"Some people are trying to kill me. I inadvertently stumbled onto an organized crime operation and now they're trying to silence me, forever."

"Who?"

"It doesn't matter," he replied. "I don't want you to get involved. I'm in DC and I just need a place to crash. Does your brother still live here?"

Samantha gave Jackson her brother's address off of King Street in Alexandria, Virginia. He was out of the country on business, but fortunately, he typically left a spare key above the front door.

Perfect, thought Jackson. He finally had a refuge. There was no way anyone could find him there.

Just as they were about to hang up, Samantha said, "And Jackson," she paused. "My family doesn't know about us. Please don't say anything if you see anybody. They've always loved you."

"Okay, and thanks again," was all he could say before clicking off the call.

The call with Samantha reminded him of the good times they had shared and, for a brief moment, he forgot about the jerk she ran off with. She had hurt him, but right now, he owed his life to her for setting him up in her brother's empty apartment.

Jackson hailed a cab at Farragut Square and asked to be taken to Alexandria.

40

Caroline was stuck in a room with no windows. The taxi had taken her through parts of the city she had never seen before, following a roundabout route so she would have no chance of assessing her location. Halfway through the cab ride, the driver pulled into a parking garage where her captor blindfolded her and forced her into the trunk.

That's where she realized her fate. Or at least felt it. Pressed next to her in the darkness of the trunk was the dead body of a stranger, some one whose identity was unknown to her.

She vomited, again and again. The stench of fresh blood was overwhelming in the confined space.

Once the taxi reached its destination, the man escorted her through what sounded like another parking garage. The only sounds she could identify were the echoes of her footsteps and the man's heavy breathing.

He gripped her upper arm with his massive hands and led her up three flights of stairs. He removed her blindfold and left the room, leaving her unrestrained. She dared not try to escape this time.

She sat on the cold floor of the tiny room, hugging her knees. She no longer felt the pain from her wounds on the right side of her head. She was preoccupied with more pressing concerns, like her life.

A single lightbulb hung from the ceiling, dimly illuminating the room. The room was cold. Caroline shivered as she tried to tuck her legs and arms into her body as tightly as possible.

The door flung open without warning, causing Caroline to cover her head in fear. By the time she removed her arms away to see what had happened, the door had already closed again.

Someone had tossed THE dead body into the room with her.

A single bullet hole in the forehead indicated cause of death.

Caroline knew the face. It was Paul—Paul the captor, Paul the bartender.

She reasoned that his demise resulted from his inability to watch her effectively. But now the tiny, cramped room reeked of his dead body.

Caroline draped her jacket over his head and upper torso so she wouldn't have to stare into his lifeless face. She could think of nothing more than how much she wanted out of the cold room.

She could hear two men having a angry conversation outside. No names were mentioned, intentionally she assumed. One of the men spoke with a mild Southern accent. The other man, whom she suspected to be her captor, spoke in crisp, sharp fragments, not wasting a single breath.

Caroline's heart jumped when she heard her name.

"She has no value to us," said the man in a crisp tone. "She should be killed."

"I'm not yet ready to dump her," replied the southerner.

"That fat, worthless bartender is dead," the captor said. "Now we need to get rid of the rest of the dead weight."

"We can't. We need her for leverage. As long as my father knows we have her alive, it's a different game. She's the wild card."

That was just the reference Caroline was listening for. The man with the slight drawl was John McAllister's son, Ron.

She fondly recalled John McAllister. He had been a father figure to her over the last couple of months. He had taken her under his wing and mentored her. It had been therapeutic for both of them. That is, until she found out there was a connection between her father and the old man.

The two men stopped talking when a few loud knocks banged on another door. She must be in an apartment. She heard the other door open. A barely audible voice was asking the two men questions.

All three men were now whispering. It was no use straining to hear the conversation. They were probably plotting where to dump her body along with Paul's.

Regardless, she assumed the worst—that these men were against John McAllister.

The door flung open again, and the man who had captured her reached down and yanked her to her feet by her arm. Without bothering to blindfold her, he marched her through what she could see was a luxury apartment overlooking the Potomac River.

Instead of exiting the building through the parking garage, Caroline was escorted down an elevator and through the lobby of the building. No guardsman was on duty as Ron and her captor led her to a waiting SUV out front.

They forced her into the backseat, sandwiched between Ron and her captor. As soon as the doors closed, the driver took off.

The passenger in the front seat turned to greet Caroline.

"I hope these men have been treating you well," said Senator Windgate.

She didn't respond. She simply tried to internalize the hatred she instantly felt for the old senator.

"I came into possession of a few of your belongings from that old shack you were living in," he continued, ignoring her disregard. "Old John didn't quite give you the credit you deserved."

The driver kept speeding along, disobeying the traffic signals. Caroline couldn't tell where the car was going, but she did know the vehicle was headed away from civilization. Her immediate future wasn't looking too bright.

"I just have a few questions about the pictures found in your closet," he said in jest. "You're too much like your father. You think you can save the world."

The mention of her father made Caroline's blood boil.

"But let me ask you this," he continued. "If you were so determined to solve the mystery of your father's murder, why was the majority of your research about something completely different? I just don't get what you want from us."

The senator's statement sent confusion throughout the rest of the car, mostly to Ron. Senator Windgate had been withholding something important from his partner in crime.

"What are you talking about? Other information?" asked Ron.

The senator ignored Ron and focused his interrogation on Caroline.

"Your father was a dirty man," he said.

"Don't you dare speak of my father," Caroline interrupted.

Her captor put his hand on her shoulder, letting her know he was alert to her trying anything.

"Your father used to work for me, Caroline."

"Liar," she cried out. "You're a liar!"

"Oh, where to begin," the senator said in mock wistfulness. "I'm retiring soon, but you probably already know that. What do you think about the 'Senate Proof' batch of whiskey to be released very soon now?"

She stared out the window, ignoring his remarks.

"Listen to me, young lady!"

His sudden lashing out caught everyone in the vehicle off guard, including the driver, who swerved into the other lane in surprise. But Windgate had Caroline's full attention once again.

"Let's get back to my retirement. You see, I would love to live very comfortably for the remainder of my years. Unfortunately, it seems like you had other ideas in mind. Tell me something: Who exactly do you work for?"

"Go to hell," were the last words she uttered before a hypodermic needle rendered her unconscious.

41

John McAllister was violating the very order he had given to his team: Do not leave the bunker. With the estate in chaos, no one dared to violate the old man's orders.

However, McAllister needed some fresh air. He left the rest of his team bewildered as he suddenly walked out the front entrance of the bunker unannounced.

Now he strolled through the fields behind the burned remains of his old mansion.

Smoke still rose from the ashes of the house. Several exterior brick walls remained intact, but the interior had been gutted. Everything of value in the house had been lost. Everything was gone.

That's why John never kept his most personal treasures anywhere near the estate. His business records, both legitimate and illegitimate, were kept hundreds of miles away in a remote storage area.

His family memorabilia, that which was worth keeping, was housed in a secure storage building disguised as a horse barn on the back of the property.

McAllister wandered through the tall grass about two hundred yards from where the mansion once stood. The orange sun was dropping lower into the sky, sitting just above the tree line to the west.

He needed to be alone. He wanted nothing more than just to have a few minutes to himself. He knew the risks. He was well aware that he might not make it back to the bunker alive. Yet, he was at peace with it all.

Part of him wished a sniper would drop him dead. But, he thought, that would be too easy. He'd never have to face the consequences of his past transgressions.

He had ruined many lives over the years. Not directly, but by supplying narcotics to helpless addicts. He had provoked drug wars among inner city gangs. So many young people had died, and all because of his greed.

But was he the changed man he claimed to be? He tried so hard to convince himself that he was.

Senator Windgate's words from their last encounter kept haunting him. *Once you go dirty, you can never come clean again.* It was so true.

McAllister knew that if he came clean, too many lives would be ruined. Lives that mattered. Lives of people who governed the nation. The trust and confidence that the American people instilled in their leaders would be utterly destroyed.

He knew it was all false. The old man couldn't fool himself. No life was greater than another. Try explaining to a mother who just lost her eighteen year old son in a drug war that his life wasn't worth as much as an elected official—especially an elected official who just sat back and collected a paycheck while doing nothing to improve society.

McAllister got out of the drug game more than two decades ago. It wasn't worth it. Too many close calls caused the operation to retrench back into the distillery business.

Distilling homemade whiskey was his hobby. Nobody cared. They would smack a fun label on the bottle and throw parties for all of their friends. It was harmless.

McAllister never suspected that Senator Windgate had continued the drug business, going behind the backs of everyone involved. Or, had he? Who else was involved? McAllister was certain that Ron was a co-conspirator. And the Chief Justice's reaction to the secret file hinted at his involvement.

There was only one way to find out.

At a steady pace, McAllister headed straight for the garage. Before his security team could stop him, he would be long gone from the estate. He was confident that Ms. Ruby could hold down the fort just fine.

McAllister picked the Ford F-250 truck. It had been Jimmy's.

In the rearview mirror, he smiled as his security team came running from the woods to the garage, scrambling to follow his trail.

X   X   X

The Chief Justice kept a nice apartment in the District overlooking Rock Creek Park. He would often stay in the apartment on weeknights to avoid the commute to and from Annapolis after putting in long nights at the office.

McAllister had already checked in with his informant to confirm where the Chief Justice was staying for the night.

Abramson answered the door in a faded Yale Law sweatshirt. The weariness of the long workweek was evident in the judge's tired eyes. McAllister couldn't understand how the Chief Justice kept his professional life, family life, and illegal life so separate and distinct.

His visible stress was proof that it was becoming too much, even for him.

Abramson welcomed McAllister into his kitchen and invited him to sit down at the table for a cup of coffee. Their relationship was a far cry from friendship, but their mutual respect was evident.

"I wanted to thank you for handing over that information," said McAllister.

"I think it was as much a shock to me as it was to you," replied Abramson.

"How long have you known?"

"I've had my suspicions for a while," answered Abramson, careful not to play all of his cards. "When Ron moved to Florida, it provided the perfect opportunity for him to oversee the importation of any narcotic he wanted. He made frequent trips along the Gulf Coast, from Key West to Texas. I knew something was up, but I never suspected he was in cahoots with Senator Windgate."

"I thought we all agreed to leave that business behind forever. Too many risks."

"By the time I was working at a law firm, I knew that I had to break ties with all of that activity if I ever wanted a legitimate shot at a judicial position."

"And now that you've reached the apex, if any of this comes out, you're done."

"Exactly," sighed Abramson.

"Who tipped you off to the investigation?"

"I think you'll understand if I keep that to myself for now."

"I can respect that," responded McAllister, disappointed not to find out the identity of the leak. "I had to ask."

"I know."

The two men sipped their coffees without saying much for the next couple of minutes. Both were strategizing a way to end all of this.

"There's something I've always wanted to ask about, but I've just never had the opportunity," began McAllister.

"Go ahead," said Abramson.

"You were there that day when Robert Peterson was murdered. You gave him a good beating, but I don't believe you shot him. Do you know who did?"

Before the Chief Justice could answer, they were interrupted by a knock at the door.

McAllister was startled. Surely Senator Windgate was not foolish enough to send someone to kill the Chief Justice of the Supreme Court in his own apartment. Armed security was only a short distance away from the front door. Not to mention, the media circus would be a disaster for all involved in the operation.

Looking through the peephole in the front door, the Chief Justice motioned for McAllister to come over and join him.

"I don't know these men," he whispered. "Are they yours?"

The old man stretched to look through the peephole, and determined the men were, in fact, members of his security team. They had found him after all. With Abramson's permission, McAllister opened the door and let a team of six men inside the apartment.

"I knew it wouldn't be long until you found me," McAllister assured his men, albeit a bit disgruntled at the interruption.

"We'll resume this conversation at a later time," he said to Abramson.

The two men then informed the security team of most of the known details. McAllister trusted the Chief Justice and now considered him his ally, however unlikely their partnership. McAllister ordered his team to guard the Chief Justice, despite the available forces from his official duties.

The battle lines were redrawn—McAllister and Abramson versus Scooter Windgate and Ron.

McAllister refocused his team on finding Caroline as quickly as possible, which was his first priority. He would willingly suffer any consequence to ensure her safety. He didn't have much more of a legacy to leave behind.

But there was a still a wild card in their plan of attack—bigger than all the others. Jackson Cole.

42

Finally cleansed of the blood and stench of death from the previous days, Jackson felt like a new man as he emerged from his first shower in several days.

He had successfully gained access to Samantha's brother's apartment in Alexandria. The old lady next door was as smitten with Jackson as most other women were. He didn't even need to rely on his backup story. It was too easy. Hopefully this was a sign that things would be turning in his favor.

Luckily, Samantha's brother was about the same size as Jackson. While not a perfect fit, he was able to assemble a presentable outfit from the man's closet—a pair of khakis and a striped polo.

It felt so refreshing to put on clean clothes.

He dumped his bloodstained clothes into the trash chute of the apartment complex.

Without a comb for his hair, he was still a little disheveled. Who cared? He was young and could easily pull it off. It's not like he was interviewing with Stephen Forrester for another job at Schneider Sims & Zelli.

With about an hour until he was should to leave for Forrester's house, he began his research into Stephen Forrester.

For all he knew, Jackson was invisible. He had already discarded the prepaid phone he'd purchased with cash. He didn't carry a single electronic device with him to the apartment. He had also watched his tracks for any followers. He didn't see a single person.

Little did he know, he *was* invisible. He didn't know what magnitude of power he wielded. He *was* the wild card.

Shaun had informed him that John McAllister was a client assigned to Forrester. There had to be some reason for McAllister to receive such personal attention from Forrester, and Jackson was determined to uncover it.

Using Samantha's brother's computer and his own hacking skills, he easily gained access to Schneider Sims & Zelli's secure network.

He quickly found the McAllister file on the firm's secure network. It was quite large. In fact, the directory contained twenty sub-folders, covering from McAllister's business—legitimate banks, holding companies, bottling companies, etc.—and personal files. Or, what looked to be personal files.

Jackson opened the first one and wondered if there would be enough time to review it before he was expected at the Forrester's?

There was nothing. An empty folder stared back at him.

Jackson closed it and opened the second one.

Another empty file.

Jackson was certain that alarms were firing somewhere notifying the powers that be that some unauthorized person was in the system.

Instead of digging further, he quickly exited the secure network to avoid being tracked. By the time someone found the network connection, Jackson would be long gone from the apartment. Or so he hoped.

Before shutting down the computer, Jackson logged into his investment account.

He wasn't sure why he thought about checking the balances. It was something he rarely monitored. However, he suddenly felt the urge to check his money.

Wiped out. All of it.

Although he didn't flaunt his wealth, Jackson took pride in his balanced portfolio that had survived the stock market collapse. He held a good mix of equities, bonds, and cash. It had all disappeared—vanished without a trace.

For a moment, he regretted trying to help Caroline. He had lost a best friend, had almost lost his own life numerous times, and now his entire financial security had vanished. And for what?

He could feel nothing through his regret, anger, and frustration.

Everything was crashing all around him, and for the first time, he genuinely doubted that he could help Caroline. He knew he was in too deep to save himself, too.

Jackson shut down the computer and left the apartment, long before he had originally intended to leave for the Forresters.

Outside of the apartment building, Jackson trashed his bag of remaining belongings in a dumpster. He wandered the streets of Old Town Alexandria for a while before hailing a cab and heading to his dinner appointment.

X   X   X

After observing Jackson wander aimlessly around Old Town, Shaun Martin returned to his car and made a phone call. Careful to remain unseen, he followed Jackson's cab on its way to the Forrester residence.

Jackson slipped the cab driver the last of his cash, and he then turned to face the stately home. Located just outside of Fairfax, Virginia, the Forresters maintained a grand home. Not a surprise, since Stephen Forrester was the managing partner of the law firm.

The large iron gate slowly creaked open when Jackson approached the entrance. His polo, about one size too large, flapped in the summer breeze while his already messy hair blew around. Jackson looked like a lost high school freshman trying to fill out his older brother's clothes.

Shaun Martin stopped several hundred yards back, obscured in the shadows. He could observe every movement in the mansion from his spot just outside the perimeter of the property.

The residence was surrounded by a ten-foot stone wall. Jackson walked through the iron gate and up the long paved drive. Fine landscaping bordered the driveway, and overhanging electric lanterns lit his path. It was very quiet—almost too quiet.

Jackson walked up the steps to the front door of the white-washed brick mansion. He still hadn't seen a single sign of life. It was all very strange.

He rang the doorbell once.

A beautiful, young woman answered the door and invited Jackson inside. She introduced herself as Mrs. Forrester. Jackson was certain that she must be the fourth or fifth in the long line of young Mrs. Forresters.

For the first time all day—in several days—Jackson felt the urge to grin.

The two shared a brief moment when their eyes met, but he thought better of it. He looked away, but he couldn't help but wonder what it would be like to be married to someone thirty years older. The poor woman. Anyway, that was a question for another day.

"You'll find the men in the parlor at the back of the house," she instructed with a melting southern drawl.

"Men?" Jackson sharply asked, stunned.

"Yes, Stephen invited a few other friends over this evening," she replied before turning around and disappearing into the depths of the mansion.

Reality struck Jackson hard. He wasn't prepared to speak with anyone else tonight. He thought Stephen Forrester would explain how he could help rescue Caroline.

Who were they? Were they really random friends of Stephen Forrester? Could they help Jackson? Or were they involved in a cover-up of Caroline's, and soon to be his, disappearance?

For what seemed like ten minutes, Jackson stood in the open foyer. He stalled as long as he could, admiring the art collection in the few minutes that passed—paintings, sculptures, and even a complete Native American warrior suit.

Mrs. Forrester was long gone, and Jackson could hear the male voices, although barely audible, coming from the back of the house.

He gave a quick tug on his khakis, exhaled deeply, and marched towards the parlor. He was forced to travel through three dark hallways, each darker than the previous one. And through each passageway, Jackson was convinced that someone would reach out and grab his throat.

In the third hallway, his borrowed loafers knocked loudly against the hardwood floor. The aroma of cigar smoke increased in intensity as he made his way toward the lighted room at the end of the hallway.

There was no laughter in the men's voices. It didn't seem like old friends getting together. It sounded like all business. In sometimes hushed tones, sometimes loud outbursts of passion, the men were clearly hashing out details of something quite a bit more serious than their sailing expeditions.

Jackson turned the corner into the room and gave a light knock on the dark wood-paneled wall.

Jackson was a mediocre law student at best, but it didn't take more than a split second to recognize the youngest of the three men in Forrester's parlor. Even unshaven and sporting an old faded sweatshirt, Jackson easily identified Chief Justice Michael Abramson.

Stephen Forrester was wearing the same suit he had been wearing in the office earlier that day, sans the necktie. He puffed on a robust cigar, confidently smiling at Jackson. He invited Jackson to come in.

Jackson knew the other man, too. It was John McAllister.

"Please come in," welcomed Forrester. "You're a few minutes early."

"Yes, sir. Thanks again for inviting me," Jackson answered.

"You know John, here, but please meet Chief Justice Abramson," said the old law partner.

Jackson shook Abramson's hand.

"It's an honor to meet you, Chief Justice," said Jackson nervously.

He had never been in the presence of such a high ranking official.

"Thanks for coming by," said John McAllister, taking the reins of the conversation. "I know you're wondering why I'm here."

"Sure," muttered Jackson. It was all he could say.

"Mr. Forrester has been my attorney for quite some time," the old master distiller began. "He has represented me in many ways, from leading deals with my banks to securing contracts for my bottling companies. He has always been my go-to attorney.

"But even before our legal partnership, we were in business together. Or rather, I should say we had a nice relationship. When I was distributing drugs left and right through this entire region, Forrester covered my back. He was the lead narcotics guy with the Federal Investigation Bureau, and I used him well."

"I already know this," interrupted Jackson.

This was a surprise to the members of the audience.

"I'll cut to the chase," interjected Forrester, trying to avoid being implicated any further than he already had been by the old man. "There are a lot of things that we've done that we regret. I use 'we' loosely, but the entire operation with McAllister and his colleagues has seen some pretty dark days. We've done our best to move beyond that nasty period. And, quite frankly, we thought we'd had until recently—until that girl appeared."

"You know, I really don't care about what you've done, or what you're still doing," replied Jackson. "I just want to find *that girl*—her name is Caroline—and then I'll leave you alone forever. I'm sure she will too, as long as you didn't hurt her."

"It's not that easy, son," began McAllister again. "There are events that, if they were to ever be exposed, would rock this nation to its core. My guess is that whoever is holding Caroline—I'm thinking it's someone associated with Senator Windgate . . ." he paused mid-sentence. He looked away, remembering how close he had been to the senator.

The old man cleared his throat and continued, "My guess is that someone working with Senator Windgate is holding Caroline until they're sure she can't spill any long hidden secrets."

Jackson was no fool. He watched McAllister closely. He was trying to give Jackson a subtle signal. Jackson was sure of it. He was desperately trying to tip his hand to Jackson without showing his cards to the other men at the table.

Perhaps the stars and moon aligned because, for a second, the old man and Jackson were on the same page. This wasn't an inquisition of Jackson. The old man was indirectly probing his longtime attorney. He needed a bit more information from Forrester, and Jackson's presence was the catalyst.

Without blinking an eye, Jackson responded, "What, like the murder of Robert Peterson?"

All three pairs of eyes looked directly at Jackson in horror. The group's dirty little secret wasn't so secret anymore.

Jackson and McAllister briefly made eye contact, but the message was clear. *Thank you. Well done.*

"What do you know about the murder?" asked a bewildered and confused Stephen Forrester. Jackson's statement nearly caused him to choke down the fat cigar.

"I know more than any of you think I know," Jackson bluffed.

It must have worked because even John McAllister looked confused at the comment.

"I'll only ask this one more time," stated Forrester again. He had regained control of the room as he slowly walked toward the young law student. "What exactly do you know?"

"I know exactly who did it," Jackson said. "I also know exactly who ordered the execution."

No one in the room wanted him to finish that thought. Yet, they all really wanted to know the answer to the decades-old riddle.

The tension was thicker than any cloud of cigar smoke in the room.

Without uttering another word, Jackson turned to leave the room.

"Stop him," ordered John McAllister.

Before Jackson could reach the doorway, McAllister's security force blocked the entrance.

I don't understand. I thought that's what the old man wanted.

Everything was suddenly cut short and Jackson saw nothing but darkness. There was no pain—simply darkness. And silence.

43

The air was cool and moist. Running water was the only sound she heard. But it wasn't from a faucet. It was fresh running water.

Caroline was freezing. She shivered as the cobwebs cleared from her head.

With her eyes still closed, she felt the bandage on her arm where she had been injected with the rather large needle. What in the world was that stuff?

The pain in her head still throbbed from the beating she had taken a few days earlier.

Caroline was a complete mess.

She tried to stand, only to find that she was much too weak to stand.

She opened her eyes and couldn't see much at all. She was surrounded by darkness yet again, but her eyes began to adjust.

Soon, she realized she was in a cave very similar to the one she had ventured into at the McAllister estate. But this was a different cave.

The McAllister cave had modern amenities including electricity, drywall, plumbing, and flooring, among other things. But here, she found herself on the muddy, damp ground.

When her eyes adjusted, she noticed that the running water was a natural stream just a few feet from where she sat.

The bright light blinded her when a door flew wide open a few yards away.

She squinted, trying to force her eyes to adjust quickly. She could hear footsteps sloshing through the muddy soil as they approached closer and closer.

Before she could identify the intruder, he grabbed her arm and lifted her completely off the ground. She was going toward the lighted doorway regardless of whether she wanted to or not.

From his pure strength, she knew it was the burly man she had already encountered one too many times. There was no reason to fight. She let her body remain completely limp as the man dragged her through the cave.

"Get up on your feet," he ordered as they reached the doorway. "Now."

Caroline obliged and stood under her own power, though still weak.

She stepped through the doorway and couldn't believe what she saw. Even more surprising was the fact that she was allowed to see it. For the first time, she wasn't blindfolded, and she wasn't sure how to interpret that.

The men either didn't care what she saw because they were to eventually kill her, or they just made a huge mistake. She tried hard to believe the latter.

It was a gold mine—the largest cache of drugs she had ever seen. This was a game changer.

She assumed the room was inside the network of caves. The sheer size of the space was impressive enough. But the magnitude of the drug stash was greater than Caroline could've ever imagined.

To the right, a group of workers dressed in Tyvek suits were cooking something—probably methamphetamine.

To her left were rows and rows of marijuana plants, as far as her eyes could see, growing under intense lighting. Beyond the plants, another group of workers, dressed in sanitary gear, sorted tablets of another substance—probably ecstasy.

Impressed with the scope of the operation, Caroline was taking detailed notes in her mind. If she were to ever escape, this place was going down. She'd see to it.

This was the cash machine. Nothing but illegal profits churned through this room. With her limited knowledge of the drug world, she estimated the value of the inventory to be greater than the GDP of some third world countries.

The old men may have liked to play with their bootleg whiskey, but this was the real moneymaker. Here were the answers that she was looking for.

The man escorted her through a large, open room for what seemed like an eternity. Through another door, a long dark hallway stretched ahead of them.

The man pulled out a flashlight and led the way. Caroline followed closely behind, fearful that if she didn't, it would be the end of her life.

At the end of the hallway, they reached another door.

"Watch your eyes," he ordered. "It's bright out there."

"Oh, how thoughtful," she quipped.

He wasn't amused.

"Let's go," he said.

It was clearly early in the morning. The grass was wet with morning dew and the birds were chirping away, hunting their breakfast between the blades of grass.

There wasn't a cloud in the sky.

But Caroline didn't notice. She was desperately trying to determine where she was. The surroundings were foreign to her—not a single familiar object or landmark.

Their journey wasn't over yet. The burly man grabbed her arm again and led her down a path, through an open field, and into a waiting town car. The man climbed in behind Caroline and locked them inside the car.

The land looked vaguely similar to that which surrounded the McAllister estate. But she couldn't be certain.

"So where are the senator and Ron?" she asked her chaperone.

No answer. He gave her a quick look, and then stared straight ahead.

"Nice guy," she replied back.

No answer again.

"How much do they pay you?"

Still nothing.

She let slip a brief mocking laugh only to feel herself gasping for air as she struggled to breathe. The man nearly punctured a rib with an elbow to the ribs.

After she regained her breath, she decided no more jokes. Even her sanity wasn't worth it.

X X X

The senator was seated at his desk in the Hart Building, which housed the majority of the Senate offices. Ron sat across from the old man as the two attempted to draft his retirement letter.

While it had not been made official publicly, it was becoming common knowledge among the political gossips that Scooter Windgate was retiring. Unfortunately for Senator Windgate, the announcement also stirred the expectation that there would be an extravagant retirement party. Of course, the folklore of the McAllister-Windgate parties and even news of the release of the special Senate Proof batch of whiskey traveled the gossip circuit.

A bottle of Senate Proof had already made its way to the senator's office. It sat in a place of prominence on his desk. A very attractive bottle, it would be displayed to garner more demand for the special edition batch of McAllister whiskey.

Windgate and Ron hoped to be in a position to fill the orders after their plan was implemented. McAllister would be long gone, and the rightful heir would be running the business. Cash would roll in from the distribution ring they already had in place. Life would be more grand than it had been in many years.

Senator Windgate and his new partner, Ron, would live very comfortably for the rest of their lives, running a drug operation like the world had never seen before.

The inside men would be paid as usual. But now they wouldn't have to hide their activities from John McAllister—or the rest of the gang.

Ron had already negotiated a sweetheart deal with a South American cartel that operated in the Caribbean. The wheels were in motion.

The arrangements were in place to get the drugs shipped to the holding center—really a cave—in Virginia. From there, Senator Wind-gate and Ron could control the details of distribution. The network was perfectly set up throughout the entire East Coast.

Ron was never interested in politics, so he would be more than happy when Senator Windgate was out of the political limelight. The senator was ready to retire, escape to a large and secluded area of land, and watch his pile of cash continue to grow.

They both knew that Chief Justice Abramson would bow out of the group. No hard feelings there. He had many years left on the bench, and he would merely be an added liability for the clan. The trick would be trying to get him to remain silent about the operation for years to come. But it was nothing that Ron didn't think money could buy. And there would be plenty of it.

John McAllister had to be forced out. He wouldn't knowingly allow his name, his reputation, his network, or his funds to be associated with such an illegal operation. At least not anymore.

"Just don't kill him," said Ron.

There was a lot of mutual dislike between the father and son, but Ron didn't want to go so far as to be responsible for his father's death. He'd soon be gone from old age anyway.

"We'll do what's necessary," Senator Windgate instructed, not a single hint of emotion in his voice.

This miffed Ron, but he couldn't say anything at this point. He was about to get filthy rich by riding the old senator's coattails.

"We're meeting the girl in an hour," said Ron as Senator Windgate put the finishing touches on his resignation letter. "Let's wrap this up."

44

Jackson opened his eyes to an unfamiliar bedroom. It had happened to him before, but this time was ominous. Holding his head completely still, he moved his eyes around to take in the room.

The room was meticulously decorated, presumably by a well-known interior designer.

Still fully clothed, he tossed the covers off of his body, sat up, and swung his legs off the side of the bed. The bright sun slipped through a crack in the curtains hitting him right in the eye.

He ducked to avoid the beam of light and climbed down from the bed. It was so tall that his feet didn't reach the floor when he sat upright on the edge.

He smelled the fresh flowers placed in a vase on the nightstand. For a split second, Jackson wondered whether he was dreaming, or dead.

If it was a dream, it was rudely interrupted when Chief Justice Abramson plowed through the door.

"Wake up," he ordered. "It's time to get going. We have a lot to talk about."

And though it wasn't Jackson's habit to even consider getting out of bed at this hour, his mind was already racing with thoughts of Caroline. He was on a mission to find her.

Abramson looked like a new man. He was clean-shaven and sported a crisp grey suit. His coal black hair was slicked back, as usual, and his black eyes pierced through Jackson.

The judge left the room, slamming the door behind him.

No doubt, the Chief Justice had already been to the office this morning.

Jackson hoped he hadn't picked up any unwanted followers on his way back to the house. The reality of the situation was quickly hammered home as he heard the footsteps on the roof above his guest bedroom. McAllister's security staff was on full alert. No unauthorized visitors would be allowed to penetrate the Forrester's fortified estate. Unless, however, there was an insider.

Jackson climbed out of bed and peeked through the windows, confirming that he was still at the Forrester's estate. The property was much more expansive than he had noticed the previous night. The mansion, with its château-esque façade, was surrounded on all sides by wide, open lawns spanning several acres.

The window didn't budge with his attempt to open it. His sense that he was a captive was confirmed when he ran into an armed guard posted outside of the bedroom. It was clear that Jackson would have a full-time escort for the morning.

Downstairs, the strong smell of freshly brewed coffee drew Jackson to the kitchen. Inside the kitchen he encountered the very young, very attractive, Mrs. Forrester. And again, they exchanged knowing smiles.

She quickly looked away before vanishing to somewhere else in the mansion.

This was his weakness—the forbidden fruit. Jackson knew it. But he also knew he had to remain focused on Caroline and find her before it was too late.

Hushed voices from the three men—Abramson, McAllister, and Forrester—brought Jackson to the breakfast room. Once inside the room, his armed escort disappeared.

They had obviously been drawing up plans for quite some time this morning, if not since the night before.

"I'm sorry about last night," offered McAllister to Jackson. "We couldn't let you go until we uncovered exactly what you knew about the Peterson murder. Are the drugs wearing off?"

"Drugs?"

"We had to sedate you just to contain your excitement over the Peterson murder," McAllister explained. "It was just a simple shot of a sedative cocktail. I hope it helped you get a good night's rest."

"Thanks, I guess," responded Jackson, just then remembering how suddenly his night was cut short.

As he pulled up a chair to join the other men, he touched the back of his neck and felt a scab where the needle punctured his skin. And to think he'd had the impression they were all on the same team.

"Seriously, regarding the Peterson murder," the Chief Justice began, "nothing can ever be said about that outside of this house."

"What are you talking about? You say you want to find Caroline, but you also want to keep the murder covered up? What's next, are you in on the conspiracy to murder her?"

Jackson was fed up with the secrecy, vagueness, and lack of help from the men. He simply wanted answers, and the three men weren't offering it.

It was early, and his mind was still foggy—from the drugs in his system.

"I'll do this without you," he answered unapologetically. "I'll find Caroline, and I'll see that all of you get what's coming."

"Relax," responded McAllister.

"No. I'm out of here," he announced as he briskly made his way out of the room.

Chief Justice Abramson jumped to his feet and caught up with Jackson. He didn't acknowledge the esteemed man, so the judge merely walked in stride with him until they had almost reached the front door.

"Look," began the Chief Justice as he put his hand on Jackson's shoulder.

Jackson stopped and faced Abramson. Never in his life could he have imagined standing face to face with one of the most influential legal minds of all time. But it didn't phase him. He could only think of Caroline.

"Go out there, all by yourself," said Abramson just loud enough so Jackson could hear. "But you don't know everything about the Peterson murder. In fact, I'd be surprised if you knew anything other than the fact that the victim was Caroline's father."

"What's your point?"

"My point is that I know more about that day than probably

anybody else you'll ever talk to," said Abramson, desperate to gain Jackson's buy-in.

"Oh, really?" replied Jackson.

He wasn't impressed. But he was intrigued to see what Abramson had to say.

"Let's walk," Abramson said, as they exited through the mansion's front door.

Jackson and Abramson strolled down a walkway that surrounded the house. From a window in the breakfast room, Stephen Forrester and John McAllister observed every move. If only they could hear the conversation.

They knew that everything would be fine as long as Jackson was in Abramson's hands. If anybody had anything to lose, it was the Chief Justice. They had lived their lives. Abramson was in his prime.

Abramson looked up and briefly acknowledged the two men in the window. He then turned his full attention to Jackson. The kid's patience was running thin, and he knew it.

Caroline was sequestered away somewhere, far from escaping. Or at least that was Abramson's best guess.

Jackson, on the other hand, was still an unknown. He had the potential for blowing the lid off of the entire group. But they couldn't keep him against his will. That wasn't the M.O. for McAllister or the Chief Justice.

Abramson had no choice but to throw out the Hail Mary.

"I was there when Caroline's father was murdered," he admitted.

Jackson slowly turned to face the Chief Justice.

Looking directly into the judge's eyes, he said, "What? How can you live with yourself? Murderer!" he shouted loud enough for someone off the property to hear.

There was no doubt that any onlookers, including Forrester and McAllister, heard Jackson. Although it wasn't news to the two men that Abramson was present at the murder, it still sent chills spiraling up their backs to hear it announced for all within hearing distance to hear.

The Hail Mary had been tipped, but it was still suspended in the air, waiting to be caught.

"I didn't murder anybody," replied Abramson calmly. "And that's the honest truth."

Jackson didn't respond. He was steaming, his face bright red, his fists clenched.

The Chief Justice had to act fast, or else Jackson would take off and destroy everything.

Abramson, quick on his feet, took control.

The two stood face to face, mere inches between them.

"Don't look now," whispered Abramson. He paused. "But can they see me?"

"Who?" Jackson asked, confused.

"John and Forrester," Abramson clarified. "Can they see me?"

"They can only see your back," Jackson replied, still angry, but controlling his tone somewhat. "They can only see my face. Not yours."

"Good," replied the Chief Justice, relieved. "This is what's going to happen."

"I'm listening," said an intrigued Jackson.

"We're going to slowly walk around the edge of the house," Abramson said, pointing with his eyes. "Just beyond this corner is where my car is parked."

"What, no driver for Mr. Chief Justice of the Supreme Court?" interrupted Jackson. He was tired of the games.

Abramson ignored the remark.

"My car is unlocked. Climb into the trunk from the backseat. I'll go report that you made a run for it, and the three of us, we'll split up to look for you."

"You're crazy," replied Jackson. "Do you think I'm stupid? You're just looking for a reason to shoot me? Why should I listen to you?"

"You're not stupid. You're desperate."

"What's your ingenuous plan?"

"As soon as I get out of sight, we'll find somewhere to chat, and I'll tell you everything I know. No secrets from me. Full disclosure."

"And you'll help me? Caroline?" asked a concerned Jackson.

"Yes," replied the stoic judge. "I promise not to hurt you. But we must act fast if we want to find Caroline. There are some things I want to share with you so you know what you're getting into, and why Caroline is so important to Senator Windgate."

"Just know that I'm doing this not because I want to," said Jackson, "but because I have nowhere else to go, and nothing else to lose."

Abramson gave an affirmative nod to the young man, and they both turned to walk toward the corner of the mansion.

Jackson's heart raced and his palms moistened with sweat as the anticipation increased with each step.

This was it. He was making a run from McAllister and Forrester and had no idea what would happen. For all he knew, a sniper could drop him any second.

An armed member of the security team caught Jackson's eye down the driveway at the front entrance. He was well positioned, only able to be seen from the inside of the estate.

Jackson's stomach knotted up.

"Stop," whispered Abramson.

He continued to gesture with his hands as if in the midst of a long-winded story, acting out his story for the on-looking men. But his eyes scanned the roof.

Another armed member was making his rounds atop the roof of the mansion.

"Count to three and then calmly walk to the other side of the car," Abramson whispered after a few seconds had passed. "Nobody will be able to see you if you go now. Hurry."

With that, Jackson took off towards the car. He didn't walk. He ran. He didn't care. Part of him wanted to draw attention so the ordeal would be over sooner rather than later. The other part of him just didn't care.

He climbed into the backseat, slowly closed the car door, and held his breath. Everything seemed like it went off without a hitch.

Slowly, Jackson raised his head just high enough to see out of the car windows. He looked around to see if he had caught anyone's attention. The man on the roof had his back turned, and the guard at the front entrance still faced the outside of the compound.

Everything appeared to be normal. Nobody panicked, no alarms sounded, and nothing was disturbed. The only sounds were natural background sounds.

The Chief Justice turned around and sprinted back up the sidewalk to the front door of the mansion. Jackson did not envy Abramson for having to give McAllister and Forrester the news that their prisoner had escaped.

This better not be a trick.

45

For two hours, Caroline was wedged next to her stone-faced captor in the backseat of a car. Her ribs ached, her head pounded, she was starving, and she just wanted to give up. She was tired—tired of everything. She had bitten off more than she could chew in her quest for the truth, and she was miserably choking on her poor decisions.

Her chaperone answered a call on his cell phone. The conversation was brief and to the point. Not a single word was wasted.

"They have a few questions for you," he said to Caroline without so much as looking at her.

He stared ahead without even a glimpse of a conscience, determined to carry out his duties.

"Wonderful," she replied.

She knew the end of her ordeal was drawing much closer. Her hopes for a rescue were diminishing by the second. Who even knew she was missing and in trouble?

She was completely cut off from the outside.

When she decided to move her life to Warrenton, Virginia, Caroline should have assessed the risks associated with her mission. After all, her father had perished there years before.

She tried diligently to separate her work on the farm from her investigative work. She knew the value of compartmentalizing. But the waters had become quite muddy. She met a nice guy—Jackson Cole. She had allowed her life to become immensely complicated. The peace and serenity of the McAllister estate should have helped her avoid the chaos; instead she lost the focus of her mission.

While Jackson and Caroline never openly shared any feelings that were deeper than friendship, there had definitely been a tension between them. She was a young, successful, and self-assured. Not to mention beautiful. Jackson was well on his way to future successes in any path he so chose, and he had the confidence to back it up. He was boyishly handsome and possessed just enough of that bad boy persona that he was begging to be tamed by a strong girl.

Caroline and Jackson had never shared any physical intimacy. In fact, when they were together, she was often repulsed by his adolescent behavior. But she knew it was all a show. He was stronger than steel, and he would always lend a helping hand. Or so she thought.

He didn't have to befriend Caroline. The random encounter at Molly O's should have been the end of their brief relationship. But he needed her company more than she would ever realize.

Caroline gazed out of the window of the back seat. She could tell the car was getting nearer to the city limits. Civilization was becoming a little more dense with every mile they drove. Recognizable food chains started to pop up. Soon they were traveling through an affluent neighborhood in suburbia.

A hard, fast right turn took Caroline by surprise. And a whisky bottle rolled across the floorboard.

Her escort reached down and retrieved the runaway bottle without uttering a word.

Upon further evaluation, Caroline saw the label—Senate Proof. It was distilled in honor of the retiring Senator Windgate.

Honor? Not so much, Caroline thought. She longed for the opportunity to take down the old man and all of the crookedness he represented.

She became confused when the driver pulled onto the Beltway, the interstate encircling the nation's capital. She couldn't imagine where they were headed. Or why they were traveling closer in to civilization.

The senator and Ron were playing with fire—they couldn't allow her to live. She could bring the whole group down for good with what she knew. And oh, how she'd love to do it.

Caroline had lost track of time for a few minutes, and before she knew it, they were crossing the Potomac River. The car continued to weave through traffic across the bridge and into downtown Washington.

Her hopes of a bystander seeing her battered face through the window diminished when she realized the windows in the town car were much too tinted for anyone to clearly make out the passengers. Most onlookers probably thought the car was chauffeuring a government dignitary.

After blowing through several lights, Caroline realized she was in an official government vehicle. At least two District police officers kindly waved as the sedan sped right by. If only they knew who was inside.

After what seemed like fifteen circles through the narrow streets of Georgetown, the car turned into a hidden alley with an open garage door at the end.

Once inside, the garage door shut behind them and the muscle-bound escort climbed out of the car.

He walked around the vehicle and opened the door for Caroline. He even extended a hand, as if to try and show a little compassion.

Caroline ignored his gesture. She climbed out under her own strength—she was stronger than she thought at this stage of abuse.

She couldn't determine whether it was her mind playing games or if it was reality, but the garage reeked of death. How many moles, bootleggers, and rivals had met their demise in this garage?

Caroline forced herself to look straight ahead as she was led out of the garage.

She closed her eyes and relished the fresh warm air as it hit her lungs. Although the walk outside was brief, she was grateful it.

Assessing her whereabouts, she noticed the backsides of a row of Georgetown brownstones. That was the extent of her field of vision. A tall privacy fence bordered the patio she was crossing with the escort.

Caroline bit her tongue and resisted the urge to scream for help. She was ready to meet her foes face to face.

Inside the back door, a woman greeted the entourage. She was warm and welcoming. There was a kindness about her. She even reached out and offered Caroline a sweater for her exposed shoulders.

Confused, Caroline shook her head. Why the sudden hospitality?

The two women's eyes connected, and Caroline immediately understood.

"How are you Mrs. Windgate?" asked Caroline's transporter.

"Oh, I'm just fine," she replied.

It was obvious to Caroline that she was lying.

Her suspicions were confirmed that the old lady was Senator Windgate's wife.

The history was probably too complex for Caroline to understand in such a short time, but her look summed it up in a matter of seconds. Sure, she seemed kind enough, but if she was the senator's wife, she had to be at least a little tolerant of his corrupt behavior. After all, she shared in all of the profits.

A not-so-gentle nudge in the middle of the back let Caroline know it was time to move forward. She was directed to the basement door and escorted downstairs.

Mrs. Windgate vanished without any further interaction. Once again, Caroline was left alone to fend for herself.

The basement was finished, but the drop ceiling gave it a dreary feel. Along one long wall was a wood-paneled wet bar, stocked with enough liquor to serve the entire Senate. It didn't take long for Caroline to realize that all of the bottles were from different batches of McAllister whiskey.

A billiards table was along the opposite wall adjacent to a set of leather sofas. That's where the men were sitting, plotting their takeover of the McAllister estate.

Guided by two hands securely steering her shoulders, Caroline was led over to a hard, wooden chair and promptly forced to sit.

She tried desperately not to show her pain, clenching her teeth as she slammed against the stiff back of the chair.

The two conspiring men stopped their conversation and turned to her. They passively watched as the bulky escort positioned her hands behind the back of the chair, securing them with a zip tie.

Caroline was no match for the man. She winced as he cinched the zip tie around her wrists. Her fingers began to tingle as the circulation ceased in her hands. She knew the man was attempting to demonstrate his control in front of his bosses. His behavior was a stark contrast from what he displayed when not in the presences of Ron and Senator

Windgate. Although he had never been friendly toward Caroline, he had never carried out his actions with the malice he showed now.

Originally, she thought she may have been able to turn the man, to use him as leverage. But that chance was obviously gone. He had something to prove.

The old senator rose from his chair. With a little bounce in his step he walked over to the huge man and patted him on the shoulder. The giant immediately stopped manhandling Caroline and walked to the other end of the room to stand guard.

Where was Mrs. Windgate? How could she let this happen in her home?

So many questions raced through Caroline's mind. But she focused her attention on survival.

"Hi there, Caroline," Senator Windgate began, as if they were old friends. "I'm sorry we haven't had the chance to spend more time together."

"Don't patronize me," she interrupted.

The seasoned senator ignored her and continued, "I wish we had more time together because I'd really love to know who you are funneling information to."

That remark took her breath away.

"Who are you feeding information to?" he asked.

"I, uh," she stumbled over her words. "What information are you talking about?"

"Let me ask you another way," said Senator Windgate. "Who do you work for?"

"You know who I work for, you old bastard," said Caroline. "John McAllister."

"Watch your tone with me, young lady," he ordered.

He was clearly frustrated with Caroline's lack of cooperation. His face reddened and his old, frail arms shook with anger. He turned his back to her, trying to control his rage. The old man closed his eyes and inhaled deeply.

Ron remained seated at the table. He hadn't moved much since Caroline was brought into the room.

"What are *you*? Some kind of pawn?" she fired at him.

Ron sprung to his feet and drew back his arm, ready to unleash a powerful smack across the girl's face.

"That's enough!" shouted the senator.

Ron stopped mid-motion and backed into his seat, still staring with hateful intensity into Caroline's eyes.

Likewise, Caroline's eyes remained fixed on Ron. He would never intimidate her. She was the bigger person, and given the opportunity, she whole-heartedly believed she could take the estranged, loser son down with a swift kick to his manhood.

"You *are* a pawn. Nothing but a minion taking orders from one of your father's twisted partners," she said.

"That's enough!" shouted Senator Windgate.

Caroline's death stare was broken when the barrel of a pistol passed in front of her eyes. She looked up to see the senator aiming the firearm as he pulled back the firing hammer.

"I will give you one more chance to tell me," he said to Caroline.

This was it. This was what she knew was coming. A lump formed in her throat as the repulsive old man drew closer to her.

"You're nothing but a liability to us, and if you won't give us some answers, you're just as good as dead," he said, aiming the pistol into her chest.

What seemed like an hour of silence must have only been a few seconds.

"Caroline," Senator Windgate began, "this is your last chance. Who do you work for? We have your laptop. We know your secrets. But I need a little more from you."

Senator Windgate raised the gun a little higher. Caroline was staring down the barrel as it aimed right between her eyes.

She didn't have to look around at the others. She could feel the tension packed into the basement.

It didn't matter. She couldn't look around—she was transfixed. She had never looked down the barrel of a loaded gun pointed at her face. She was less terrified than she thought she'd be. In fact, she wasn't terrified at all.

Caroline could feel the fear emanating from the direction of Ron and from her strong, masculine chaperone at the other end of the room.

She was still alive. No bullet had been fired. And she knew that as each second passed, the chances of the gun taking off her head rapidly diminished.

Killers never hesitated when they wanted to kill. They just did it. Senator Windgate had lost his window of confidence. She knew he'd never pull the trigger. It was too important to the senator to uncover where she was feeding information.

What was he talking about?

A knock on the basement door from the top of the stairs abruptly broke the silence and the tension in the basement. The cramped room seemed to take one enormous exhale as Senator Windgate lowered the gun and turned his attention to the stairs.

Ron cursed in the background, but Caroline could only hear his muffled grunts. She was focused on trying to identify the newest guest to arrive at the party.

Deliberate, slow footsteps walked down the stairs. This was, no doubt, a man of great influence.

As the shined black loafers came into view, Caroline began to panic. She knew those loafers.

As the man became visible to his waist, there was no doubt in Caroline's mind who was joining the party.

The slow, deliberate footsteps continued down the stairs until the man came into full view.

There was no denying it. She was finished—figuratively and literally.

Stephen Forrester was an imposing figure anywhere he went. But today, his presence sucked the air out of the Windgates' basement. Always neatly dressed, he was a bit disheveled today. Something was wrong. But the great Stephen Forrester could never be shaken, so what was going on?

Caroline couldn't help but wonder what had happened.

The surprise on the faces of Ron and the senator couldn't hide that his visit was unexpected.

"How nice of you to join us," said Senator Windgate as Forrester reached the last step.

Forrester walked up to the group, leaned his head back, and puffed out a cloud of cigar smoke. When he looked back down, it was clear that he had a story to tell.

But first, he acknowledged Caroline's presence.

"Caroline," he said in his deep rumble, making his way over to her.

She was speechless. She didn't know what to say. Or think. She hadn't seen or heard from him in quite some time.

"Senator," he addressed the old man, "the young man escaped our custody."

Caroline's heart raced. She knew he was referring to Jackson. So he *had* come after her and had been caught during his heroic attempt.

For a brief second, she was relieved. But she quickly became concerned for Jackson's well-being. Not a care for her own desperate situation, but Jackson—he didn't deserve this.

She was so caught up in her worries for him that she missed most of the details Forrester was sharing with the rest of the team. But, she was able to catch the highlights.

Jackson had escaped from the Forrester estate. He didn't seem to know any of the damning details, so while his capture was a high priority, it wasn't essential for the Windgate clan.

John McAllister and Chief Justice Abramson split up to search for the young man. They would check in soon.

Caroline realized the domineering managing partner at Schneider Sims & Zelli was standing directly in front of her. Her distant thoughts were broken when he spoke to her.

"Agent Peterson," he began. "It's been a long, long time. I see that you've outdone yourself this time."

"Go to hell," she snarled. She couldn't look at him.

"You just couldn't leave it alone, could you? You fell right into our little trap."

She seethed with rage. Had she not been bound to a chair, she would've ended the man's life with her bare hands. He was the epitome of everything she hated. He was the reason for her father's murder. He was the reason for so many other things in her life.

And now, finally with the chance to confront him face to face, her hands were tied.

46

Shaun Martin had been sitting in his car about a block from the estate's front entrance, biding his time while he waited for any kind of movement or excitement.

Then it hit.

Two black SUVs, surely loaded with top-notch surveillance equipment, blasted out of the front gate. Turning so abruptly they nearly went up on two tires as they entered the street, they sped down the street on a mission.

Shortly afterwards, John McAllister and his team exited the grounds, heading in the opposite direction. It didn't take years of experience for Shaun to realize that they were sending out a couple of search parties.

A few seconds after McAllister left the estate, Stephen Forrester's car exited the front entrance. He was alone—no one else in the car. Forrester turned in the same direction as John McAllister, but was not nearly in the same hurry.

Just as Shaun started his car to leave the scene, the gate to a hidden entrance in the estate opened and the silver sedan exited.

Shaun knew the sedan to belong to the Chief Justice, and he was certain that neither the Chief Justice nor Jackson had already left the estate, so he began to tail the judge.

The silver sedan navigated through the heart of a residential subdivision in Northern Virginia. The tinted windows, which were so dark they were probably illegal, made it difficult to see that there were even any occupants in the car. But Martin knew he was following the correct sedan. Abramson and Jackson were on the move, and it was very apparent to Jackson's former mentor that they didn't want anyone on their trail.

The escape from the Forrester estate must have gone as smoothly as they could have hoped.

As Martin followed the silver sedan deeper and deeper into Northern Virginia suburbia, he worried that he would be noticed. Then Abramson pulled into the parking lot of a local coffee house.

The parking lot was empty, and from what Martin could see, the coffee house didn't have a single patron. He pulled behind the building to avoid being spotted.

He reached for the briefcase in the back seat and pulled out his laptop. Before long, he had connected to the video surveillance camera on the building in order to monitor everything the patrons said—the only patrons being Jackson and Abramson.

Although he had deviated significantly from the original plan, everything was falling into place. Martin had the two people he needed isolated from the rest of the group.

x   x   x

Not much had been said during the car ride. Out of character and visibly nervous, Chief Justice Abramson's head swiveled in each direction, doing his best to identify any would be followers.

He never saw Shaun Martin.

Jackson rode along silently, pondering his fate and what he would possibly uncover in a conversation alone with the Chief Justice.

Jackson was a mere law student, constantly studying opinions drafted by the great legal minds throughout American history. Now, he was being chauffeured by the current Chief Justice of the US Supreme Court, and the last thing he wanted to talk about was the law. He knew Abramson also shared that same sentiment.

When the car pulled into the empty parking lot of the coffee house, the Chief Justice motioned for Jackson to follow him in. Abramson was not any more in the mood for conversation.

Inside, there was one barista on duty. Probably not too far removed from high school, the cute girl was clueless as to the identity of the man accompanying Jackson. This was exactly how Abramson wanted it. Obscurity. And the freedom to speak freely.

"I need you to be completely honest with me," opened Abramson. "Can you do that?"

"Do I have a choice? You probably know more about me than I know about myself," responded Jackson.

"Not so much," said Abramson. "And that's the problem. We—I'll explain who *we* is later—are trying to uncover something big. And you got in the way. You poked your head into some business that you should've never been exposed to. But, it's not entirely your fault."

"I'm not sure I follow what you're saying."

"You found yourself in the middle of one of the highest profile undercover drug operations ever," Abramson continued. "This has been going on for quite some time now."

Jackson wore his poker face well—he was not shaken. He wasn't even sure if Abramson was telling the truth. There was no way to be sure.

"So what are you trying to say?"

"First of all, you're lucky to be alive right now. Secondly, John McAllister is a good man. And had he not been at the Forrester's, you probably wouldn't be around right now."

"Are you serious?"

Although Jackson had been on the run for weeks, he hadn't come face to face with the possibility of getting killed. There had to be some truth to Abramson's words even if he didn't know exactly how much.

"Yes, I'm as serious as I could possibly be," answered Abramson. "Had John not been there—even if I had only been there—it would've been c'est la vie for you."

Abramson paused to let reality sink in for Jackson. After a few seconds of silence, the lone waitress brought the beverages to their table. It gave Jackson a chance to exhale and regain his composure. He tried to organize his thoughts.

Was he in trouble? Yes. Was he in danger? Yes. But Jackson was still more concerned with Caroline's well-being. He was already in too deep, making it an easy decision to keep plowing away.

"Okay, so I could've died," Jackson said. "I get that. I'm fine with that. I want to know what I stumbled upon, and what, if anything, that has to do with Caroline Mills, or Peterson, or whatever her name is."

The Chief Justice nodded his understanding.

"I could've forgotten about this whole thing a long time ago," Jackson continued. "Caroline was abducted in Kentucky where, by the way, my best friend was murdered. I didn't have to chase her down. But I have nothing left in my life right now, and all I want to do is help."

"I'm not sure she needs your help," responded Abramson.

"Whatever. Why did you bring me here if you're not going to tell me anything other than that my life was, or is, in jeopardy?"

Abramson had no other choice but to tell the truth. This would mark the first time that he would divulge information about the operation with an outsider.

It was the fair thing to do—for everyone involved.

The Chief Justice pulled out a folded, sealed envelope from his back pocket. He placed it on the table between them.

"Do you know what this is?" he asked Jackson.

"Not a clue."

"This is my resignation letter from my post as Chief Justice of the Supreme Court," said Abramson. "It could be hours before I hand this over. Or it could be days. It all depends on your friend, Caroline."

"What the hell are you talking about?"

Abramson displayed a warm, surrendering smile. The time had come to disclose everything, even if it was to a young, wayward law student.

He gently blew on his coffee and then took a sip.

"When this happens, when I am forced to resign, most people will think this will be my lowest, most shameful point in life. But I know it will be one of my proudest moments. No one will understand, but the risks I have taken over the past few years, and the backs I have stabbed of the people who helped put me where I am today, I will be proud of those things."

Jackson found himself listening intently to the Chief Justice. It was clear he genuinely wanted to do the right thing in his life.

"Your friend, Caroline," Abramson changed directions to a more serious tone. "She's in trouble. Big time. But don't you worry, she was fully aware of the risks she was taking."

"What risks?"

"Caroline is a federal agent, Jackson. She's been trying to uncover and destroy the McAllister-Windgate drug trade."

Jackson slumped back into his chair. Suddenly, he didn't have a clue who he was trying to help. Yes, there were plenty of details about Caroline's past that he didn't know. But never in a million years would he have guessed that she was working for the Feds.

"A long time ago," Abramson professed, "John McAllister wasn't the man he is today. He ran the East Coast's most profitable, most powerful drug trade. Cocaine, heroin, marijuana, pills, you name it, he ran it. McAllister was the brains behind the operation.

"His father and grandfather made a fortune running bootleg liquor and distilling their own whiskey, especially during Prohibition. So it made sense that the heir would find another way to run banned substances for money."

"That's insane," Jackson said, shocked by the revelation. "I would've never guessed that old man was capable of that."

"Oh, he's capable of almost anything," Abramson responded. "Both illegitimately and legitimately. He's run some of the most successful businesses Virginia has ever seen. He's a brilliant man, Jackson. He just got caught up in the greed and the thrill of sidestepping the law. It's that simple.

"But then he became friends with Senator Windgate. McAllister and the senator hit it off immediately—this was a long time ago, back when Windgate was a teacher without a dime to his name. But Senator Windgate is another very sharp man. With McAllister's deep pockets and their brilliant ambition, they amassed a fortune and increased their drug territory to cover the entire East Coast, from Key West to Boston."

"So I still don't get what this has to do with Caroline?"

"Actually, you do," said Abramson. "You know about Robert Peterson's murder, and you know that I was there that night. But what you don't know about Robert Peterson is that he was a federal agent, too. He was the FBI's first attempt to penetrate the operation. And his loss was an embarrassing failure on their part."

Jackson was so tuned in to the story that he failed to notice that someone else had come in the coffee house.

The Chief Justice turned his head to identify the other patron and then returned his attention to Jackson.

In a much quieter, less spirited voice, he continued, "Nobody within the FBI realized how well networked the McAllister-Windgate operation was. They had people in every government agency, especially within the investigation and enforcement units. That's why they were able to operate so freely."

"So they had moles inside the department, and I'm guessing one of them was Stephen Forrester."

"Bingo," said Abramson. "Now you're starting to figure things out. Well, it gets even better. Forrester headed up the investigation arm of the Bureau, but more specifically, he was in charge of narcotics. Everything went through him and the buck stopped there."

"Then how did Caroline's father get assigned to investigate the drug operation?"

"This is where it gets interesting," said Abramson. His eyes lit up as he recalled the conspiracy. His own passion even surprised him. "Senator Windgate was, and still is, one of the biggest proponents of the War Against Drugs. He worked hand in hand with the head of the entire FBI, not Forrester. Rumor had it that Scooter was having an affair with the head man's wife—"

Jackson cut in, "So in retaliation, Forrester assigned someone to bring down the senator and his little operation."

"Exactly," confirmed Abramson. "You see, in that inner circle, there weren't many secrets. They all knew about the drug operation—probably because they were all getting a nice chunk of change to keep quiet.

"The fatal flaw, and the subsequent demise of the investigation and Robert Peterson, was that nobody realized how tight of a hold McAllister and Senator Windgate had on the Bureau. Unfortunately, Robert Peterson was an agent reporting directly to Forrester. When he was pulled from under Forrester's direction and reassigned, Forrester did a little bit of his own investigating and alerted everyone to what was going on."

"Caroline's father never had a chance," responded Jackson, shaking his head.

"No, he didn't," answered Abramson. "Senator Windgate got word that Robert had worked his way into the party that night. He told McAllister about it, and they argued about how they wanted to handle the situation. McAllister wanted to welcome the man into the party and try to flip him. Nothing like a wad of cash to flip an agent and gain yet another mole. McAllister even approached Robert that night at the party to try and get a feel for the man.

"However, Senator Windgate had other plans. McAllister immediately shut down the notion that they should kill the undercover agent. He never resorted to violence. People will try and say that McAllister used to order hits on rival drug runners. Not a chance. The order for any murder, from the hands of the McAllister-Windgate drug trade came directly from the senator himself. So Windgate took matters into his own hands and gathered Ron, myself, and the local bartender, Paul. Ron and I roughed up the man a little as we escorted him out of the party. We were just college kids doing what we were told. We didn't want to hurt him too badly, just let him know that he wasn't welcome there. Nothing too terrible. Of course, our orders came from Windgate, not John."

"Then who killed him?"

Abramson slowly pulled back from the conversation, carefully tiptoeing around the subject. He needed a few seconds. He had never disclosed the truth to anyone else, ever. Then he closed his eyes, swallowed hard and turned back to Jackson.

"Senator Windgate killed Robert Peterson," he announced, lifting years and millions of pounds of stress from his shoulders.

There it was. The truth finally came out. But all of this was news to Jackson. Did Caroline already know this? He wondered. Could it be part of her plan to get inside the group, as part of a much larger investigation? Was she really an agent? Was Chief Justice Abramson telling the truth?

Caroline once told Jackson that John McAllister hated Abramson. The young law student had no clue whom to believe. At this point, he was taking everything with a grain of salt.

"How did they find out about Caroline?" he asked Abramson point blank.

"That answer, I don't know," he lied.

Before Jackson could further question the Chief Justice, Abramson's cell phone buzzed. It was a voice message.

Abramson's face portrayed his confusion as he listened. Jackson waited patiently for the news.

"That was John," Abramson said. "Everyone has been summoned to the McAllister estate. And I guess that means you'll need to come with me."

"What's going to happen?"

"Everything," responded Abramson.

X   X   X

Outside the back of the coffee shop, Shaun Martin heard and recorded the entire conversation. He had enough evidence to take down the Chief Justice and ruin his career forever. But he respected the man. And he would guard the recording of that conversation with his life.

Shaun dialed a number on his cell phone.

"We're heading to the distillery," he announced.

47

Late afternoon brought long, dark shadows across the meadows and horse fields behind the ruins of the McAllister mansion. Smoke no longer rose from the destruction, but a pile of bricks and memories still remained.

John McAllister sent everyone home from his estate—Ms. Ruby, his security detail, and even the snipers. The old man had no idea what was in store after he summoned the members of the operation to the estate, but he did not want any outsiders, even if they were part of his staff, around for the fallout. Things could go down peacefully, or things could go up in a round of gunfire.

The sun was now below the western tree line, suffusing the sky with a soft orange glow. A cool breeze lifted McAllister's gray hair. He strolled around the back of where the house once stood, thinking about all of the memories from the family's land.

An old maple tree down by the lake had provided much needed shade on the hot summer days of his childhood. He heard the leaves gently rustling in the summer breeze, and he began walking toward the tree.

McAllister's mother and father lay peacefully side by side on the lake side of the tree. And on the other side was a headstone for McAllister's late wife.

As he approached the lake, tears welled in his eyes. The corners of his mouth turned up as he thought about her warm, beautiful smile and her tender touch. How he missed her. She had been the Southern belle of his dreams.

Deep down, McAllister knew it wouldn't be long until they would be reunited once again. But he also knew he would have a lot of answering to do.

Why did you get involved in drugs? How could you do such a thing? And Ron? How could you let him end up that way?

The old man was ashamed of how he had acted in the past thirty years. Her life had been cut way too short, leaving him all alone with a rebellious teenage son to raise.

At first, he had been angry. He blamed his misery, misfortune, and sadness on her death. But then he became engulfed in the web of illegal activity growing beyond his established whiskey distilling operation. He profited on any poor soul who would partake in his poison. And he didn't think twice about it. Not for a long time.

The whiskey business was fun. He would always honor his political friends with a special batches of the whiskey. Everyone in the group loved the camaraderie it produced.

But before long, he was deeply involved in illegal schemes and, unfortunately, he taught his son to live that way: greedy, opportunistic, and uncaring. To prey on the poor, prey on the needy, and prey on the ignorant.

Thankfully, the group decided to cut short their first drug run after the government tightened its reigns and tried to bring all of the dealers to justice. It was during this lull in activity that McAllister reflected on his actions. And he vowed to quit the drug trade.

What a surprise to find that his son and closest business partner were back at it again. And all behind his back. He actually couldn't be too disappointed that the whole thing was about to crash, destroying the monster he had created.

He knew full well that Caroline was an undercover federal agent. He knew her story, and he knew her father's story. Maybe that's why he invited her into his life with open arms.

Slowly but surely he left openings for her to dig deeper into the operations, giving her a chance to uncover whatever it was that she was looking for. McAllister also gave the young girl a chance to explore her father's murder and find peace with the tragic loss early in her life.

The old man knelt down beside the headstone of his late wife. Tears ran freely down his cheeks. His life would've been so different if only she had been around.

Once upon a time, he had dreams of making the world a better place. How far he had fallen. He had riddled society with poison.

She had loved him unconditionally. And all he wanted was to hear her say that everything would turn out just fine.

McAllister gingerly made his way down from his knee and lay down beside her, underneath the old maple he remembered so fondly from his childhood. He was tired.

He closed his eyes, praying that he would take his last breath right then and there. His breathing became lighter and he dreamed of a warm summer day out on the lake.

Before he knew it, he was soaring over the mansion. It was standing once again.

A much younger Ms. Ruby was chasing a toddler—it was Ron— around the back yard. Ronnie was running towards the lake, occasionally looking behind him to see how fast Ms. Ruby was closing in. Before the young boy got too close to the lake, she scooped him up, giving him a scolding and a smack on the rear. The child laughed.

And so did McAllister, floating high above it all.

Mrs. McAllister watched the scene from her spot inside the shaded gazebo. She sipped iced cold lemonade. She was more stunning than he had ever remembered.

Those were the days.

John McAllister's eyes remained closed, and he slowly lost sensation in his body, barely able to feel the coolness of the Virginia twilight and approaching dusk.

His breathing was even shallower now. The old man was just cognizant enough to will himself to pass on to the other side. He was so close.

His wife was standing there beckoning him closer. Inch by inch, he moved toward her, reaching out to touch her. His hand was only inches from her hand—so close. The light around her kept getting brighter.

And then it was shattered.

The screeching sound of tires skidding in the gravel at the front entrance of the estate awakened McAllister from his trance.

He opened his eyes and found himself looking straight up into the old maple, gazing up at the same branch he had looked at throughout his life. He turned his head and looked at his wife's headstone.

He had some unfinished business to attend to.

"Not yet, sweetheart," he whispered. "I'll do better this time. But don't go too far. I'll be back soon."

The old man crawled to his knees, and then clamored to his feet.

In the distance, Abramson's silver sedan barreled toward the ruins. John McAllister winked at his wife's tombstone, just as he always had winked at her when she was alive, and made his way to the top of the hill to greet his guests.

48

John McAllister led the trio, with Abramson trailing close behind. Jackson brought up the rear as they hurried down the dimly lit hallway. Titans of national politics and other friends of the estate stared quietly from portraits and photographs on the walls as Jackson hurried to keep pace. Unsure what to look for, he failed to notice the picture of Caroline's father

Abramson and McAllister said little to each other.

McAllister had met the men on the site of the mansion and then quickly motioned for the two guests to follow him down to the caverns. Jackson speculated about how the mansion burned. He didn't have a good feeling about any of this.

While the hallway was dark, Jackson could see that the massive room at the end of the hall was well lit. A grand ballroom in a hidden cave in Warrenton, Virginia? Things became more strange by the second.

The mounds of corn had been removed. The floors were swept perfectly clear. White tablecloths covered what must have been fifty round tables, each large enough to seat ten guests. A stage at the far end of the ballroom had been set up, ready for a live band to entertain guests throughout the party.

Curtains hid the racks of barrels along the rocky walls of the ballroom—plush red curtains, as nice as could be found in any lavish hotel or theater. Gold cording and tassels lined the curtains, highlighting the giant gold "M" embroidered in the center of the fabric.

Before he sent them home, McAllister had instructed his staff to prepare the ballroom for what should have been Senator Scooter

Windgate's retirement party and the dedication of the Senate Proof batch of whiskey. Jackson had no idea what the ballroom looked like during distilling season, but its current state was very impressive.

Still feeling apprehensive, Jackson wandered over to a table and picked up the centerpiece, a bottle of McAllister whiskey featuring the Senate Proof label and the dates that Senator Windgate had served in the United States Senate.

McAllister was the first to break the silence.

Leaning against a chair at the table where Jackson stood, the old man said, "The whiskey hasn't aged nearly long enough, but it serves the bastard right."

He paused and looked around at his masterpiece.

Then he continued, "He is cutting everything short. There is nothing in that man but evil. He must be stopped before he ruins any more lives."

"John," Abramson interrupted, trying to redirect the old man's attention away from Senator Windgate. His face showed his concern for McAllister.

"It all ends tonight," said McAllister, ignoring his longtime foe. "We'll hunt them down and end everything. They'll kill Caroline if we don't do something soon. She'll meet her end the same way her father did."

Chills crept up Jackson's spine as the two men openly discussed Caroline's fate. There was a determination in McAllister's voice that Jackson had never heard before, from anyone. Abramson must have heard the same thing because he didn't attempt to calm the old man down after that. The nation's most powerful judge simply stood down and listened to McAllister's ranting.

"I will kill the Senator," he boldly proclaimed. "I'll pull the trigger. I'll take the fall. I don't have much longer to live, but I won't allow him to ruin my son's future—or Caroline's—any longer. I will kill him."

The rapid succession of gunshots sent the three men diving for cover behind the tables in the ballroom. The shots echoed through the cave. The bullets hit the stage at the far end of the room.

Jackson looked down the darkened hallway just in time to see the flashes from another round of shots, this time even closer.

Several bottles of whiskey shattered, sending shards of glass over Jackson and Abramson.

"That won't be necessary, John," announced a deep baritone voice.

Stephen Forrester and Senator Windgate emerged from the hallway into the light of the ballroom. Both men had guns drawn, aiming in the direction of the three men.

"Hey Judge, I never realized you were in on the action," yelled Forrester before unleashing another flurry of shots, this time hitting the table Jackson and Abramson hid behind.

McAllister hadn't moved since the second round of shots. He was still, face down.

"John," Abramson whispered urgently, trying to get the old man's attention.

No response.

Then they saw it. Blood pooled slowly on the floor beside McAllister, but they couldn't tell where he had been hit.

Abramson peeked around the side of the table. Forrester and Windgate hadn't moved any closer. They were standing firm, waiting for one of the three men to make a move.

And then he did. The Chief Justice sprung over to McAllister's side, somersaulting to dodge any gunfire aimed in his direction.

Jackson was paralyzed from fear. He couldn't move. He had tucked his knees up under his chin and wrapped his arms around his legs. All he could move were his eyes. He was watching Abramson tend to the wounded McAllister.

Forrester and Windgate fired shot after shot at McAllister and Abramson, only stopping to reload. The attackers weren't advancing any closer, but the bullets sprayed around McAllister and Abramson, with the deafening shots rattling around the cave.

The Chief Justice's dramatic actions took Jackson by surprise. The longtime rivalry between the two men had been put aside, and Abramson was risking his own life for an old foe who didn't have much time left.

Jackson watched as Abramson rolled McAllister over on his back. Despite the gunfire all around him, Jackson was relieved to see that the old man was speaking.

Abramson looked over to Jackson and pointed to his shoulder indicating that McAllister had been hit there.

The piercing sounds of the shots made it too difficult for Jackson to hear what McAllister was saying, but it appeared that he wasn't mortally wounded, as Abramson helped the old man sit up and stay behind an overturned table.

Suddenly, there was a terrifying silence. Both Abramson and Jackson leaned around the edges of their tables to see what was happening.

Forrester and Windgate had disappeared back into the darkness of the hallway.

Jackson saw it as his only opportunity to reposition himself. He took a deep breath, said a little prayer, and crawled to the other two as fast as he could.

Luckily, only one of the shooters fired at him. The air above him crackled as the bullets raced just over his head.

"As long as I can hear them, I'm still alive," he kept repeating over and over again in his head.

The three men were battered. Jackson and Abramson had cuts on their hands and arms from the glass of the shattered bottles. Wooden splinters from the tables were randomly piercing their shirts. And McAllister's wound continued to bleed profusely, despite Abramson applying firm pressure.

"Here, I've got something," McAllister said, gesturing toward his pocket. The excruciating pain kept him from reaching for it.

"Which one?" asked Abramson.

McAllister grimaced as he pointed to his right pocket. The blood had already soaked through his shirt, and was now soaking his jacket.

Abramson reached into the pocket and pulled out a Glock 19 Compact.

"It's loaded," grunted McAllister, as he leaned his head back against the table in severe pain.

"You ever used one of these before?" Abramson asked Jackson, offering the gun to the young man.

He shook his head back and forth. "No." He wanted no part of that.

While Abramson and Jackson were discussing the gun, McAllister had managed to pull out two magazines full of ammunition from his other pocket.

"You might need these," said McAllister as he handed the extra ammo to Abramson.

Abramson slipped the magazines into his pockets. He paused and looked at the old master distiller and the unfortunate young man. A maniacal grin formed on the Chief Justice's face and the light sparkled in his eyes.

McAllister and Jackson remained still. Confused.

"What's the world going think of this?" he boasted. Those were his last words before springing into action.

With his gun raised more confidently than a gung-ho marine, the Chief Justice stood tall, firing shot after shot into the dark hallway.

Abramson placed one foot in front of the other as he marched steadily closer to the hallway's entrance. No shots were returned.

With each step, Abramson fired another round. As he approached the last table between him and the hallway, he stopped. With the barrel of the Glock still pointed down range, the obviously seasoned shooter kicked over the table and quickly took cover behind it to reload.

Down to two magazines.

Jackson continued to apply pressure on the old man's wound.

"It looks like it came out the back," said Jackson as he took a closer look at McAllister's shoulder.

"It will be okay," whispered McAllister. "I never thought it would burn this bad though," he said as he squeezed his eyes shut.

"We'll get you out of here," Jackson responded not too confidently.

McAllister said nothing. There was nowhere to escape. The end was near, and he knew it.

Just as the Chief Justice was about to stand up over the table's edge and begin firing, they all heard her voice.

"Don't shoot!" Caroline screamed out.

Everyone could hear the sounds of her struggling against someone restraining her and trying to cover her mouth. They could hear her scratching and clawing, wrestling. They became louder as she approached the ballroom.

Two shadowy, struggling figures appeared as they approached the lighted ballroom.

Finally, Caroline and Ron emerged into the light.

Ron had a tight grip around Caroline's neck. She kicked at his shins to no avail. The more she pounded her elbows into Ron's doughy sides, the tighter his hold became around her throat. Her efforts to escape weakened as she began to visibly feel the effects of the stranglehold.

None of the three men were prepared to see Caroline in this condition. Her once beautiful blonde hair had turned a filthy brown. Her face had been beaten and her eyes were swollen. Crusty, dried blood was glued to the side of her face from her eye to her ear, and into her hair. Her lip was busted open from taking a few punches to the mouth.

Caroline was exhausted. She was done struggling. She couldn't fight anymore. She looked starved and weak, too frail to resist.

Ron used Caroline to shield himself. He stopped as soon as he came into the ballroom, giving himself plenty of opportunity to retreat if necessary.

"It's over, old man," he hollered.

Jackson's attention turned to McAllister who simply shook his head. What had become of his son? His wicked ways were destroying everything McAllister had worked so hard to build. A nice life, prestige, honor, power—all of it was going down the drain.

The hallway lit up brighter than a fireworks show as grenades exploded one after the other. A flurry of gunfire sent everyone scrambling for cover.

Incomprehensible shouts and screams filled the ballroom as the walls shook from the thunderous gunfire.

Barrels upon barrels of aging whiskey were spouting their contents as bullets punctured the curtains and the wooden sides.

The sickening smell of blood and whiskey filled the grand ballroom.

Jackson found himself with both arms wrapped around the master distiller, courageously shielding the old man from harm.

Looking over his shoulder, he saw the Chief Justice curl into a fetal position in order to stay out of harm's way. The table Abramson hid behind was shredded from the bullets.

The pops and thunder of the grenades and guns were never-ending. Bullets continued to fly into the ballroom, but that didn't stop Jackson from watching the entire thing unfold from his spot behind the table. He watched everything. It looked like a slow motion action scene in a movie.

Ron's body was sprawled out, motionless at the entrance to the ballroom. Blood had pooled around his entire body. There was no doubt he was dead.

Jackson looked desperately around the room for Caroline. He couldn't find her. He panicked. His heart raced and he felt the blood rush to his cheeks. His stomach dropped and the nausea hit him hard.

So many thoughts ran through his mind in the few seconds of panic. He had unnecessarily risked his own life to save a friend's—only to find out that she was a federal agent, embattled in her own investigation that had turned sour, at least according to the Chief Justice.

A hand touched his shoulder.

He jerked his head around to see Caroline's battered face. She held her finger in front of her mouth instructing the two men to keep quiet.

Jackson was speechless, but relief quickly set in, relaxing his body for a moment. Caroline had escaped the mayhem, for now.

"Is he okay?" she mouthed, pointing to McAllister.

"I don't know," Jackson mouthed back.

She pushed her way in to get a better look at the wound.

Jackson eased out of the way, careful to stay hidden behind the table. He checked on Abramson who was still curled up behind what was left of his cover. He made eye contact and nodded to Jackson, acknowledging that he saw Caroline attending to McAllister.

"He's lost a lot of blood," she said, returning Jackson's attention to her and McAllister. "We need to get him some help. Just stay down," she ordered.

Caroline kneeled, observing everything from behind the table. She was in obvious pain, but she was in full form, ready to protect the two men from harm.

She pointed to Chief Justice Abramson and gave a thumbs-up. He returned the gesture. He was still fine.

Auburn colored whiskey ran across the ballroom floor. The place was a disaster. Bullets were still piercing the barrels, followed by a steady flow of liquid reaching the floor.

Everything McAllister possessed had been destroyed—his home, his distillery, his family—everything.

The gunfire eased up and the shouts became a bit more clear and audible.

Jackson exhaled and rubbed his eyes as he heard the voices of what he thought were federal agents securing the scene. One by one they announced the all clear.

"Agent Peterson," called out a familiar voice.

Whose voice was it?

"Agent Peterson," the person called out again, this time inside the ballroom.

"Over here," she responded, standing up and waving her arms to grab the man's attention.

Caroline grabbed Jackson's hand and placed it on McAllister's shoulder to continue applying pressure to his injury.

The mysterious identity was revealed when Shaun Martin came around the table to check out Caroline and the old man.

"Mr. McAllister, we're here to help," said Shaun. "Everything's going to be just fine."

Shaun requested urgent medical assistance into his radio before turning his full attention to McAllister's shoulder.

While tending to the wound with some heavy gauze, he grinned widely at Jackson, fully aware that the young law student was astonished at what he was witnessing.

"I'm not even going to ask," said Jackson.

Shaun smiled proudly at the remark, but his concern, and rightfully so, was on providing the medical attention that McAllister needed.

The Chief Justice had walked over to the group. He placed a hand on Caroline's shoulder.

"I'm so sorry, Caroline," he said. "That was much too close."

"No biggie," she responded. "I'm fine and Senator Windgate has been placed under arrest. He'll be facing plenty of federal drug charges, murder charges—the whole shebang."

"He's still alive," grunted McAllister as medical staff arrived to help.

"He'll never know a free day again, John," answered Caroline. "I'll make sure of it."

She swallowed hard as the lump formed in her throat when she continued, "And he will also finally be charged with the murder of a federal agent, my father."

Chief Justice Abramson put his arm around Caroline to comfort her. But she didn't need it from him.

After the medics had wheeled McAllister away on a gurney, Shaun helped Jackson to his feet, shirtless, bloody, and exhausted.

"Stephen Forrester and Ron McAllister didn't make it," he said.

"I'll break the news to John," said Caroline. "I think he'll appreciate it if I am the one to tell him."

"We have a lot of debriefing to do," Shaun said to Caroline and Abramson. "I suggest we get started so the Chief Justice can get back to work.

He turned to both Jackson and Abramson, "After we're done, you two were never here. Do you understand?"

Jackson nodded his affirmation while Abramson closed his eyes and breathed a heavy sigh of relief.

"Thank you," Abramson said to Shaun. "And I mean that in the most sincere way possible."

"No. Thank you," he replied. "This operation would've never happened without your help."

49

Caroline looked out of her office window and watched the rain pour onto Constitution Avenue. It had been two weeks since the showdown at the McAllister distillery, and she eagerly awaited her lunch date. She hadn't seen Jackson since the crazy events, and she was anxious to see what he had to say.

He was running late, and it was now thirty minutes past the time he was supposed to show. With an afternoon full of scheduled meetings, her window of opportunity to reunite with Jackson was narrowing.

Her heart thumped with anticipation when she heard a knock on her office door. She skipped over to the door and opened it, ready to welcome in Jackson.

It was Shaun.

Caroline didn't attempt to hide her disappointment. She invited him into her office with a mere wave of the hand.

"You're healing up nicely," began Shaun.

"Thanks," she mumbled. "I'm finally starting to regain some feeling in my face."

"That's always a good thing," he chuckled. "Still no sign of Jackson?"

Shaun knew how excited Caroline was to see him. Shaun was also looking forward to explaining his role in the ordeal as well.

"Nothing," she replied. "Maybe it was all too much for him. I just hope he's okay."

"I'm sure he's fine," consoled Shaun. "He didn't have to search for you. He could've just walked away and forgotten about everything. But he went back for you. That says something."

"I know. He was brave. I admire that."

"How did John McAllister take the news that Ron didn't make it?"

"He was devastated," she said. "He couldn't believe that Senator Windgate survived the whole thing and Ron was the one who didn't make it."

"Trust me," replied Shaun, "I wish it could've been the other way around."

"Me, too."

"Well, hey, it's good to have you back in the office for awhile."

"Yeah, I definitely need the break. I'm sure you're happy to be out of the field, too."

"Nah, I enjoyed being a lawyer for a couple of years," he joked.

The two agents turned their heads toward the door when they heard someone approach.

"Knock, knock," announced Jackson.

He was dripping wet. His wavy, brown hair was plastered to his forehead. The rainwater dripped off of his bare arms onto the tile floor. His white, cotton polo shirt was glued to his body, almost completely translucent.

"No umbrella," stated Shaun, reaching over to shake his hand.

"Funny," Jackson replied, giving Shaun a good handshake.

Caroline walked over and gave Jackson a hug that lasted for several seconds.

When she finally pulled away, the front of her suit was soaked. But she didn't care.

"It's so good to see you," she said, beaming from ear to ear.

"You too," he replied, smiling broadly back at her. "Oh, and you too, Shaun—er, whatever your name is."

The three shared a good laugh.

Caroline and Shaun were both relieved to hear Jackson laugh about everything. He had been a rock throughout it all, even with his life in serious danger.

"So, I want the whole scoop," Jackson said. "What happened? What was going on? Who was who?"

"You absolutely deserve some answers," said Shaun. "And yes, you can call me Shaun. That's my name. Maybe."

Only Shaun and Caroline laughed.

Caroline jumped in and asked, "What do you want to know?"

"Everything," Jackson responded.

"Well, we can't tell you every single detail," said Shaun, "but I think we can fill in most of the blanks."

"Okay, spill it," said Jackson.

"I'm sure you know by now that Chief Justice Abramson set up the whole sting," Caroline began. "He had had enough of the illegal crap that was going on, and he was tired of watching a fellow public servant profit off of an illegal drug trade."

"The largest drug trade we've ever busted," interrupted Shaun.

"The group began cutting Abramson out of the loop a few years ago," continued Caroline. "It wasn't anything personal. They just knew because of his status that he would be a liability. It makes you wonder why they didn't give the old senator the same consideration.

"Anyway, he got a little hot under the collar, especially when Ron spilled the beans that they were back in the drug business. You don't even want to know how much money they were bringing in."

"Sure I do," said Jackson.

"Let's just say that they netted nine digits in the last two years," answered Shaun.

"The poor old senator," Caroline said. "Charges just keep adding up. Tax evasion."

Shaun took over the story, "Abramson was well aware that Caroline had followed in her father's footsteps with the agency. He knew there would be no sweeter justice for her, and for him, than to see her take down the group. This was his brainchild, of course, with the input of many agents."

"I had no choice but to take this assignment," said Caroline. "It was a chance to bring closure to my father's murder while also bringing his killer to justice. I had no idea the scope all of the other activities—the drugs, the gambling rings—any of it."

"So Abramson went behind everyone's back to bring the whole operation down," clarified Jackson. "But what about John? He seemed to be out of the game."

"He was," Caroline said. "He snuffed me out from the beginning though. He's smart. I think he wanted everything to stop, too. He had a pretty good hunch that his son was up to no good. But he didn't suspect the senator was behind anything. He thought it was Abramson all along.

"But one day, Abramson showed up at John's with a folder. Actually," she said as she paused to search around her desk, "here it is. Abramson took this file to John to show that he was behind an investigation into Senator Windgate, Forrester, and Ron. And my name was in that file, too.

"John didn't quite know how to take it. On one hand, he was upset that Abramson would implicate him, his son, and his family business. On the other, he did not want to be associated with anything that the senator was doing. It hit John hard—finding out about the ongoing drug trade and finding out that Abramson was the mole that set them all up."

"I don't think Abramson was ever the same after seeing the senator murder Caroline's father," said Shaun.

"You're right," she confirmed. "He wanted to break free from the entire group after that, but he was already in too deep. But once he decided to launch this sting, he was able to turn one other key inside man. Agent Willie Stewart."

Shaun took up the story again. "Abramson actually sent Stewart to rescue Caroline when you guys went to Kentucky, but he never made it back. By that time, word had spread that Stewart had switched sides, and Senator Windgate had Stewart killed. Abramson didn't know if Caroline had been discovered at that point, but he didn't want to risk it, so he tried to get her pulled out of the field. But, of course, that didn't happen. She was abducted so the cronies could figure out what to do with her."

"I'm surprised they didn't kill me on the spot," Caroline said.

"Agent Stewart had it coming," said Shaun. "First, he was a dirty agent, obviously. Second, do you remember Philip Waters, the guy I tried to set you up with for a summer job?"

"Yes," answered Jackson.

"Well, he was going to perform some tax audits of the drug trade. Stewart found out about that little operation and informed Windgate of what was going on."

"So they killed him?"

"Yes," replied Shaun. "You're fortunate they didn't find your name associated with Waters, or you would have never made it out of Forrester's house alive."

Jackson found himself a little overwhelmed with everything again. There were too many intricacies to the story. Jackson was just glad for a happy ending.

"So you went undercover, too?"

"Yep," answered Shaun. "A few years ago, when Abramson first came to us, we had to do our research and lay the groundwork for Caroline to be able to really get in deep. We found that Forrester was Windgate's real right hand man, so I worked for six months to get hired for a position directly under Forrester. Ever since then, I've kept a running tally of all of his doings. Lucky for him, he didn't live to face up to all the charges he racked up."

"Wow."

"Well, I have a meeting to get to," announced Shaun. "I'll leave you two alone."

He shook Jackson's hand before disappearing from Caroline's office, leaving them alone together for the first time since they were in Kentucky.

An awkward silence hung in the air as Caroline circled around behind her desk. She grabbed a towel out of her gym bag and tossed it over to Jackson.

"Here, you might need this," she said, looking at the rainwater pooling on her floor.

"Thanks."

Jackson ran the towel through his hair before drying his arms and legs. His sandals squeaked as he slipped them off to dry his feet.

"You didn't have to risk your life for me," Caroline said. "Really, you probably shouldn't have. But, thank you for coming after me. That was courageous of you. I'll always remember that."

"I wanted to," he responded. "I needed to. But I never would've guessed you were an agent. You were, are, much too beautiful for that."

Caroline blushed.

"Thanks. That's sweet."

"So do you want to hang out sometime?"

Caroline smiled and said, "That would be nice."

"But no more secrets. You have to tell me everything."

"If I tell you everything I know, you'll never sleep a peaceful night again," she answered. "But what about all the other girls that Jackson Cole loves to chase?"

He laughed.

"Let's just say that I look at life a bit differently now," he claimed.

The thunderbolt outside jolted Jackson out of his chair.

"But that's not to say I don't still get jumpy at gunshots, or thunder," he said sheepishly as he settled back into his chair.

Caroline cancelled her meetings and the two of them chatted and laughed the afternoon away before heading out to dinner together. And later that night, they took Max on his first real walk since returning home.

50

Two weeks had passed since Jackson and Caroline attended McAllister's funeral. On that hot August afternoon, he was laid to rest underneath the old maple tree, right beside the love of his life. The old man was finally reunited with his wife, surely relishing every moment of the reunion. The entire family was back together—husband, wife, and son.

In the summer months since the sting, McAllister had donated his entire estate to the Commonwealth of Virginia. The caves were to serve as a museum to showcase the role the region played during Prohibition. A replica of the mansion would be constructed to showcase the plantation style homes that once dotted the Virginia countryside.

Jackson's thoughts of the McAllisters shifted as he heard the sounds of a marching band. He was back on a familiar bench on Notre Dame's campus. Directly across from the law school building, he sat in his spot, once again waiting on a girl.

On this sweltering Midwest afternoon, the sun reflected off of the golden statue of Our Lady atop her perch on the Golden Dome.

There was a buzz in the air as the campus swarmed with fans and friends of the university. The Fighting Irish were less than two hours away from kicking off another football season of high hopes and aspirations.

Could this be the year? Domers always thought so.

The band had already started its march across the beautiful campus. Making their way down the God Quad, the chorus of the fight song drew nearer to Jackson on his bench. The crowd was growing as fans gathered to catch a glimpse of the marching band before they made a hard left turn and headed toward the football stadium.

But Jackson couldn't focus on the band. Instead, his gaze was fixed on a beautiful woman. Her blonde hair swept over her right shoulder as she looked back at him from her spot in line. Her green shirt proudly featured The Leprechaun on the front. Her legs were toned and tanned, and Jackson couldn't help thinking how lucky he was.

His eyes never left her as she approached. In one hand she carried a cold drink, moisture beading on the plastic souvenir cup. In the other hand, she carried a hot dog she'd bought in front of the law school building from a student group fundraiser.

It was a perfect day for Jackson—he didn't have a care in the world. The past few weeks had been some of the best of his life. And how ironic that he ended up right where the whole adventure began a few months earlier. Where one dream ended, another was just beginning.

"Are you ready to go to our seats?" Caroline asked.

Jackson didn't respond. Instead, he just smiled, soaking in the scene. Reflecting on a life that had changed so much in just a summer.

"Hey, I'm talking to you," she said again.

"Yeah, I'm ready," he said as he stood up from the bench.

He took the drink from her and took a sip. He stretched his arms over his head before saying, "Okay, let's go."

As the couple walked around the campus, surrounded by the joyful sounds of a college football Saturday, Jackson reached over, grabbing her fingers with his.

"So why haven't you been back to a game since you graduated?"

"I've never been assigned to a case here," Caroline responded.

"Whoa! So I'm an accessory to another case?"

"You'll never know," she replied, batting her eyelashes at him coyly.

With his radio earpiece in place, Shaun Martin observed everything from his hidden surveillance point atop the law school.

He was truly happy for his partner, but only as long as her love interest didn't interfere with their new investigation.

Before long, Shaun was tracking his new suspect down the quad. It was back to business as usual.